i

Charity's Fire

How do you survive when worlds collide?

CRAIG MATTHEWS

Charity's Fire

Cover by: CM Creations

Editing by: Larry Giroux

Formatting: Nancy Kuykendall

Proofreading: Tracy Jones

Visit for news and information on this and other exciting titles.

I began this project as a Christmas gift for my brother and sister-in-law. That short story ended up being the first chapter of this novel. Before I was even done, the thought was planted in my heart this story could end up being a book swirling with life and death, faith, selfishness, challenge, and insecurity. I prayed throughout this work God would be glorified in it somehow as I wrote it with my kids in mind, all six of them!

This labor of love is dedicated to the glory of Jesus Christ alone, with the hope that it will bless all who embark on its journey of faith and peace.

CRAIG MATTHEWS

Thank you Connie for your love and support all throughout this process. As well as Bob Taylor for your ever present encouragement, Ryan for challenging me to be a better writer and Karen for making my thoughts understandable to humans! Larry for all that you do for the kingdom. Joy for your incredible ability to encourage everyone in your orbit.

I am blessed by you all so very much!

Craig Matthews

January 2024

CHARITY'S FIRE

The cast of characters (nicknames) and some terms.

Craig and Connie (Con)

Bruce and Diana (Nan)

Frank Kenneth Draper

Chuck Powell

Larry, Wendy, Mary, Melissa (Boo Boo), and Megan (Sunshine) Shields

Angelic Warriors:

Captain Amadan, Sargent Gilboa (Gills), Tic, Ollie, Bigs, Helek, Bapps, Iggy

Dark Warriors:

Commander Cryptis, General Von Jamin, General Slubus, Hateed,

Leech - Anchor setting, soul-eating demons.

Whisperer – (Fly) - dragonfly-looking demons that relentlessly accuse.

The Herd - small rat-like demons.

Archers – tiny, fast demons that shoot fiery darts.

Reaper - Angelic-like demons that answer directly to the HE.

Some Terms:

Angelic Warriors call believers "Shiners"

call some believers "Flickers" because their faith was under developed

call unbelievers Vanu

call Dark Warriors the "Cast"

Dark Warriors call believers "Carne"

call unbelievers "Prode"

call Angelic Warriors "Pluck"

CRAIG MATTHEWS

Contents

ACT I

ONE

A LITTLE CHARITY

At the edge of the horizon, hiding behind a strip of blackness, death was coming for us, and we had no clue of its demands because we were mesmerized by our ignorance, captivated by pride, and lazy in thought— we were on vacation. Still, I am getting ahead of myself and the story surrounding the day I left this world.

The notable part of that fateful day began as gentle blue water caressed the sandy southwest shore of the heavily forested island. The sun was high in the sky, blazing and glaring off the tops of the rolling waves of the cove, making it difficult to maneuver the boat through the rocky inlet. Most hull-eating obstacles were submerged in the water, half-hidden in the sandy lakebed by the slightest covering of blue-green algae, making them hard to locate from the pilot's seat. The growth also made the sandstone boulders slippery as an ice cube in three feet of water. I stayed aboard the craft with half of my shirtless body hanging over the bow. The burning fireball of the noonday sun reflected off the water's surface— directly into my unprotected eyes. I could not see.

"Oh, for the love of some of those polarized sunglasses the large-mouth bass fishermen buy from late night infomercials," I thought. I assume the mouth reference is to the fish, not the men. My shades were in the front seat of our car, at least fifteen miles behind us, melting into the dashboard— useless. While squinting and trying to block out the soul-piercing reflections with my right hand, my internal grumble choir singing out of tune, I searched intently for rocks hidden beneath the lake's surface.

"Go Left," I shouted back to the long-haired captain as I caught a glimpse of another rock. I pointed with my arm to get her attention. The boat responded, missing two beige boulders by a couple of feet. I was impressed. She was good at controlling her "Baby," as she called the well-kept craft. She was so confident that she piloted with one hand on the wheel and the other on a cold drink wrapped in one of those dark blue slip-on insulated keep-my-beer-cold covers. Which, by the way, was wearing out at the seams from another summer of heavy activity. She had one hand on the throttle, the other on the wheel, and the ever-so-present beer was stowed in the cup holder to her right, well within striking range.

"You're good for fifteen feet," I said, my face still pointing down into the crystal clear water.

"What?" Diana shouted at the back of my bright orange swimsuit.

"Stay straight," I said, turning my head so she could hear while both of my hands chopped at the wind. Realizing she still could not hear me over the motor and the music, I repeated myself.

Aah, the music. Another wonderful Jimmy Buffet song blared in the background. A couple of his songs were tolerable. An hour into Margaritaville tunes, and they were already feeling stale. It had one of those band channels through a satellite radio, and it was all I had heard since we left the dock. Not even a single commercial interrupted their Buffet bliss. It was not my boat, so I kept silent on the musical selection, choosing to enjoy the water, the company, and the warm summer air. Until I was drafted into Her Majesty's service on the close combat support team, searching for those U-boat boulders hiding in the sandy depths.

For the last three hundred yards, I hung over the bow searching. My chest rested on the short chrome rails of the boat, leaving a bright red upside-down "V" across my tan-less midsection. We weaved left and right, approaching the empty beach. We could make out individual trees and shrubs from the forest wall that rose up out of the water before us. Our target was a white sandy beach in the area dead ahead. It was not a large beach, twenty feet wide and a hundred feet long.

The reflection of the bright white sand caught our attention from over a mile out in the lake, and knowing the island was uninhabited raised the romantic draw for the four of us. It was unanimous— our picnic lunch on this beautiful

Michigan summer day would be on the beach of a deserted island. The afternoon would include at least a million pictures to remind everyone connected with us that we were having a blast, and they were stuck at work, mowing their lawns or some other mundane task.

"Hey Craig, grab the anchor from beneath the seat cushion." The blonde sea captain said from below her trusty pink and white sun visor. She loved those topless hats and possessed half of the visors known to mankind back at their cottage on the mainland.

"Got it!" I unstuck my chest from the metal rail and rolled back onto my knees, grabbing for the white vinyl seat cushion that covered the cubicle where the stainless steel anchor lay waiting for deployment. The white nylon rope was neatly spooled around itself, the work of an experienced deckhand.

Bruce, the tidy deckhand, was responsible for this handiwork. He is my brother-in-law, married to Diana, the captain, my wife's sister. I have known him for 40 years. He was digging through a compartment under one of the seats in the stern. His long gray ponytail hung beneath his Daytona Beach cap covering most of his impressive back tattoo. The artwork is the Punisher skull from the American Sniper movie, wrapped by an eagle and flag, painted between his shoulder blades. Shirtless, he sought to maintain his stellar suntan. His laid-back appearance was interrupted by his desire to be busy, in motion, and accomplish something. He worked hard maintaining their A-frame lake cottage and his home north of Detroit. He craved neatness, organization, and order. At this moment, he struggled with a steaming pile of chaos.

"Right!" I barked with authority, pointing my hand. We glided right and missed a couple of small rocks and then a stray cloud covered the sun, making weird shadows across the lake.

———◆◆◆———

Meanwhile, soaring high above the lazy scene circled the afternoon watch detail. The assignment was another way to pass the time on the other side of the Curtain. None of the team members were familiar with any of the Shiners they had been assigned to that day. No one could figure out the duty's importance, yet none complained. It indeed was a beautiful day on the lake. The warriors could have pulled a more dangerous gig in some God-forsaken place. They had served in several war-torn combat zones before. Round and round, the six of them circled without a care. Still, many desired to be back home, and the boredom increased the longing. The world was a fantastic creation, yet it still paled compared to home, even if home was at least another full rotation away. They all agreed this assignment was "cake" duty. They had to fight the pull of wandering thoughts.

As the red and white boat below drifted through the cobalt-blue waters near the island, no observable threats appeared in the immediate area. The team was well-rested and in good spirits. During these times, complacency tried to weasel its way inside, even in the best units. Going through the motions of guard duty without full attention can end up causing havoc. The enemy lusted for these opportunities.

Captain Amadan, the leader of the circling band of warriors, knew his team was drifting from eons of training regimes and countless battles. Many good soldiers had suffered under the command of leaders who became hypnotized into letting their guard down. He was determined to fight that tendency. The team assigned to him that day was more than capable. He had served with most of them on different occasions. Many were veterans of hundreds of battles, and only two were new to his command.

Remembering the briefing earlier in the day at the Joint Operational Command Center, the JOCC to everybody in the sector, he was unsure why the threat level was so elevated when none of the typical signs had been tripped. It could be that little skirmish from last week, or someone inside the JOCC was hyper-vigilant and did not want any mistakes under their watch. So, this was his mission. They were honored to carry it out, even if it was just watching over four Shiners as they played on a boat.

"Let's look alive here!" Amadan barked to shake the watch team. "Gilboa, put some eyes on the assets, danger close."

"Sir." The winged soldier responded and streaked through the sky, diving low over the water within twenty feet of the boat. Braking hard, he came to station about five feet above the lake, causing a slight ripple on the surface. He circled with intention, scanning the water first, then the beach, and finally the surrounding area. His intense focus caused him to glow a brighter shade of yellow, which he knew made him visible to the enemy. Still, he saw nothing dangerous around the four souls aboard the watercraft.

"All clear, Cap," he reported.

"Widen your search to one klick," Amadan responded.

"On it," Gilboa chirped.

"Tic, check with JOCC on the latest weather," Amadan said.

"Roger Cap," Tic said and tuned into the JOCC.

"All clear on the weather front for fifty klicks out, Cap.

Something felt off to Captain Amadan and an uneasy feeling surfaced inside of him as he recalled the elevated threat level.

Two

Charity Landing

The landing was a few yards off as the boat grabbed the bottom violently. Something crunched beneath the waterline, and immediate curses were expelled by my brother-in-law. Curses that were based on experience. I am confident he sensed his wallet just took a beating.

He has often told me while sitting around a campfire on their beach, "The two best days in any boat lover's life are, first, the day you buy your boat and the second best day, is the day you sell the damn thing." This line was delivered with his belly laugh that followed most of his stories. Even if you did not know him, you knew his stories had been well-travelled, rehearsed like a veteran comedian on tour. They were smooth, paused at the correct times, and funny.

At that moment, Bruce was not in the mood to laugh. The sudden violence caused him to tumble backward, knocking his hat off. I hit the bow railing pretty hard, catching myself with my hands. Captain Visor knuckled the wheel, and my quiet wife spilled her bottle of ice-cold water down her chest with a yelp. Then, in a split second, even the radio went silent.

"Lift the prop!" Bruce shouted, and before the words passed his lips, Nan was on it, slipping the boat into neutral while pressing the hydraulic lift switch and killing the motor. The buzz from the rear of the boat sounded just as Bruce stood and then he slammed his left knee while getting onto the white diving platform. As he scooted rearward we could all hear metal grind against a rock beneath the waterline. Bruce launched himself into the water from a seated position and the grinding stopped as the boat's stern rose at least four inches from the sudden weight reduction.

"Connie, move to the front of the boat!" Captain Nan told her younger sister.

This move was to get the stern out of the water further to relieve contact with the rock I had not located. A wave of insecurity and shame washed over me as I extended my hand to my bride. She was navigating past the tan Yeti cooler, trying to move it with one foot. Those coolers do not slide easily, by design, so she stepped up on it and grabbed the windshield that was opened up in the middle fifteen minutes earlier. Releasing my hand, she plopped harder than expected onto the hot cushion, laughing embarrassedly. After all our years together, many things could be communicated with a particular look, a head tilt, a glance, or a glare.

More muffled curses came from the back of the boat as Bruce tried to peer through the out-drive to the propeller protection plate. I glanced over the rail's edge to check for rocks, then jumped over the side to help steady the craft and look for any damage my negligence may have caused. In my haste, I forgot to let go of the anchor rope and got a nasty rope burn around my wrist as the anchor fell from my hand into the boat.

"Are you O.K.?" Connie asked, peering over the side.

"I'm fine, just stupid," I said as I rubbed my wrist. "Is the boat alright?" I asked, hoping I hadn't just gouged the shiny white fiberglass— that would have pushed Captain Visor's anger button.

"It's fine," Connie said, sliding the chunk of steel away from the edge. She was making a face with an exaggerated expression, indicating the unexpected weight of the anchor. Connie can be funny, and I love our ability to laugh at life together. Her beautiful brown eyes lit up as she laughed, reminding me to relax.

"Hon, can you see what is broken?" Nan asked Bruce.

"Not really. But as far as I can tell, the prop looks fine." Bruce responded, somewhat calm now, having put eyes on the outboard drive.

"Craig, can you see the plate on the front side of the propeller?" Bruce asked me as I showed up on the scene. I moved closer while he tried to lift up on the diving platform. The platform was a purely practical addition to the boat. It made getting out of deep water accessible, but also made checking for damage more difficult.

"It looks like it is bent sideways," I said after tucking my head beneath the diving platform above the cool water. I was in the water now, so I committed and slid beneath the landing platform to feel the plate. It was bent and torn to the side as if two of the four bolts that held it on the shaft had given way. The steel plate was still solid but was folded into a weird "L" shape.

"Take a look," I told Bruce as I stood up and grasped the round metal edge of the platform to lift.

After a few seconds, he came out and agreed. It was still attached, which was good, but it would mean that we would have to take it easy on the return trip. The bent plate would want to act as a rudder pulling the boat to the starboard side.

"That prop was like three hundred bucks so I'm glad. The prop saver is only thirty." Bruce said more to reassure himself than to anyone in particular.

"I guess it did its job!" Nan said.

"Man I am sorry, I missed that dumb rock." I said to him.

"Accidents happen, Dude." Bruce said with a long, drawn-out "u" sound. He was smiling now and looking over his drippy, wet sunglasses.

"Start it up, Hon," he said to the now calmer captain.

"You guys get clear of the prop," she said, and she looked back to make sure we were out of the danger zone. Then she cranked the Volvo six-cylinder over. The naturally aspirated motor was a finicky beast, often taking long cycles on the starter to pop to life. Once it was running, it ran well. This time, it perked up right away. She lowered the prop a bit to ensure no vibration, indicating internal damage.

By this time, we had drifted so close to the shore that Nan turned the motor off, and we walked the boat in a few more yards. Now up on her knees, Connie handed me the anchor over the side of the boat, and I threw it out and set it in the lake bottom. Then I cinched up the rope to the tie down on the bow, crossing it over itself several times to secure it.

After all the excitement, our stomachs told us it was lunchtime. When examining the beach, we decided it would be best to have our sandwiches on the boat and explore the island after lunch. The beach was beautiful in its natural glory, but that meant there were only a few clear areas. Instead of hauling the heavy cooler out of the boat, we ate on board and enjoyed the sun.

Unfortunately for me, the radio went back on. Connie asked to have the channel changed to some classic rock station, which offered immediate relief. As far as I was concerned, it could have remained silent and given us time to take in all of the beauty in front of us— an afternoon uncluttered even by sound. I wanted to bathe in the scene for a time and let life's stresses wash away.

Far out in the middle of the deep waters, they gathered in secret. Huddled low on the lake bed to ensure anonymity, the four ancient warriors plotted another move in their long war. They ensconced aboard the multidimensional interstellar warship named Shogun. The meeting was to finalize plans for a secret offensive in the Lake sector on Terra. They wanted to open a second front in the region. Recent significant victories in other adjoining sectors had emboldened the leaders to press the apparent advantage they had taken over their bitter enemy, the Pluck.

Commander Cryptus was concerned that pride, the damnable type, was pushing the agenda to extend themselves beyond their means. Still, he would only consider that possibility when he was alone. As he laid out the audacious plan, he was convinced the other Generals needed to see a bold and confident leader, not some wavering fool.

"Remember this action is not to be an all out frontal assault like on the beaches of Normandy or Inchon. Those were devised to be the decisive turning points of Carne wars, whereas this concoction is designed to be merely a minor necessary diversion before the final invasion." He paused and looked up to consider another thought. "So often, the outcome of wars can be determined by a simple action," said Cryptus to the three others.

"Like Judas taking the silver?" Suggested Hateed.

"Vaguely," responded Cryptus as he pulled open his long traveling garment and sat down at the opulent table. He invited his brothers to follow, gesturing with his long spindly arms. As Supreme Commander over the Lakes region, his position was well-established and firm.

"A bit more like Hannibal acquiring the directions and knowledge to be able to march his war elephants and troops through the Alps to conquer Rome." He sat back, impressed with himself and his analogy.

"Explain to us your plan, mighty Cryptus," said the shorter, angrier, and pale Major General Slubus, with his tongue planted in his slimy cheek.

"General Slubus, we will use multiple distractions to get a Herd within ten klicks of the Mark to inflict enough critical damage on the Carne— so much so they will be removed from battle before the invasion begins!" Cryptus said with all of the drama and flamboyance he could muster.

"The key is coordinating a believable distraction against the vile Pluck long enough to deliver a swift and devastating blow to the actual target, the Carne Mark.

"TEN klicks! How will we accomplish that?" Insisted the General.

"Multiple distractions," Cryptus replied, enunciating every syllable to embarrass the upstart leader.

"What are these distractions, Commander?" Slubus said, as his black eyes bulged forward now inches from Cryptus, an obvious challenge.

"I have summoned The Herd from Europe, which will arrive shortly."

"The Herd? The five-million-strong Herd. The Herd? All the way from Prussia?" General Slubus was skeptical, and it showed all over his mangled face as he settled back, put in his place by the Commander's scheme.

"They were resting in Prussia after their magnificent deployment in Syria, my young General," Cryptus said, with more than a bit of derision.

"Now HE, whose name is unmentionable, has allowed a movement of this magnitude of critical resources halfway around the world— here to the Lakes?" Slubus pressed back.

"Yes, General Slubus. HE sees the potential of this operation as having devastating long-term implications. HE has put the entire Herd under my command,"

Cryptus now beamed with pride. The final nail was driven into Slubus' insubordination.

"They are moving in complete secrecy gentlemen, and are arriving within the hour."

"Commander! What an extraordinary honor, Sir!" Slubus was becoming more convinced that Crypus was not as incompetent as he had suspected. Taking the underling position now would serve his own desires well. Slubus knew the appearance of compliance often satisfied the insecure.

"Tell us more, Commander," said the impressed Hateed. This would be his first mission with the legendary Herd and he lusted after the opportunity.

The quiet four-star General Von Jamin raised his eyebrow in approval.

Stirring at the newfound possibility, the four drew their tattered heads together to share the details without uttering a word. At the exact moment of the Generals' confab, The Herd began their stealthy arrival in the deep waters of Lake Huron, just a few miles north of where the four tattered warriors gathered and less than fifty miles from the red and white boat.

THREE

CHARITY'S SECRETS

The sand was mucky as the four of us waded to shore. Feeling like Robinson Caruso or Gilligan, I was excited to explore. The beach was littered with tiny bits of gray driftwood, and some larger branches stuck out from the fine white sand. The sun had warmed the surface to the point we were glad we had our water shoes on. Well, Nan had a pair of those funky sock-looking contraptions on her feet, and Con had her ever-present summer wear, flip flops slapping her heels as we walked up the beach. Bruce tried to do his Ricardo Montalban impersonation from the Fantasy Island television show. It fell flat but did take us back.

The line of trees and undergrowth was thick on this part of the island, so we decided to move south and skirt around to see if there were better access points into the interior. The sandy beach gave way to dark gray rock that looked like granite, but I am not a geologist.

"Careful, these are slick," Bruce warned.

We began to form a single file line as we walked through some short green plants that looked like blueberry bushes. Then came the wild rose, which wanted to cling to swimsuits and legs. We cut through a stretch of sand-covered ground and pushed through the underbrush to the southern shore. This side of the island looked utterly different. Void of sand, it was littered with boulders— the type you had to step up on. The annoying rocks reminded me of the northern part of Isle Royale in Lake Superior. That trail had beat the crap out of me twenty years ago. Of course, I was carrying sixty-five pounds of a house on my back in the form of a green Kelty backpack.

15

"I'm gonna walk out in the water," Connie declared, and we all agreed. Walking through the chilly lake waters would be slow but not any slower than the progress we were currently making over the boulders.

Another ten minutes and an opening into the island's interior presented itself. We went ashore and up a ten-foot rise over sand-covered sandstone, with intermittent patches of beach grass, which appeared desperate to hang on to the land. The trees were more mature here and it opened up even further as we moved in. The ground felt like I was walking on a moist sponge. It was as if moss had grown over water-soaked sand without being wet. We gained what appeared to be the high ground, some twenty feet above the lake. Nan pointed out a ridiculous number of birds in the trees and on the ground about fifty yards in front of us.

Cormorants, the fish-devouring birds nested on the island in significant numbers. We all grew quiet as we noticed the sheer volume of hundreds, maybe thousands of birds squawking and carrying on. We invaded their turf, and they were protesting. We stopped as the stink hit us in the face— like a putrid wave.

"I think we found their toilet." Bruce quipped.

"Yuk!" Nan said.

"It stinks!" Connie chimed in.

"Gag." That is what I felt and said.

"Let's move back toward the shore, the forest gets pretty thick up ahead." Bruce noticed.

As we walked around the toilet toward the island's southeast corner, we entered a clearing.

"What the heck is this?" I said.

"It looks like a pen." Connie said.

"That's the barrier that goes around construction sites," I said, trying to figure out what it was doing in the middle of a deserted island.

"What?" An exaggerated facial expression is all Bruce could come up with.

"Craigy, what would it be doing out here?" Nan asked in her older sister's voice.

It was laid out in a perfect rectangle, twenty feet by ten. Somebody had taken the time to lay it out in this precise pattern.

"I have no idea," I said.

As we approached the pen, a massive pile of bird carcasses was strewn about the entire area. By now, the birds were bleached from the sun and were just piles of feathers and bones. Hundreds of dead birds, like a plague, had swept through a few months ago. We all spread out over the area, playing murder investigators, trying to piece the puzzle together to come up with a reasonable explanation. Then Bruce found some key evidence.

"Hey, look at this!" he said, motioning us toward his position about twenty-five yards east of the pen, at the edge of a more heavily wooded area.

"Holy crap!" Nan said.

"Wow!" Connie replied.

In front of us on the sandy ground, there must have been five thousand spent shell casings. Bruce picked one up and flipped it over. He tossed it to me and said, "Rim fire twenty-two long rifles." Referring to the caliber of the spent brass.

"Somebody stayed out here for days just killing these nasty birds?" I questioned.

"Could have been the DNR," Nan said.

"What? The state government who says we can't harm these fish killers, are out here smoking them by the thousands?" Bruce asked.

"Them or maybe some fishermen?" Connie said. Her dad had been a game fisherman for over sixty years. He hated that these birds consumed four times their weight in fish every day and were considered endangered.

"Obviously this is a huge nesting ground for them," I put out there.

"Look over there!" Connie pointed northeast. The trees were dying in large sections like they had been poisoned.

"That may be all the bird crap poisoning the ground." Bruce guessed.

"Man, it stinks up here. Let's move back by the water," I said and I started moving away.

The girls started up a conspiracy conversation about what was behind that whole scene in the middle of the island. We decided to circumnavigate the atoll to check out the rest of the mysterious place. We had to return to the water and waded through a knee-deep lake.

As we turned north on the island's eastern side, as far away from the boat as we could be without notice, the wind changed direction. The waves were rougher on this side and we splashed each other for a few adolescent moments. That ended quickly, with all of us laughing, huffing, and puffing for oxygen. Playtime gave way to searching the area for rocks and shells, oblivious to time, like a proper vacation.

I was thankful I had put a tan t-shirt on before we left the boat, along with my ever-present Tigers cap. Bruce was sporting a black "POW-MIA" never-forget shirt— which may not have been the optimal choice, considering the sun. He was a sweaty guy anyway, so he peeled it off and stuffed it into his back pocket. Connie and Nan were still only in their flowery swimsuits, having applied an extra layer of sunscreen. Everyone carried a bottle of water, and soon we had a couple of exciting trinkets.

Connie's water was soon gone, and the bottle began storing her new trophies. She even drizzled some sand into the opening. I just shook my head. "Whatever," I thought as I wandered away, seeking some treasures of my own.

———◆○◆———

As the four Shiners made their way toward the beach, Captain Amadan had Sargent Gilboa swoop down again, this time low into the trees, out in front of the assets. Gilboa took a position in a cottonwood tree, scanning the entire area with intense eyes for a full minute.

"Still Clear, Cap," Gilboa said as he fought back the urge to yawn. He dialed back his eyes so no lowlife Cast could locate him.

The warm sun on his face felt great. It was almost as if he was on vacation with the Shiners.

"I could get used to a little more of this kind of detail," he thought. The birds all around him were making a ruckus. He assumed they were fussing about the Flickers walking around on their island. Although they did not appear to be Flickers in the real sense. This was the first time anyone had paid much attention to these four, which would make them genuine Shiners. Flickers always needed attention, like watching babies run blindfolded beside a cliff. All the Warriors on this team had yet to be rotated in to watch over these four. He assumed only Cap knew the backstory of these folks.

Holding steady about one klick above the island, the five soldiers in the squad were almost rocking themselves to sleep with the constant circling. They had definitely checked out mentally in the sleepy summertime afternoon air.

It was the perfect time for a summertime surprise.

Four

Charity's Fire

"**B**OOM!" A thunderous crash roared and echoed across both heavens.

Amadan shouted for the teams to go RED. Scanning the horizon to the southwest, Tic picked up the scent.

"Cap! Four and a half klicks, southwest! Looks like a serious insertion into the bay."

"How many?" Shouted Amadan.

"Could be hundreds or more!" Biggs yelped.

"Tic, take Ollie and Biggs and check it out. Full alert. NOW," he said with just enough seriousness to communicate a proper amount of immediacy without a sign of panic. The warriors needed to be focused, not afraid. The three warriors shot off to the southwest, leaving the Cap with Private Helek.

"Gills, amp up but don't let yourself be seen, in case this is a ruse to get us exposed," Amadan, the smooth, whispered to the Sargent below.

"Helek, get the encryption word out to JOCC that we've had a major insertion into Saginaw Bay four and a half klicks to our southwest. Tell them to get a Ready-Squad activated on stand-by to make the Shift." Amadan was cool under pressure. It exuded confidence in the whole team.

"Roger Captain," Helek replied in an excited tone.

"Easy Private," Amadan reassured the young warrior. "Tell the JOCC to have the Ready-Team Shift to our location and not the insertion point, something is smelling rotten."

"Yes Sir," came the taut reply.

"Rotten like a Rat, Cap?" Gilboa chimed in.

"You got it Gills."

The Shogun was in perfect position, in complete stealth mode, invisible to the Pluck scum. Cryptus was furiously scanning the sky. He knew a first-rate Pluck Watch Detail would be assigned to these special Carne. He needed to have intel on that particular day's protocol concerning over-watch on the assets. Back and forth, he swept the sky with his visor, as did another two junior officers on the bridge. High, low, inside, outside. Nothing.

"This Squad is good," he thought. "They're patient," he said.

"Come on, show your pathetic lit-up faces," he said, fighting to see through the blinding sun. The visor was a considerable help most of the time. Still, the high afternoon sun proved to be more than a match for the newest technology.

"Send the second team," he barked suddenly.

"Go Team Two," a young Lieutenant yelped into the comm.

They were fully committed now and had to push hard no matter the Pluck response. He knew he had them outnumbered at least ten thousand to one, if not a million to one. This squad could not hold out against such power! A sadistic laugh began to develop inside him, imagining the disgusting Pluck being ripped limb from limb by the infamous Herd.

The second BOOM lit up the sky to the southeast this time.

"TIC! You get back here ASAP. Send Ollie to the new splash. Biggs you stay on station at the first contact, amp down, we need stealth, then advise," Amadan barked.

"Gills, get at the Ready!"

"Half a klick out Cap," Biggs reported.

"Four klicks out," Tic said confidently.

"Eight klicks to new splash Cap," Ollie snorted.

"Roger," Amadan replied.

"At the Ready," Gilboa replied and drew his sword. Leaping from the tree, he shot over the water, taking a position directly above the oblivious Shiners. Half smiling, he was amazed at how wise Shiners can be, knowing things that he could only dream of and yet, at the exact same time, how ignorant they are. Those four souls had no idea what was coming. Come to think of it, he only knew from experience what could happen in situations like this. Rarely, if ever, does the Cast throw two distractions at us in one attack.

"Hold on kids," he whispered to the group below him.

Helek, send the encrypted message.

"JOCC Emergency Shift now! Repeat, Danger Close!" Amadan whispered, knowing the Cast were close to finding their Mark.

"There!" Cryptus was pointing. He almost jumped out of his boots when he saw the lone red Pluck trooper leap from the tree on the island's west side and then flash to the northeast. He recognized the soldier,

"Sargent Gilboa! We meet again." He marveled at the thought of revenge as a seething hatred boiled to his face.

"Release the Herd, General!"

Five million pissed-off demons exploded out of the lake into the storm, which was building with an intensity that soared above the energy of the bulging blackness.

FIVE

CHARITY'S STORM

For some reason, I looked northeast into the lake.

"Hey!" I shouted louder than I intended. I repeated it because we had drifted apart thirty yards or more. I pointed to the black clouds.

"Crap! We gotta get back NOW!" Bruce shouted, running toward their craft. We could almost turn west and return to the cove, but we were far from the boat. The girls looked as worried as I felt.

"Move. Let's move now!" I yelled and pushed my wife in the direction we needed to go.

Usually, Nan was a runner, but she had been struggling with plantar fasciitis. Her nerve endings in and around her heels were inflamed, making running painful. She was trudging through the water, now thigh-deep and waist-deep on Connie. The three of us held hands as we fought hard through the lake. The sunlight dimmed— covered by the clouds that lead the storm. As I glanced back, I tried to estimate how long we had.

"How did I miss this?" I thought. The incoming storm looked violent. Deep black clouds and a thunderhead that soared into the stratosphere. The clouds appeared like they touched the lake, which meant the rain was torrential.

"We don't have very long girls!" I said.

"What does that mean?" asked Nan.

"Five or ten minutes, maybe," I said.

"Oh, God, help us!" Connie prayed out loud.

Meanwhile, Bruce was making progress as he turned west and took an approach nearer to the shore. He looked back, and Nan waved him onward. They must have thought that if he could get to the boat and get the canvas top up, we would have enough time to get close enough to get aboard somewhere between here and there. Then we could high tail it out of the way of this monster nor'easter or at least get to the island's leeward side.

It was a nasty storm, and it was coming on us quickly right out from the center of Lake Huron. I had once experienced a storm like this off Lake Superior in the Upper Peninsula, and the seventy-mile-an-hour straight-line winds almost ripped our tent out of the ground.

"GO! JUST GO!" Nan yelled ahead, frantically waving her arms at her husband. He took off again, rounding the bend of the beach ahead of us and out of sight.

"Hey, we do not want to be out in this water when that lightning gets close, we have to move up by the shore so we can get out when we need to." I roared, pointing over my shoulder.

We struggled through the thick water, while gasping for the humid air to fill our lungs faster than it could.

Connie was falling behind. As I turned to check on her, she went down hard with a splash, unable to catch herself. We raced back the fifteen feet to help her. She was rolling around on her back, grabbing her left foot while keeping her face above the water. Nurse Nan jumped into action. Connie was in searing pain. Trying not to scream, she held her injured ankle as Diana came alongside.

"Where is the pain?" As she reached for Connie's ankle.

"Let me see it. Did you feel a pop?"

"Yes." Connie said, clinching her teeth.

Nan tried to maneuver the ankle a bit, checking for a range of motion— which sent Connie yelling at her sister.

"Sorry, Sorry, just trying to figure out if you broke something." She said.

"Well the good news is that it doesn't look broken, just sprained. The cool water is great for it."

"But we can't stay here!" I said.

"Let's get on each side of her and we can help her out of the lake," Diana said. "We need shelter!"

"Natural shelter. A pine tree, at least. That could give us some time." I said, thinking out loud.

I knew being under a tree, on the top of a hill, or even down in a valley were never good places to be in a thunderstorm, but we had to try.

"Maybe Bruce is at the boat." Nan said hopefully.

"Even if he is close we would have a few minutes before he could get around to us. We have to get to the beach and I will run and look for shelter inland."

"Let's get you up, Con," Nan said, helping pull her arm. We got her to her feet, each of us under an armpit.

"Hold your foot up behind you and we will help you walk." A long rolling thunderclap put an exclamation point on the thought.

After awkward moments, we began to get the hang of the five-legged bag race and made good time as more thunder breathed down on us. At the island's northeast corner, I left the two sisters on the grassy beach as I raced through thickets and underbrush, wildly looking for shelter. We needed a place to hide.

———◆◇◆———

Meanwhile, Bruce reached the boat on the other side of the island. He grabbed the ladder on the stern to climb aboard when his heart viciously seized from the frantic prodding. He fell, striking his head on the corner of the dive platform— splashing face-down in the lake. Blood rushed from the five-inch cut on his forehead, staining the gray water red as his lifeless body floated alone in the waves.

———◆◇◆———

A massive gust of cold wind slammed into the beach, driving sand and water into the faces of the two sisters as they waited for rescue. Turning away from the assault, they decided to get up and start moving. Fear proved to be a good, albeit temporary, pain reliever for Connie's already bruising ankle. Nan steadied her younger sister as they hobbled down the beach together toward rescue. The wind blew their hair sideways and sand into their eyes and mouths. Spitting and swearing, they marched on, not wanting to look back and face the truth of the storm.

"HEY!" I shouted.

"Have you seen the boat?" I asked as I approached them running.

"What happened to you?" Connie asked after seeing my legs, arms, and face scratched up and bleeding.

"Ran through a thorn bush." I had not bothered to stop and look.

"I found a spot that will work, but we need to go now."

A previous gale had torn an old tree out of the ground. The extensive root ball and trunk could offer some protection. I knew we could not be on this beach when that storm hit.

"Bruce could be coming with the boat any minute now!" Nan protested.

"That is true Diana, but we are not going to outrun that storm," I said, pointing back to the wall of water that was maybe a mile away.

"We have got to get some cover before it hits. Bruce is a smart guy and he will do what he needs to do to be safe. We have to move now!"

"Alright." She conceded, and we started moving away from the shore. I took Connie's left side, and Nan shouldered under her right. I searched for an easier way to the fallen tree. We stepped into some warm and murky water.

"Go right," I said, "around those trees, then left."

Connie groaned a bit.

"Sorry, honey, but we have to keep moving. We do this first, then we figure out what to do. I know it hurts."

"I will be alright," she said, forcing a half smile.

Two minutes later, and there it was. I pointed with a nod. They both were unimpressed and communicated with nothing more than an indignant frown. A talent they had learned from their dad.

"Hey, it's not the Holiday Inn, but it is better than the beach," I said.

"It's better than the boat too," Nan said, afraid for Bruce on the open water.

"He'll take the boat to the leeward side of the island to wait it out," I yelled to be heard.

I broke a couple of branches out of the way, and we climbed beneath the log, which may have been two and a half feet above the ground. Connie, being claustrophobic, protested for a moment until there was a CRACK of lightning! Followed immediately by the roaring BOOM of thunder! The storm was upon us.

Trees all around us bent over in response to the ferocity of the wind racing over the island with a deafening roar. I started praying out loud while my mind was transported back to another storm I had endured with my two boys. It was so bad that we all stood under my poncho after discarding our external frame backpacks next to a tree. I had asked God to protect my sons then and protect us now.

The sisters were crying now as their faces filled with terror. The power of nature's wrath was evident as trees broke around us. Debris flying through the air. The loud strikes of lightning hit so close they were shaking the ground. A plastic garbage bag was lodged in a tree ten feet away. I rolled out, jumped, and grabbed it before it could race away. Fighting back to the hugging, crying, praying girls, I pulled the bag apart at the seams and tried to wrap it around the three of us as we hunkered down in a heap.

"Jesus, we are yours, please help us now!" was all I could say. I prayed that way many times before, but verbalizing it in front of others was rare.

I was shivering from the cold rain and soaked swimsuits, but the real reason was the pile of raw fear. Connie was in the middle, and Nan and I were on either side. We clung desperately to each other for warmth and security.

"Father be close to Bruce right now," Connie prayed, and Nan sobbed.

———◄O►———

The red and white boat separated from its anchor as the surging winds shot over the island. The searing gale brought the bow up and drove the propeller into a boulder, causing it to twist and capsize. Bruce's motionless body was being driven out into the lake when it caught on a rock at the end of the peninsula, at the very western tip of the island. The growing swells washed over it. The boat was never coming.

Six

Unseen Charity

Bruce, the fundamental part of him, had separated from the body he had been so intimately connected to for over sixty-seven years. His identity was no longer concealed from the real world behind clothes, careers, possessions, or even his skin. He felt naked as he hovered above the water. Laid bare in the truest sense of the word, he felt no pain in his chest or from the gash on his forehead because he was no longer joined to a physical body. That part of his old self was face down in the lake.

The storm was raging, but he was not affected in the least. He recognized what was happening— for the first time, he finally understood. He could see unlike any other time in his existence. He could hear the cries of the three people below. He could discern their unspoken prayers as they hid beneath the plastic and tree. Instantly, he was hovering above them, but he had not made himself go there. He was ushered there by an unseen hand, like he was meant to watch for something to happen, waiting as the story unfolded before him.

He could sense a warm presence above and over his shoulder, and he wanted to turn and look, but his "eyes" were glued to the drama below. In an instant, he could see gigantic winged creatures swirling through the air between him and the ground. They were magnificent. Soaring and swooping, they furiously fought in the middle of the dark storm. Swords flashed like lightning, meeting other forces veiled in the darkness. Bruce tried to shield his face with his hands to protect himself from the flying debris, but he did not have a head, arms, or hands. The debris passed through his very essence— as if it was happening in a different dimension that shared the same space. He was not himself, and yet, at the same

31

time, he was the most authentic self that he had ever been. No hiding, no pretense, and surprisingly, no guilt, fear, or shame. He was fully present and was allowed to watch a glorious spectacle.

A growing realization washed over him like a force was moving through his essence and into him. The sensation carried a warmth but more than just a feeling of heat. It differed from what the storm had forced through him, which produced no interconnection. A sense of love seared through him. Love unlike any he had experienced before. Pure, unmistakable affirmation. It was as if he had sought this genuine connection all his life. It was as if all the deficits of every single day of his existence had been summed up, and the entirety of that longing was now a single grain of sand lying at the bottom of the deepest ocean. Covered in this pure, unfettered acceptance.

Washed in this intense grace now flowing in and through his being, he realized that this was what he wanted from the start. What a glorious revelation. All the way back to his mother's breast, this is what he sought. It was so crystal clear to him in this magnificent instant. This always had been what he desired and now possessed for the first time. All his longings, groaning, striving, fighting, and escaping had been satisfied in a miraculous flash. Satisfied is not the sudden reality— maybe filled to all the fullness is closer to the truth. He knew he was precisely where he was supposed to be at that moment in time. This had been the place and time for his departure and had been decided before the foundations of the world were laid. From his new perspective, everything was perfect.

Another flash and boom. A significant tree was pushed over in the gale, landing on the shelter with a thud. While the tree fell, Bruce saw a flashing sword shove it a few inches to the left, leaving a burn in the bark.

Crack! Boom! The lightning was still on us as we held each other tighter. Rain poured over our heads and backs, soaking everything. The wind was fierce, tearing the old plastic bag into bits.

"I love you guys!" I said. "We're gonna be alright."

Suddenly, a dry-rotted branch from another oak tree crashed down and thudded Nan across her right shoulder and the back of her head. She went limp, toppling face-first into the mud and water that had gathered from the deluge. The blow bent her in half, and the weight of the fallen wood pinned her to the ground.

"NO!" Connie screamed from the bottom of her soul, grabbing for her sister. Pulling at her face.

I jumped up, pulled with all my might on the limb, and dragged it off to the side. Connie scrambled to turn her sister over, screaming and crying. I brushed the blonde hair from her face, then leaned in to feel the carotid artery on her neck.

"She is alive! There's a pulse!" I said.

Then I heard a sudden, deep, unmistakable crack. The hair on my body stood up with the flash.

There were now only two left on the island. Bruce knew the battle had taken place as it should.

A light was floating up through the trees in the darkness below. All Bruce could see was a back. The other was allowed to see what was happening in the battle below. Bruce knew this person. He did not have to see their face to know who climbed into the heavens to join him.

SEVEN

CHARITY'S PAIN

I stepped out of that world. There was no momentary pause as I moved up over the scene like I had walked out of a dark room into the light. Not an overwhelming light like the reflections off the water just a few hours before that had caused me temporary blindness, but an illumination where I could see everything around me. This light, this newly revealed but ever-present light, caused me to see magnificent things. Like a switch flipped, and I could see a world teeming with life, hope, and a Presence— even amid the storm. Swirling angelic beings shot past in majestic violence, tremendous swords lifted high over their heads. Their piercing eyes fixed on a dark foe. A battle raged on all around me, of which, five seconds before, I was oblivious.

I could see my wife try to protect her sister and hear her screams of agony as the falling tree drove my scorched body into a pile of broken bones. It was strange to see yourself, or at least your once visible self, from outside your own body. There was no struggle to get back or fix the girls' situation. I knew it was all within the realm of the love gripping me. Even in the chaos, I was at peace, or in peace— that may be a better description. I felt a tide of what I could only describe as love wash over me as I watched Connie struggle, scream, and curse against the raging wind.

She now held her sister's head, protecting her unconscious body, rocking back and forth, afraid to look at the broken tree next to her and the corpse she had married forty-two years ago. It was too much. She wept uncontrollably as the storm raged. Inside her heart, she asked a question that I could somehow hear. The whole universe heard— "Where are you, God?"

At that exact moment, I drifted higher, away from the swirling fight, rising next to someone familiar who had been watching the scene unfold. In that second, I heard— the universe heard— the booming whisper, "I Am Here." For the two on the island, it was muted by the storm.

I felt a loving hand rest on my shoulder, and as I rested my now flesh-free hand on it, my index finger dipped into the nail-carved hole in its palm. The rushing realization made me jump inside.

"Jesus, you are here in the middle of this!" I said without using audible words and turned to look. His deep eyes gazed into mine, and I was undone. Joy, miraculous joy, washed through me as he embraced me.

As I looked past Jesus' shoulder at Bruce, his smile was glorious, and we were ushered away. Glancing back toward the girls in the rain below, a slight ache arose inside our hearts. At that moment, Jesus said to his brothers, "I will never leave them or forsake them either," and we soared above the fray.

EIGHT

COLD CHARITY

"You should not have stood up!" Connie screamed. "You should not have stood up!" And again. And again. She was rocking with her sister's head in her lap, screaming into the wind. Blood was oozing out onto her forearm from Nan's skull. The blow from the tree had been swift and almost deadly. She could have been rocking her dead sister's body if it had been just a few inches left. But she was alive. She could feel the heat from Nan's core warming her legs when everything else was soaking wet with the cold wind and rain. She bent low several times to make sure there was still breath. Reaching over with her right hand, gently stroked her cheek and whispered in her ear that she loved her.

"Come back, Nan. I need you here with me," she said, trying to push the words through the sobs. Connie pressed gently on her neck, searching for her carotid artery just to make sure there was still a heartbeat. There was, yet it was weak. She was trying to understand if it was subdued because she was in shock or Nan was. Connie had endured the Red Cross first aid training every year for over twenty years because her job required it, and now was finally good for something real. Several years ago, she had used it to help a choking student but had never been in a desperate situation like this. Connie knew she needed to pull herself together to give them a chance to survive this swirling hell.

"Nan! Wake Up!" She found she gained more control of her mind by insisting her sister come to her. Reclaiming her thoughts from the shock that she had been swimming in for at least an hour was empowering. It was akin to forcing yourself to wake up after a nightmare, grasping for reality, fighting the fog.

37

The rain slowed to a steady soaking. The wind was almost gone, and the sky was no longer angry black, just a thick, sullen gray. The clouds were moving quickly out of the northeast, and the temperature had fallen dramatically from an hour ago. Emotion got the best of her for a few moments as she pondered how much had changed in just a few ticks of the clock. So many things could have been different.

"Bruce!" She said out loud in response to a sudden, powerful thought. Where was her brother-in-law? Maybe he would soon find them and bring the boat. He would know what to do with the pile of bones within three feet of her. She entertained the idea of reaching out and touching Craig's brown leather sandals. She picked out his footwear for him as a Father's Day gift just last year. His legs were gray now, no longer twitching like they had after the tree violently landed. The sound she didn't want to remember, but would never be able to forget, was the hollow crunching thud with a simultaneous groan through a forced expulsion of air. The sickening noise made her want to vomit again. It haunted her, making her feel like she had lost contact with reality. She would have melted into the forest floor next to him if she hadn't forced herself to focus on Nan. Now, she had to peel her mind away from the sadness to save her sister.

"Nan! Wake Up!" she shouted. Her legs had become numb, and the muscles in her back were beginning to seize up from leaning over to keep the rain out of Nan's face. Looking down, she noticed Nan's arms and legs were turning blue. Connie knew she had to try to get her out of the rain, but for the moment, she began vigorously rubbing her sister's bare skin, barking at her to wake up. Noticing the log that they all had sought shelter under initially, the one Craig had torn his face off to find was almost a couple of feet wide. She needed to move Nan back under. Sliding herself out from under her unconscious sister, laying her head down ever so softly. Swinging herself up to her knees as her ankle screamed in pain, she yelped and bit her lip. Working quickly to carefully straighten her sister out and positioned herself above her head so she could pull her by the armpits back under the downed tree. Tugging, heaving, and yelling in anger, she got Nan's body lined up below the rugged brown bark of the dead ash tree. Noticing the bark was pulling away from the trunk relatively quickly, she began tearing pieces off and covering Diana's blue legs. Connie wanted to protect her from the rain. More bark for her right side, then she just laid herself on Nan's left side to protect her and to warm her own frigid frame.

"Come On, Nanny. Come on, we can do this. You need to wake up so we can find Bruce and get back on the boat. When we find him we can get into some warm clothes hide under the canopy and figure out what to do. I need you to help me figure out what to do. Please Jesus, help us!" Tears reappeared, flowing from Connie's red eyes onto Nan's shoulder. Connie placed her hand on the back of her sister's head into her blood-soaked hair.

"Mimi would not have liked your hair-do," she whispered into her familiar ear, allowing one corner of her mouth to rise in a pseudo-smile. She was harkening back to their precious grandmother, who had passed a few years ago. Mimi invested considerable time, money, and energy to ensure her hair always looked just right. That gene, some might say a gene flaw, had been passed along in earnest to her three granddaughters.

"It feels like you have stopped bleeding Nanny but you have a huge lump on the back of your head! I think it is even bigger than the one Dad had on his head—you remember his bump." Referring to the benign growth under her father's scalp that had to have removed a few years before his death.

"I really miss him, Nan. I know you do too. I wonder if he's met..." her voice trailed off. Thinking about that was much too painful. Going down that road would be entering a whirlpool of despair and would do nothing to help her. But the pull toward the bottomless pit was strong. It was an easy place to return to, familiar territory. She had spent significant time living there, and it wasn't pretty.

At that moment, a nudging in her soul took her back a few years to a Sunday School lesson she had taught to a group of fifth graders. It was so long ago. How could she remember that here in the middle of this? Still, the words flowed from her lips, bubbling up out of the depths of her soul, "Humble yourselves, therefore, under the mighty hand of God so that at the proper time he may exalt you, casting all your anxieties on him, because he cares for you. Be sober-minded; be watchful. Your adversary the devil prowls around like a roaring lion, seeking someone to devour. Resist him."

She repeated it as a growing light inside of her revealed the truth of her situation. Hope flickered inside her like a small candle in a distant window. Now she shouted the scripture verse into the wind, lost in the moment and clinging to its promise.

"I'm so cold," Nan whispered.

"DIANA!" Immediate tears flowed from Connie.

"Thank You, God! I thought I had lost you too!" Suddenly, hope rushed in to fill the space between them.

"My head hurts Con."

"A tree branch fell on you and knocked you out cold. I think it hit your shoulder first because you already have a nasty bruise," Connie could barely contain herself.

Diana looked past her sister's intense hug, trying to focus her blurry vision and reaching up to feel the knot on the back of her head. That is when she saw her brother-in-law's gray legs and torso. From this angle, the fallen brown tree covered his shoulders and head. A wave of horror tore through her heart as she grabbed onto her little sister.

"Oh my God! What happened? When? You've been here all alone!"

They both wailed as waves of sorrow and fear crashed on the shore of their wounded hearts.

It was too much, and Nan suddenly pushed away, turning her head, and wretched out her lunch. Her skull felt like it wanted to explode. Wiping her face, another genuine fear pierced her soul.

"Where is Bruce?"

"I don't know," Connie said as she lay in a heap, sobbing and freezing.

The rain had slowed to a sprinkle as grief drove the two together. The sisters held each other like when they were young and shared the same bed, hiding under the covers during a thunderstorm. Although Connie claims those times made her feel claustrophobic, she needed her Nan closer than ever for the warmth, sure, but more for her presence, confidence, and connection. Nan had always been a central part of her life. In a split second it took her back to a simple time, an era that made sense— because this island's reality had become so surreal.

Neither of them measured the time they spent under that tree. Yet, someone kneeling right next to them added up all the tears. His righteous arms were wrapped entirely around them in their grief like they had grown in length according to their need. Their loss gripped his heart, and he cried for their ache.

———————◄O►——————

Unbeknownst to the sobbing sisters, a score of immense warriors held a perimeter around the intense battle scene. Most of the eighteen-foot-tall creatures had yet to sheathe their seven-foot-long swords. Those offensive weapons were four inches thick and a foot wide at the handle. They throbbed with an internal energy that shone like transparent chrome. Several were dripping with a thick black tar-like substance, confirming contact with the agents of the dark. Each warrior had a battle-scarred shield that clung snugly to their left forearms. They gleamed like polished gold In the sun and were smeared with the black, gooey substance. Their gigantic wings spanned thirty feet and were held at the ready, waiting to soar back into formation if need be.

Two soldiers inside the circle were being tended to by several tiny magnificent creatures. The Serfs, as they were affectionately called by the troopers, were covered in what can only be described as hair that looked as if it was floating in water. These golden green creatures were all busy sewing up wounds on the warriors with an intense lime green light emanating from wand-like devices in each of their eight hands. There were several large gashes on Ollie's arm from what appeared to be bite marks. Biggs had a significant right shoulder laceration that would undoubtedly lay him up for weeks.

Captain Amadan thanked the wounded warriors for their gallantry in battle, assuring them that the two Shiner transfers were on him while placing an affirming hand on their backs.

"This one is on me, boys. This one is on me," he said while the sad realization moved deeper inside him. Amadan insisted that the rest of the unit, which was now made up of members of two Ready-Squads plus a couple of escorts who happened to be in the sector, plus his own troopers, stand at the ready, secure the perimeter and be alert for any signs of the enemy. After all, this was Cast's domain, and they could inflict severe damage if they returned with the massive herd that had just rolled over the island. Amadan was seething and angry at himself for missing the signs of the attack, and he knew he would have to answer for the mistake. Two Transfers on an otherwise calm day would cost him something, and he knew it. He silently prayed it wouldn't be a demotion back to San Francisco.

"Please God, not that again," he whispered.

However, there was a growing consensus among the winged brothers, with the unspoken thought that most of the fighting for this day was behind them. Still, they remained vigilant in the search, not wanting to be caught off guard. Scanning in all directions with their disproportionally large eyes, which had turned red with righteous indignation during the action, they were now beginning to cool to an intense purple. Aware of the kneeling King in their ranks, they were decidedly alert to their duties. A pure other-worldly focus drove them as they began to calm down from the battle, secured by His presence.

<hr />

The rain was gone, but a light breeze pushed the chill deep into the two shivering sisters.

"We have got to get up off this ground before we freeze to death," Connie whispered.

"My head is pounding," Nan said as she reached back to feel the knot on her swollen skull. Her shoulder was aching, and a wet scab was entangled with her mud-covered hair. She leaned over and rubbed her grieving sister's back to try and warm her, but this made her feel light-headed and dizzy. She knew she must have a concussion and concluded that walking around would be difficult.

"How is your ankle?" she asked.

"It is sore but I think the fact that I am freezing has kept the swelling down." Connie said, slowly touching her bruised leg.

"I lost my flip-flops."

"I have to go find Bruce," Nan said, now more determined to take some action. Crawling under the tree to the other side, she tried to stand up and nearly fell over, reaching for the log. Connie crawled through and got to one knee. She stood up next to Nan, clutching the tree with her uninjured foot as a base. Connie let out a slight groan as she tested the injured ankle.

The breeze made them shiver as they stood, trying to get their bearings. Shaking violently, they knew they had to move around to warm up, or hypothermia could incapacitate them, even on a summer day. They held onto each other, one dizzy, the other limping, and trudged away from the smashed body under the tree. Forcing their way through the thick underbrush, they fought hard for every step. Shivering, hobbling, grabbing, and pushing branches to forge a path. Their filthy swimsuits were taking a beating from the thorns, broken twigs, and brambles.

Warm tears fell down Diana's cold cheeks as she considered the fate of her husband. This certainly wasn't like Bruce to take so long. He was always prompt. She knew something had gone wrong and tried to brace herself for the sobering reality of whatever awaited her.

This pain took her back almost seventeen years to another waiting time. She'd gotten a call from her frantic mother at two in the morning. Dad was missing. It was in the same lake a hundred miles north of here. He and his buddy Al went out in the evening trying to take advantage of an early Steelhead fishing season when a horrendous storm raced across from Canada. No one knew where they were. The Sheriff's Department and the Coast Guard searched the icy waters. The waiting went on for three days before the bodies were found. Diana couldn't allow herself to emotionally go there right now.

"Not now, not now!" she whispered to herself. Fighting against the desperation, she wiped her face with her grungy hand and kept moving forward.

"I have to keep going," she thought. Her wounded head and shoulder pounded with every heartbeat. Her breath smelled like puke, and dirt was smeared everywhere. She held her sister a little tighter now.

"How are you doing, Nan?" Connie asked.

"One step at a time, Con. One step at a time," Nan said, trying hard to focus on the here and now while fighting blurry vision.

"Is this the way back to the beach?" Connie wondered aloud— directions were never her strong suit, especially now, walking through a fog of trauma.

"Its an island, we will get there one way or another," Nan said with a half smile.

Another five minutes and they pushed through the last thickets and spilled onto a narrow sandy beach. Disoriented, they stood looking out into the angry lake with the cool breeze against their faces. The rain had stopped. The water was a thick gray as low pregnant clouds overhead were pushed along by a northeast wind. Small whitecaps dotted the entire horizon as water splashed their filthy feet. They had only been on the island a few hours, but it had felt like an eternity. Everything ached. Physically, mentally, emotionally, and spiritually, they felt like they had been through a supernatural hurricane and lost.

"Let's go left, Con, I think that is the way to the boat," Nan said, fighting through a stale brain.

"Come on, Bruce has to be just a few minutes away," Connie said to inspire her sister.

"If he is just sitting there drinking a beer, I am gonna be so ticked off," she said, hoping it would be true.

"He probably has his feet up, listening to the the radio and wondering where we are," Connie said with a grin.

"I'd kill him," Nan said with an indignant tone and realized it was the worst thing she could have said.

Connie squeezed her sister tighter around the waist and leaned her head into her.

"I am sorry, Con. Sorry for the whole mess," Diana said, tearing up again.

"Let's find Bruce," was all Connie could muster. She desperately tried to keep a tight lid on her emotions, but her head wanted to explode. Connie felt like her heart was dragging in the sand behind them as they walked down the beach. She tried to pick it up and lock it away but didn't have the strength. Part of her wanted to curl up beside her husband and go to sleep with him by that tree. The pain in her ankle reminded her that she was alive and needed to be brave for Diana. They would have to be strong for each other.

Progress was slow along the beach; minutes felt like hours as they stepped over driftwood and rocks through the soggy sand. Numbness had set into every part of them as they approached the cove where the boat had been anchored.

"We get around these trees up ahead and I think the boat should be there," Diana said.

Nudging the cedar branches aside, the shallow cove was in front of them, but no red boat was anchored twenty-some yards off the beach. Bewilderment rushed through their minds. Instantly, a million questions shot into them like a jolt from smelling salts. Diana let go of her sister to speed ahead, scanning furiously down the beach, out in the lake to the west. Her brain was moving too fast, pounding, reeling, flailing. Her eyes were searching everywhere and seeing nothing. Her vision was a little blurry, and more so with the running. The ingrained image of her boat was not registering anywhere.

"DIANA!" Connie shrieked.

NINE

CHARITY'S DISASTER

Nan spun around to look at her yelling sister, who she could barely recognize in her current state of mind. She was pointing out in the water. As Diana focused her attention, she finally realized the hull of her baby sticking up through the lake's surface. Horror swept through her like a mighty wind, driving her to her knees. She wrapped her arms around herself and screamed with primal fury. Connie finally caught up to her and threw herself on her sobbing sister, trying to comfort her with her presence; not knowing what to say herself, she held on, cried, and cried out to God with all the pain surging through her.

"Jesus, help us. Please God, come close," she whispered into Diana's sandy ear and God's heart.

The bridge of the Shogun was a complete disaster. Many crew members had been knocked to the deck and tried to recover their bearings amid the numbing confusion. All the carnage had happened so fast and had come out of nowhere. Smoke now billowed out from every instrument panel high and low, swallowing the entire area in an eerie tan fog. Lights flashed from emergency beacons on the interior walls, enhancing the dramatic effect. It was chaos as everyone pushed to fend for themselves. On the edge of complete panic the crew was clawing, shoving, and fighting for life.

Commander Cryptus had a large gash across his knotty forehead that was oozing thick black tar. It was running into his left eye, causing searing pain to shoot through his head. Grasping for the navigator's panel directly in front of him, he wiped at his newest battle scar, knowing that he had to regain composure to control the growing mutiny of panic. Pulling himself up, he choked out a cough that felt like a lung had been suddenly and irrevocably displaced. Stammering to regain his voice, he finally spoke into the chaos.

"Return to your posts, NOW!" he bellowed so loud the floor of the ship shook. "This is how the enemy wins every time! They want us to turn on each other and think of only ourselves. Well, that ends right NOW!" He screamed so loud his voice broke with an adolescent squeal.

"You two, get the extinguishers and begin putting the fires out," he said as he pointed to the nearest sailors. Reports from every area on the ship began barking out over the intercom, and none offered any hope.

"Reactor room reporting...," the comm broke up slightly, "we have lost all power and have switched to back up."

"Weapons off-line, sir," barked another.

"Shields destroyed," and on and on the reports came. "Hull breach in sector six," piercing the Commander's dark soul with wave after wave of bad news.

"You," he barked at a lowly, bent-over sailor coughing next to him, "find the main breaker and kill the power."

"Sir, that will lock us all on the bridge!" said that panic-stricken junior officer.

"DO IT NOW!" Thundered Cryptus with disgust.

"What was the weapon the Pluck used against us, Commander?" Asked another shaken sailor through a half-stifled cough.

"It wasn't a Pluck weapon that disabled this ship... it was Carne," which was decidedly worse for the Commander and the Herd. The newest and most technologically advanced ship in the entire fleet lay disabled at the bottom of the lake.

"Prepare to abandon the ship," Cryptus said as he lowered his gaze in defeat; this was his only move.

In that instant, a disturbingly maniacal thought gripped the dejected Commander. The ship may be lost, but that didn't mean this battle was over.

"Send every Archer we can muster to that damnable island and destroy the two Carne left!" The booming sadistic laugh echoed throughout the corpse of a ship.

Within moments, panic reigned supreme in the crew's lives as they were forced to leave the safety of the doomed Shogun, exposing themselves to the soul-severing swords of the ruthless Pluck. The other-worldly screams pierced the silent lake bed as they scurried out of the escape hatches toward the surface in utter terror.

"Nan, think about it. All we know right now is that the boat is upside down in the lake. We don't know anything more than that. We have got to pull ourselves together. I will go out to the boat and check it out. Look, there are some things washed up on the shore down there. You go get them; we may need them to stay on this island tonight. Grab everything you see." She reached over, gently took her sister's face and looked deeply into her bright blue eyes. "We can do this, Nan, if we do one thing at a time. We must focus, even one minute at a time, one thought at a time."

"You are right, Con; we can cry later," Diana said as she got to her feet, wiping her face. "Let's go out to the boat together," as she grabbed Connie's hand and made their way into the water.

"It feels warm!" Connie said as they leaned forward into the inland sea, leaving a sandy, muddy plume in their wake as they swam toward the wreckage.

"I feel nasty," Con said to her sister.

"You've got mud on the whole side of your head," Nan pointed out.

"Gross," is all that came out from Connie's lips as she felt the nappy hair, which forced her to duck under the little waves and scrub the dirt free. Diana did the same, trying to avoid the massive lump on the back of her skull.

Two hundred yards of casual swimming relaxed them. The waves of grief subsided as they had a new momentary focus for their thoughts.

"We have to grab everything we can, Connie," Nan stated as the lake deepened to about four feet. The ribbed white hull was getting close. They began swimming through an oily surface film.

"I smell gas," Connie said.

"Don't get it in your mouth," Nan replied.

"Or your eyes," Connie said.

Walking became the more accessible mode as they used their hands to push the floating film away from them.

Diana's baby was entirely submerged except for about a foot of the white hull sticking out above the water facing south. The weight of the iron motor kept the stern firmly ensconced in the lake. It bobbed with the rhythm of the cove as the torn anchor line snaked away from the scene like a white water moccasin. A hollow clunk sounded from the diving platform, banging into a boulder.

"I am going to take a look, Nan," Connie insisted. She thought if Bruce's body was somehow lodged beneath the boat, she should be the one to find it instead of her sister. Nan understood and acknowledged with a curt nod.

Grabbing a deep breath, Connie dove under the side of the boat and came up in the middle between the inverted seats into an air pocket. It was eerily dark as only a dim gray light was reflected through the water. The Yeti cooler greeted her by banging into the back of her head. It stank of fuel. So many things were floating around her now. All this stuff was hard to make out in the low luminescence and a foreign context.

Everything was upside-down, and orienting her mind around this new reality proved difficult. Her eyes burned, and she couldn't breathe through her nose, which caused her to cough.

"Are you alright?" Came the muffled question from her concerned sister.

Looking around, she did not see what she was so afraid of finding floating with the debris. She knew she had to be the one to search and was desperately fighting to hold down her fear of tight spaces.

"It's dark in here, Nan. But I don't see Bruce," she said.

With the all-clear, Diana joined her sister in the dark underbelly of the ill-fated craft. A deep sadness once again washed over her, seeing her baby in such a state.

"We can't stay under here very long Nan," Connie said.

"Let's grab everything we can and shove it out on the beach side so we can gather it up," Nan said, taking charge.

The Yeti had to be opened, and water was let in so it would submerge beneath the side of the boat. Diana felt her way to the storage compartment in front of the seat next to the pilot's chair. She knew that everyone's essential belongings lay inside. As Nan opened the lid, keys, change, phones, and other heavy objects headed to the bottom.

Reaching in, she felt all around the lunchbox-sized area and grinned when her hand fell on top of a metallic object she knew was from her brother-in-law's pocket. She remembered he had given her his ever-present black work knife at the dock for safekeeping. It was one of those you could replace the blade with a fresh throw-away whenever needed. They both needed fresh air, so they escaped the boat's captivity.

"Con, I found Craig's knife!" Then she realized those words might sting her sister.

Connie was happy and holding another real treasure for the duo— a lighter.

"We may need this too," she said.

After several round trips from the beach to the boat, they had recovered almost everything they could find, even a couple of water-logged phones off the bottom. Connie had located the blue jeans and sweater she had brought along on the day trip in case she got cold later in the evening. Everything was drenched in oily lake water but would dry someday. Nan had found Craig's gray Detroit Tiger hooded sweatshirt and her thin black shorts.

The latched Yeti was a treasure trove of goodies, including two leftover sandwiches, seven light beers, five bottles of water, four individual Cheetos snack bags, four Nature Made Fig bars, and even some Chex-Mix in a Ziploc bag. They drained the water from the cooler to preserve the remaining ice and tried to rinse the oil from everything. They hung the clothes after ringing them out as best as they could in a couple of bushes on the beach's edge. They placed the coveted knife and lighter on the top of the cooler, trusting that they would remain safe, as they ensured the latch was secured.

One more foray out into the sea, and they could then figure out what to do next. Connie's "one-thing-at-a-time" mindset had helped them focus on what was needed, pushing off the grieving and questioning to a future moment. A different moment. They had to retrieve whatever was left of the canopy for shelter. The fact that it was bright red could be a factor in getting someone's attention to the reality they were alive on the island.

Ten

The Cost of Charity

"Cap, we have movement a half a klick north," Gilboa chirped.

"Take Ready-Squad One and go!" Amadan commanded the Sargent. The seven soldiers pulled hard at the air simultaneously with their immense wings, causing an immediate downward blast that sent several of the hairy Serfs flying in all directions. The few that could hang onto something were flapping horizontally in the sudden hurricane-force gale. If the situation had been different, Halek would have had more than a few jokes to toward the determined medics.

"Tic, you're my commander of Ready Squad Two; get at ready," Amadan said.

"Sir," was the only response required as that team powered up.

"Halek, get comms up, one-klick observation post," Amadan insisted. This sent the warrior to an altitude of one kilometer above the fight to observe what Gilboa's team was doing and keep the JOCC informed of the situation as it developed. He dialed up his transparent camouflage and headed for the brightest spot in the sky.

Amadan pointed at the escort closest to him, who had shown up during the previous fight, "What's your name, soldier?"

"Sargent Bapps, reporting for duty Sir," the young warrior had gone rigid in attention.

"Haven't we served together Bapps?" Amadan asked.

"Yes Sir, Croatia, about twenty turns ago," Bapps was obviously impressed with the Captain's memory.

"Right," the memory was accurate in the Captain's mind.

"You," pointing at the other much beefier escort.

"Private Igor Lirionov, Iggy is what everyone calls me, sir."

"Alright, Iggy. You and Bapps here have Shiner duty. You need to understand—nothing touches those two!" Amadan was insistent, eyes blazing red as his gaze burned through the two warriors.

"Roger," Bapps snapped.

"Sir," Iggy said. They swooped low, drawing their swords, tempting any filthy Cast maggot to try to get close to their Shiners. The two sisters huddled on the beach, crying in each other's arms.

"Cap there must be several hundred or more coming out of the lake!" Gilboa barked.

"Go Tic, NOW!" Amadan shot over the communicator.

"Gone," Tic said as the seven of them launched out from around the Serfs, which sent half of them flying, causing a chorus of high-pitched squeals as they fought to regain their orientation and dignity in the sudden wind.

Ollie drew his sword from the sheath, pushing the remaining metallic green medics away. Due to his deep shoulder injury, Biggs had to abandon his shield and grab his weapon with his left hand. Both were ready to jump into the mix at the Captain's word.

"Hold on boys," Amadan said calmly to the two eager veterans.

"Engaging now Cap," Gilboa grunted over the comm.

The communicator sparked to life with reports from the battle and from Helek floating above. The Cast sailors were no match for the ferocity of the winged warriors. Swords flashed like exploding magnesium, and limbs flew off in all directions as the wounded fell back into the water, trailing black plumes into the lake. Shrieks and blood-curdling curses were coming through every warrior's comm unit from the massive damage they inflicted upon the retreating, light-ly-armed Cast sailors.

"This is a good day!" Some over-enthusiastic warrior shouted.

"Sir, they are abandoning a ship on the lake bed," Tic barked into his comm unit.

"Send two in to have a look-see," Amadan chirped.

"Roger Cap," Tic said and commanded two from the Ready Team to swoop in.

"Helek, ask JOCC if they have anything on Cast ships operating in the sector," Amadan said. "And Helek, ask them to ready a Jumper, just in case."

"On it," Helek responded with his words, and inwardly, he lurched with the seriousness of the command. A Jumper.

"Dang," was all he could think.

"Shogun, the side marking say it's the Shogun, Cap." Tic relayed this from his two guys who were investigating the ship.

"Relay that to JOCC, Helek," Amadan insisted.

Two seconds later, "JOCC just Shifted in another Ready Team Captain, directly to the ship," Helek replied. "It's the newest ship in the Cast fleet according to Command and they want the third team on site to have a look-see."

"Roger that," Amadan smiled as the massacre rolled on.

"The ship is on fire!" Someone barked into the Comm.

"I confirm the smoke, Cap," another voice said plainly.

In that very second, at least a thousand tiny arrows were launched from every direction toward the Shiners wading in the lake, even from beneath the two girls. There was only so much Bapps and Iggy could do to intercept the flaming missiles and the streaking little rats everywhere. The warrior's swords cut through a dozen or more at a time, and flapping wings knocked several hundred off course, but there were just too many to stop.

Reaching the boat, the women moved to the far side for the first time and found the canopy floating in the water. It clung to the hull by a few snaps that had held, and the rest flapped through the lake like a graceful jellyfish billowing in the waves majestically suspended between the gray surface and the sandy bottom. Nan reached up and unsnapped the final three buttons.

Connie held her mouth as she noticed a body face down in the water about thirty feet away. She gasped and reached for Nan.

Diana noticed the horror on Connie's face and turned to identify the source.

"NO! NO! NO!" She screamed and began to run through the water to him.

Connie let go of the other end of the canopy and pushed through the water as tears ran down her face. Her heart broke in that instant all over again, this time for the pain that her closest friend in the world was now feeling.

Nan yelled and ran to Bruce, hoping for a miracle and knowing people didn't breathe under the water. He was face down, slumped over a rock that was just breaking the water's surface. She knew he was gone and threw herself at his cold, lifeless body, wailing against reality. Connie drew up behind her and hugged her sister as they wept in a heap.

"This makes no sense!" Nan screamed. "Both of them are dead, why?"

"Father, we don't understand this. We hate this. Help us, God, please help us," Connie prayed over her sister and for her own sanity. Insanity had come knocking.

A few minutes later, as they turned his body over, they saw the open wound on his pale forehead. They closed his eyes as Diana rubbed his face.

"Pooch, why did you leave me?" That was all she could say as she kissed his cold, wet cheek. "Why did you go?" A deep groan welled up inside of her.

As a hospice nurse for thirty years, Diana was well acquainted with death. Perhaps better than most, she understood that death is a part of life on this planet. No one escapes this sobering reality. Over the years, she had talked to thousands of people about losing someone close. Offering comfort and compassion to the suffering was a central part of who she was and what she identified with as basic human kindness.

The closest experience to losing Bruce had been the tragedy of losing her beloved father. Being able to finally see her dad's body lying on that gurney was both challenging and healing at the same time. It took the Coast Guard three agonizing days to find the bodies just fifty yards from shore. Unfortunately, their tan bibs and coats blended with the sandy lake bottom. The search and rescue teams had gone over the top of the two men at least ten times before a helicopter discovered their inverted bodies bobbing off the lake bed. She had wondered more than just a few times how it would have been different if the bodies were never recovered. She concluded that the healing process was better with closure because open wounds of unknown varieties can drive people crazy. So, in that thought, she was thankful for the grace of knowing and seeing what was left of her Bruce.

"We can't leave him out in the water Nan," Connie whispered to her sister, sitting beside the corpse.

"We have got to get him off of this rock," she replied. "You know its funny Con, he always said that he wanted to be buried with his butt sticking up in the air."

"That is why he has that tattoo of the red lips on his rear end," Connie smiled.

Nan laughed out loud. "That is how we found you Pooch," she said to him. "Telling the world to kiss you where the sun don't shine!"

They both laughed out loud and started crying all over again. Bruce was gone, and he left them to clean up the mess.

"Kinda makes me mad, Nan. Craig and Bruce get heaven, and we are stuck on this stupid, stinky island without even a boat to get home in," Connie said through tears.

"You're right Connie, it makes me mad too," Nan replied.

"Now we have to bury them both without a shovel," Connie pointed out.

"I think we have an oar stowed on the boat in the side compartment by the pilot's seat. We can use it as a shovel," Nan thought again. Planning how they could make it for a few days or longer. Who knew how long they would be stuck in the middle of the lake. A penetrating and stifling spiritual darkness settled in around them. Desperation pushed at their soul. Fear was triggered in their hearts, and they reached out and clung to one another as the invisible arrows found their target.

ELEVEN

CHARITY'S CEMETERY

How Cryptus and most of his executive staff escaped through the slaughter was something he didn't understand. The entire executive staff had exited the Shogun through the escape portal on the western-facing side of the ship. Trying to keep the Shogun between them and the Pluck, hoping for some cover. They had clawed undetected along the lake bed for several hundred yards before some of the junior officers' panic got the best of them. Two younger sailors shot straight up into the sky, hoping to find more cover in the clouds. They were immediately cut in half with the same massive glowing sword strike. The pile of body parts fell into the lake, and the thick black blood muddied the waters. Cryptus, seizing the opportunity, stepped into the plume and let the current slowly carry them away from the murderous scene, undetected by the Pluck.

An hour later, the six took shelter in the dingy, dark bottom of a hollow metal lighthouse in the middle of the bay's shipping channel.

"Oh the irony of hiding in a lighthouse," smirked the arrogant General to no one but himself. He used the time to concoct his elaborate alibi to avoid responsibility for the loss of the Shogun.

"Certainly," he mused, *"the War Counsel could understand the plight of the battle with the fog of war and all. Two Carne targets transferred would count for something,"* he thought and hoped. Besides, the archers were waging a competent hit-and-run terror campaign on the remaining targets. Yes, he knew he was grasping at straws, and Cryptus also knew he was still in one piece. "Besides," he quipped, "ships are built quicker than Generals."

"Pull, Nan, pull," said the grunting, pushing sister as they tried to dislodge Bruce's body from the rocks.

"Why is this so hard?" Diana shot back.

"Wait, wait, wait," Connie insisted.

They both were breathing hard and beginning to warm up a bit from all the exertion.

"It always looks so easy on T.V. Soldiers just lifting their friends up over their shoulders like a bag of rice," Nan said.

"Well, they would be much younger and in better shape than us Nanny," Connie said, breathing heavily.

Both were standing with their hands on their hips and trying to catch the breath that seemed to allude to them.

"Hang on! Fight with all your might!" The miniature voice squealed out to his cohorts as the tiny Cast troopers fought to salvage part of this disastrous day's events.

"The commanding General gave us direct orders to disrupt, annoy, and attack in any way possible these two Carne scum. We will fulfill our orders today. We will fight these two imposters with everything we have!"

A less than half-hearted cheer arose from the panting group.

"We should launch some missiles, we are so close to them we could hit them easily," one voice whispered among the group.

"The Pluck are too close, you idiot! As soon as we launched they would pulverize our brains into the bottom of this lake," the first tiny soldier shot back. "Now shut up. We need to dig in so we can wear them down and later tonight we can attack when the conditions are in our favor!"

"Let's try the both of us getting on the same side and pushing under his armpit to roll him off of the rock," Connie said.

"I am just so tired Con. My head is pounding, I couldn't find the little First Aid kit on the boat to get some aspirin. I know I have a concussion from that stupid tree branch. I know we can't leave him out here either, I am just so tired," tears welled up again as she gently rubbed her temple. Connie reached out and hugged her bruised sister.

"Father, we need your help," she prayed out loud. "Could you send us your Spirit to give us the strength we need to do this. We hate this Lord, and we know you are here with us in the middle of our disaster. Please God we so desperately need you. Don't abandon us, give us courage to face what is in front of us in this moment. In Jesus' name I pray Father."

"Amen," Nan responded.

Fifteen minutes later, they each had an arm and made the final heave up to the top of the beach. The boat canopy, which had a small tear, a couple of white seat cushions, and the oar were all daisy-chained to Bruce's leg with the remnants of the anchor rope and were just reaching the beach.

"I will get the canopy and the rest of the stuff up on the beach; you take a break," Connie said to her sister. She reached down and untied the former anchor rope from around Bruce's blue leg and began to tug the canopy ashore until the seat cushions and oar were all up out of the water together. Limping to those rescued items, Connie untied the rope and threw them onto the shore beside the cooler. Tears again welled as she looked at Diana.

"Where did all of these tears come from?" she wondered.

"I don't cry," Connie thought.

Connie watched as Nan removed Bruce's black POW-MIA t-shirt from the back pocket of his swim trunks. She shook the sand out, kissed him on the cheek, draped his favorite shirt over his face, and gently patted his chest affectionately. Hanging her head while sobbing, heavy tears dropped onto his lifeless body.

"Waa, waa, waa," Connie thought while gathering the rope. The tears rose up over the edge of her eyelids and spilled. That is how she often teased Craig whenever he got emotional during a movie or song or sometimes during a silly commercial. He was always so quick to shed a tear. Connie smiled at the memory. Limping back up the beach, now on the other side of Bruce's body, she started quietly digging with the oar.

Knowing they needed to get the body underground so the flies and creepy things wouldn't begin to eat the rotting flesh, she pushed the silky soft sand away with the sturdy white plastic oar. It was slow going but better than just using your hands to claw at the sand. She had hoped to get the hole deep enough to cover Bruce before she hit solid rock or even water. The almost silent digging and the not-so-quiet sobbing continued for at least an hour before Connie opened the Yeti quickly to get a bottle of water to share between them.

"Here Nan," she said in a quiet tone. "You need to drink some of this."

Nan had been laying her head on Bruce's mid-section and sat up slowly. She mouthed a silent "thank you" to her sister while taking the cold bottle. Noticing for the first time the hole Connie was standing in was past her knees.

"Wow, Con, you have been really working," she said, pointing with her chin while wiping sand off her face and head.

"The oar really helped it go faster."

"This really tastes good. I guess I was thirsty," Nan said while passing the half-empty bottle back.

"We have got to start thinking about getting more water since there are only four left," Connie said as she put the lid back on the thin plastic bottle.

"You need to drink that. You've been working hard, and it doesn't make sense to get dehydrated now," Nan put on her nurse's hat.

"Too late, I already am," she replied.

"Drink it," Diana said with all the authority of the oldest sister.

Connie downed the water in two big gulps and resealed the lid.

"We need to bury him, Nan," she said.

"I know," came the sobering reply.

When they forced his body into the hole, they said goodbye after Nan's final kiss on his cold, sandy face, then replaced the t-shirt. Both sisters began pushing sand over the corpse, figuring this would be a temporary solution and not his last resting place. Putting sand over the body was challenging because everything inside of them wanted Bruce to breathe again, making the simple task impossible. The sobering reality was striking for both of them.

Nan talked about the two grave plots Bruce had recently bought from a close friend living down the street from the cottage. Those plots were only twenty miles from the beach where they were digging sand. They both admitted they had expected to outlive their husbands. Still, they never would have guessed in a million years they would be physically burying them, especially on a day that started in a boat on a beautiful summer morning.

Fifteen minutes later, they had accomplished the burial. Diana simply lay on the top of the pile. Connie prayed in hushed tones over them both and sat rubbing her sister's back as she wept.

"I have been praying so much today, God. Just thank you for listening to me. I am sorry I have been so distant for way too long. I feel ashamed that it took a day like this to wake me up again. I am angry. I don't understand any of this. But thank you for waking me, Father," Connie was barely whispering, even unheard by Diana. While her head was bowed, she noticed the bright blue-green hue that had gathered at her ankle, which was throbbing after all of the efforts of the burial.

"We have got to do something about making a camp Nan," she said to her now quiet sister.

"I know Con, five more minutes then we can go," she said with a muffled voice because her face was in her arms directly over the middle of the sand pile.

"I am going to go and and try to find a place somewhere close," she said. "Take your time."

"OK," was the only reply.

"Bye Bruce," and Connie was off on the hunt.

TWELVE

CAMP CHARITY

"Captain Amadan, excellent job, Sir!" Said General Sikes in a booming voice as he slapped the Captain's back with an exuberance Amadan had never witnessed.

"I am recommending you, Sir, for an immediate promotion to Major! The way your team captured the ship, stopping the self-destruct detonation with only ten seconds remaining, was an extraordinary act of courage," said Sikes. He was proud of his men, and his short stature seemed to lengthen as he paced back and forth. As the Commander of the Lakes Sector, he had the power to promote warriors as he saw fit.

"Sir, that was the valiant work of Sargent Gilboa," the new Major proudly responded.

"Sargent Gilboa, front and center," the General requested.

"Sir, yes Sir," Gilboa responded by snapping to attention, heels clicking together.

"Thank you Sargent for your bravery, as soon as the paperwork goes through you will become this sector's first Sargent-Major. A well deserved promotion!" The General warmly embraced the tired warrior.

"Thank You, sir, that is very kind," replied the embarrassed and decidedly uncomfortable Sargent-Major.

"Warriors, the treasure trove of enemy information our Intel teams are gleaning from that new ship will help turn the violent tide in this sector. The work you have done here today is noteworthy and deeply appreciated. We expect to discover many secrets as we pry into her underbelly," he said. "Hopefully, circumstances will warrant you to get an extended leave from here in a few week's time. Keep up the good work Major Amadan," The happy General saluted, turned, and departed with his team in a flash, even before the return hails from Amadan's warriors were recognized fully.

"Good job boys," Amadan said proudly. "Let's remember we still have got a couple of Shiners to watch!"

"Looks like they are even brighter now." Helek pointed out the increased glow covering the sisters.

———— ◆◇◆ ————

Connie stretched out the canopy over the anchor rope she and Nan had strung between two trees. It was going to be plenty big enough for the two of them. The ground was sandy on the top of the wooded incline they were calling home for the night. It was only fifty feet as the crow flies from the "graveyard" beach. Still, they had to skirt around the thickets like they had done when they first arrived on shore— walking several hundred feet to get to the spot. The women had cleared out an area and moved all their worldly possessions to the hill over the last few hours. Then Connie was busy making a shelter out of the canopy. After she had pulled the wet and sand-covered tarp over the rope, then found four sturdy sticks to hold the ropes up. They had taken the braids apart from a piece of the anchor rope to use, so she used the three parts of the new smaller cord to tie down the tarp's corners, stretching it out tight so rain would roll off.

The deconstructed seat cushions were hanging from a few branches unzipped. The inner foam had been wrung out and the vinyl covers were allowed to dry in the cool island breeze.

Nan had hauled some dead wood for a fire and a dozen or so rocks for the fire ring. Connie thought she was off looking for some birch bark or pine sap to start a fire, while she was left to tackle the tarp. It was getting late in the evening, and they both knew building a shelter was their top priority, and the fire was a close second.

Diana was searching for the bark and sap, and she was also carrying the oar. She was on a mission back to the original fallen tree shelter on the other side of the island. She hoped to cut through the forest instead of walking around. Knowing her sister could sleep better if Craig's body had been covered like Bruce's had. She knew it was the right thing to do, even though there were more pressing things to accomplish back at camp. Nan didn't want her sister to have to come over to bury her husband tomorrow after a bunch of vultures or other rodents had chewed into it. It would be hard enough to get the broken tree off later, so for now, she was determined to cover Craig with as much sand as she could dig with an oar and a headache.

About ninety minutes later, an exhausted Diana rolled back into camp.

"Wow, Con! Look at you! It looks amazing," she said to her sister, who was arranging the rocks into a circle for a fire ring.

"Building blanket forts and tents with the grandkids really helped," she said rather happily. "Did you find it?"

"It looks great, and yes," Diana said as she put down a couple of football-sized pieces of white birch bark, one of which had several globs of sticky pine tar.

Within half an hour, the fire leaped from the ring as the two girls warmed themselves while splitting a turkey sandwich from the cooler. They also opened one icy light beer and shared it between them.

"We better ration these," Connie said, while taking a swig from the slender white can, not knowing how long they would endure on the island.

"At least we found a spot that doesn't stink from all of those dang birds," Diana said.

"Hey, I wonder if we could find a nest that may have some eggs, I mean if we had to," said Connie.

"Eggs would be great, we'd have to figure out a way to boil them," Nan said

"There has to be something on the boat we could use for a pan," Connie said.

"What about some empty cans in the fire?"

"Yes, I think it could work!"

"We could even eat the stinking birds if we had to Con," Nan said.

"I think I would have to get a lot hungrier to do that," Connie replied with a scrunched-up face. "Besides, someone will be looking for us real soon, right?"

"Yeah. With the white hull sticking out of the water should give someone a clue," Diana said.

The two hugged side by side in front of the fire, watching the mesmerizing flames and saying nothing as the day replayed in their heads. The fire's warmth and the flames' dance gently rocked them to sleep on the ground. Their limit for accomplishments had been found. It was all they could possibly do in one long day.

The morning came with the same cool northeast breeze as the sisters spooned under the canopy. The fire ring in front of the tent by a couple of feet had gone out many hours ago from a lack of fuel.

The birds began stirring before the sun rose; even though seeing a sunrise was impossible because of the rolling low clouds, the loud birds knew what time it was.

"Nan, I am freezing. Let's get that landscaping fabric over by those dead birds to wrap around ourselves," Connie had thought of the idea in her sleepy, cold head and figured it couldn't be too far of a walk.

"It could help."

"It can't be too hard to find."

"It looks like the forest opens up over that way," Nan said, sitting in the makeshift tent and pointing southeast.

"Last night, when I got the bark, I went and covered Craig's body up with sand so the animals wouldn't get to him," she finally confessed to her sister as she stroked her morning hair.

"Thank you, I wasn't sure what to do and didn't have the energy to even think about it," she replied.

"Let's get walking so we can warm up some," Connie told her sister. "Or, I guess, I will just hobble along," she said as she touched her deeply bruised ankle.

"That looks bad, Con," Nan said as she got into a better position to examine the injury. "It doesn't appear swollen, which is a good sign."

"It's just sore," she replied, "and it looks nasty."

"I think the lake water was good for it," Diana said.

"How is your head?" Connie asked and made Diana turn to show her.

"Well, I woke up. That is the best sign, I guess. The headache is still nagging but not as strong," Nan said, not wanting to worry her.

Twenty minutes later, after revisiting the putrid toilet smells, the hugging sisters returned to the scene of the bird massacre and began pulling up the short wooden stakes attached to the pen's woven black plastic material.

"We could burn some of this to get someone's attention, like a signal fire," Diana said.

"It would probably burn really dirty,"

"HEY!" What in the hell do you think you two are doing?" Connie and her sister screamed, stumbled back, and nearly fell at the sight of two heavily armed men approaching them.

ACT II

Thirteen

Stoned

Stopping the old green Chevy pickup, Frank Draper was ushered back thirty years as he peered at the ancient white farmhouse from inside the dingy truck. The gravel road and the ditch alongside it were exactly as he remembered them.

"How many times did I mow that stupid ditch?" He wondered aloud.

"Probably hundreds," answered himself. Frank huffed, then took a long draw on the can of ice-cold beer. Draining it like an elixir, he violently whipped the can out the passenger window into the same ditch he still hated to this very day.

Reaching deep into the brown shopping bag on the bench seat next to him, he broke off another beer, freeing it from the round plastic restraints that held the six-pack's shape. Cocktail number four went down easier than one through three because the decision to surrender against the pull of his latest and greatest addiction had already been made. Of course, he knew that choice was decided back at the grocery store fifteen minutes ago, plus knowing he was coming back here, he gave in and bought two six packs for his afternoon road trip down depression's memory lane.

The two gigantic red oak trees still guarded the ends of the long porch, although they desperately needed some pruning. The pale gray metal roof on the house and porch looked much more rusted now, with extended brown areas running from peak to gutter in some places. It looked like someone had taken the time to dump pails of brinck-red paint down the roof on purpose— but in no particular order.

The decking on the porch had been recently replaced. Frank could tell because the wood was still too green for his liking.

"Why don't people stain that?" He asked angrily as the bubbly potion began taking effect, thickening his tongue.

"Don't seem like anyone is home. I'm sure they wouldn't mind me having a little walkabout," he convinced himself as he grabbed the plastic ring that held the first six-pack's final two beers out of the crunchy bag. Looking up and down the road, his head was in a little swirl, just as he liked it. His entire being warmed to the oh-so-familiar journey.

"Yum" was all he could think as he rounded the front of the faded blue hood, patting his good girl— like the truck was his pet dog and closest friend. Discarding the now empty can, he flicked it into the ditch and started into the driveway.

Suddenly, Frank could hear his kid brother and sisters yelping and screaming, playing on the tire swing which hung in that yard. The thought made him smile for a nanosecond as he kicked up some dust from the stone driveway with his well-worn brown cowboy boots. The drive was split in two by a trail of groomed grass and weeds up the middle.

"At least they had kept the lawn mowed," he thought while noticing the tree still had a short piece of sun-bleached rope wrapped around a branch much lower than he recalled.

As he made his way up the drive, he noticed the big barn behind the house. The enormous sliding doors came into view, and he could see they were still intact, but the outside wood of the building was turning a weathered gray. His father's voice echoed over time and made him shiver in fear. Cracking beer number five was his answer to that old feeling.

"Shut up, old man! You're dead," he whispered to the wind over the lid of his drink before taking a long, satisfying swig.

"You can't hurt me anymore, Pa," he said as the childhood wounds festered. This pain was driving him still after all of these years, and, in fact, his old man was continuing to hurt him. His dad's regular beatings had driven the life out of him almost thirty years ago, but he thought he was in control now— as he staggered toward the house's back door.

Dropping empty can number five, he didn't bother to take the plastic holder off this final beer as he cracked the tab on good old number six. Grabbing for his front jean pocket with his free hand, he found the little metal tin of mints—except there were no mints left in it, only two joints. His last two. Setting his beer on the wood porch next to the back door, he pried open his red and white "treasure box," as he liked to refer to it.

"I'm gonna have to stop at the dispensary on the way home and get me some more medicine," he laughed out loud as he sparked the lighter to life. Knowing it was improper to smoke his weed inside someone else's house, Frank remained outside, drawing the intoxicating smoke as deep into himself as possible.

"Man, I love this sch-tuff," he said, making up his own words. He closed his eyes and lifted his chin to the sky to exhale.

"Does life get any better than this?" He wondered and sat down as the buzz kicked in. Finishing the smoke, he swigged down half of the beer and got to his feet. He needed to take a leak and decided the best place was right where he was standing, so he unzipped and relieved himself next to the green porch.

Walking up the creaking steps, he looked around before he tried the door. The screen squealed in protest, a loud metallic cracking sound in blatant opposition to his presence, as he tried to be as gentle as he could while he pulled. Turning the knob of the weathered wooden white door, he pushed in, stepped through the entryway, and instantly back into time.

"Holy crap! Still looks the same," he said, taking notice of the kitchen. He had difficulty distinguishing what his eyes told him and what his mind reminded him of. Hearing his mom's voice, he was pulled by it into the next room where the dinner table was waiting. Except it wasn't the dinner table, his diner table. It was all screwed up.

"HEY!" Someone yelled with genuine authority. Simultaneously, the unmistakable sound of a pumped shotgun echoed off the plaster walls, racking a live round into its empty chamber.

"What are you doing in here?" Said the man's voice from behind him.

The room was spinning quite a bit for Frank now. Startled, he tried to turn around to face the angry voice and the gun, but he moved too fast, overestimated his distance to the low couch now behind him, and stumbled. He let go of good old number six as its remnants crashed to the floor, flinging its contents in a foamy spray.

"Wait, wait, wait," he stammered as he threw his hands into the air. "I live here man, I mean I, I used to live here— when I was a kid."

"Well, you don't live here now, do you, dumb ass?" The angry voice said as the butt of the shotgun met Frank's forehead with lightning speed, driving him backward, cowboy boots over his head, flipping over the end of the beige living room couch. All of the lights went out.

Fourteen

Easy

"Ha ha ha ha ha ha, check out the Prode, down in the farmhouse," said Mortic while pointing. He was an immature slimy black Leech. The whole group laughed raspy belly laughs, some almost losing grip on their tree branch and falling.

"He just got his face pummelled by the burly dude with the gun," responded another Leech, holding its slimy midsection with his four short arms and howling with glee.

"This may be another fine opportunity to help him realize his full potential," said a third, yet much larger bug-eyed worker, Leech, as he flashed his shiny wrist device, so everyone could see the honor badge of his new promotion.

"What do you mean?" Asked the second to the third.

"Tonight, we will schedule a visit from a Whisperer to his jail cell to tell him just how great he really is," said the third to the group of twelve with a new tone of authority.

"By great, you mean screwed, right?" The whole group of Leech roared in raucous laughter again as they peered through the rusting metal roof down on the bleeding man in the tattered cowboy boots.

Resting in the treetops was usually an acceptable way to recover stamina after a long morning of travel. To have happened upon this fantastic drama was more than one could expect. Then having the entire comedic episode explode below you like some sort of Broadway play was the absolute best way to recover from an arduous day of walking.

"Hey check that new Looker mo-bob of yours and see how many Anchors this guy already has," said another squeaky little voice while pointing back to the giant bug-eyed Leech.

"Anyone know who he is?" Asked the authoritative Leech in return.

"Let me get close to see his driver's license the Cop has in his hand right now," said Mortic. After a moment, he reported, "Francis Kenneth Draper," while squinting his sick slotted eyes.

"Hang on a second," said the bug with the Looker device on his arm.

"Francis K – E - N," he said each letter as he typed it into the keypad. This was his first official search on the new Looker, and it was painfully slow.

The entire group of sadistic mutants leaned in closer to try and see what he was doing, hoping to get the information first because being first was the necessary ammunition to be funny and sarcastic before anyone else— which was the genuine desire of the whole lot of them. At least, that is what they thought of themselves as accurate when they were not in the employ of some Prode, chewing away at their heart. In these in-between traveling times, a good joke at the expense of some stupid human was music to their ears. If they actually had any ears, that is.

"Wooo, we!" Said the big Leech as the information from his Looker sprang to life. "Looks like he has ten, no, eleven Anchors set firmly in place!"

"Wooow," was just one of the exaggerated responses to the new information.

"He is only one or two away from completion," said another while whistling through a significant gap in their long front teeth.

"Lucky Prode will be going to Apollyon before too much longer," whispered a fourth Leech in admiration.

———◆○◆———

"Hey Francis, wake up," said the Sheriff Deputy to the thin, gangly man sprawled out on the floor with his wrists firmly fastened behind his back into the shiny chrome handcuffs.

Another deputy arrived on the scene, holding his hat as he entered the room. "Everything under control, Ron?" He asked the junior deputy who was slowly patting the suspect's cheek that wasn't covered in blood.

"Yes, Sarg," was the reply. Ron, a massive hulk of a man, continued, "The homeowner says this guy broke into his house as he got out of the shower upstairs. He threw on some shorts, grabbed his shotgun, and found the perp standing in his living room, claiming he lived here. The homeowner said he was afraid the guy was really messed up and may become aggressive, so he cracked him with the butt of his gun, driving him backward, which caused him to flip over the couch, knocking him unconscious. He told me, Sarg, he didn't want to kill him, in that moment anyway."

"Who is the perp?" Asked the sergeant as he glanced around the room in typical Police fashion, taking a detailed mental inventory of everything.

"Francis Kennith Draper," said the deputy to his older boss.

"That's Frank Draper?" Asked the mildly surprised sergeant as the moaning began from the floor.

"Frank? Hey Frank, can you hear me?" Inquired the sergeant as he moved around the couch toward the groan. "Frank, can you tell me what you are doing back in this house?"

"He, he, he slug, slugged me in the face," muttered the bloody man.

"Why are you in this house, Frank?" Now, a much more insistent Sheriff asked.

"It's my house Sheriff. Well, I mean it was— when I was a kid. Why am I in cuffs?" He wanted to know as he was beginning to become more awake.

"Because we are trying to figure out what happened here, Frank."

"Do you want an ambulance to come and check you out? You're bleeding from your head."

"No ambulance, Sheriff, I'll be fine."

"Have you been drinking, Frank?" Before he even asked, the Sheriff knew the answer to that riddle, as the parade of strewn beer cans had already testified.

"Maybe a couple of beers," he replied, flexing his face to somewhat soothe the sore wound above his eyebrows.

"You smell like marijuana. Do you know anything about that?" Asked the deputy from behind him. He bent down to help Frank to his feet.

"If you mean my medicine Sheriff, then yes I had a dose or two today," Frank said.

"Where and when did you do that?" Asked the older cop.

"Well, outside, of course. I'm not stupid enough to do it in the man's house," Frank said.

"What does the home owner want to do with him, Ron?"

Ron glanced over to the wall at the silent man and said, "He explained to me that he doesn't really want to press charges, but he can't have him come back here."

"Alright Frank, we are going to take you in for drunk and disorderly, trespassing and misusing your medical marijuana card," the Sargent decided. "What we're not going to do today is charge you with Breaking and Entering, which would be felonious. That, sir, would put you in prison for two to five. You are catching a break today, Frank. I guess because Easter is a few of days away, and this guy is being kind. So, if you can behave and not cause us any trouble, then the rest of this nonsense can be dropped. You need to thank the man who owns the house."

"You mean the guy who split my head open?" said Frank.

"Yes, that's who I am talking about. He was within his rights to put you down."

Looking around the room, trying to focus his eyes, Frank finally found the burly guy standing up against an outer wall, listening to the entire exchange.

"Sorry man, I never meant anything. I just have a lot of memories of this old place.... I wasn't thinking," said the humbled man.

"Hey, don't come back here. Get yourself some help, dude," said the confident, dark-haired man. "If you break in here again, they will be zipping you up in a body bag."

"Come on Frank, you're weekend plans have changed," said Officer Ron as he led him out.

"Oh he will get thirty to ninety days and nights of luxury, first-rate accommodations in Huron County's finest ho-tel," smiled the older Sheriff as Frank was led away.

The Looker Leech, who had completed the search, told three of the junior members of the band to grab onto the bottom of the Police cruiser so they could follow Mr. Francis Draper to his new temporary housing unit at the Huron County Sheriffs' department over in Bad Axe. Some of their services may be needed later that evening. As he said this to them, he submitted an official request via his device for a Whisperer to meet those three at the detention facility.

The trio of Leech had managed to grab hold underneath the dusty black Police Cruiser and steal a ride back into Bad Axe. They had all agreed that walking those twenty miles would have killed them. As their Mark got processed into the facility, two of them managed to get in position to follow him to his cell while the other set up a locator beacon for the Whisperer to hone in on. The Psychological Operation Soldiers, or "Psy-ops," flew and looked like dragonflies and were supposed to be on scene within the hour. Most of the Leech sarcastically called those winged soldiers "Fly ops" and widely regarded them as strange.

Ninety minutes later, as the inmates ate dinner, the four tiny soldiers wiggled their way into position, clinging to the ceiling above bunk number twenty in the "B" block. Waiting was always the most trying aspect of any mission. The Whisperer seemed nice enough but had grilled them with questions since he arrived. Once in a while, the Leech would exchange knowing glances while the "Fly opp" droned on.

"Hey, get at the ready!" Chirped a suddenly frightened Leech who was closest to the bunk wall.

"What are you talking about?" Asked another.

"I just caught a glimpse of a Pluck Warrior," said the first.

"Here?" said the second with more than a bit of skepticism.

Fly opp said, "If he is here alone, he must have seen us and wanted to warn us of his presence. Otherwise, the Pluck would have just run us through with his sword. He must just have a protect order."

"What's that?" asked the second.

"It means he is watching over one Carne as his prime directive," replied the Fly, "they usually aren't assigned to protect the Prode."

"Is that good?" wondered the first aloud.

"It's good for us because as long as we don't mess with his Mark, he will leave us alone. We won't see him anymore, I am sure. I have had several operations over the years where this has been true. So, if we just do what we came to do, he will do the same." The intelligent little Fly reassured the frightened trio.

A few hours later, as the group of nineteen Prode and the one Carne climbed into their bunks, the Fly was ready to begin his attack. He hoped it would ultimately result in one of the young Leech driving another Anchor home. Being the Whisperer who brought Completion was a great honor, after all.

Having previously downloaded all the info onto his mini-Looking device, he had studied up on Mr. Frank Draper. He was now familiar with his many glaring deficiencies from back in his childhood. He would strike as soon as quiet time began at the jail. He briefly tested his twin wings, ensuring they were ready for the ambush.

"All right! Pipe down in there," came the gruff command from an enormous Deputy.

"Show time," said the Fly to the others as he jumped into action. Diving down to Franks's left ear, he began to whisper.

"Idiot, idiot, idiot, idiot, idiot. You are such an idiot, Frank. Here you are, back in jail. Stupid, stupid, stupid, stupid, stupid."

Zipping over to his other ear, he continued with, "Dumb, dumb, dumb, dumb. Little Frankie Draper has been puffing that magic dragon lady again. Idiot, Idiot, Idiot, Idiot, idiot. Worthless, worthless, worthless, worthless, worthless. You proved how dumb you are because you are back in jail!" On and on and on, the attack continued relentlessly.

"You have two kids and have never seen them, you are such a loser!"

As the group of Leech watched, they grew enthusiastic about working with such a capable and talented Fly. Clapping their hands and smacking their minuscule lips, they could hardly hold back the growing excitement at the meal awaiting them.

Frank Draper's eyes became a little misty as his thoughts went down the same old rabbit hole in the darkness of that large cell full of twenty stinking losers. He rested the inside of the elbow of his left arm over his eyes and hid in his private darkness so that no one would see him cry. The attack went on for hours, and he had no way to make it stop this time. Usually, a few beers or a joint would make the voices of doom stop talking. But tonight, and for many nights in the future, he couldn't turn them off as long as he was stuck in this cell.

He heard his father's voice calling him stupid and an idiot. His first boss told him he was worthless before he fired him, joining the chorus. Memories of his father punching his face in a drunken rage raced back into his head. His mother's body was in her casket. His father left him the day he watched him drive off, never to see him again.

"I don't deserve a dad," he remembered saying to himself a million times after he had left them. "I am worthless," he muttered, joining the demonic choir.

The three little Leech slid down his bent arm onto Frank's face. There, they split up. One would gain entrance through his exposed ear, one through the new cut on the forehead, and the third through his tear-soaked eye. As they got into position, they waited for the Fly to signal.

Within five minutes, the signal came, and they all moved with haste and stealth through their access points. The priority tonight was to secure all of the Anchors set in place over the years and, if an opportunity opened, to drive one more Anchor home. Drilling the hole, setting the stud, attaching the chain, and securing the bolts on each end of the chain would be the procedure.

Entry was simple. It was a well-worn path taken by hundreds of valiant Leech before them. Locating the Anchors only took a few moments as they sloshed around the compartments inside Franks's heart. So they set about the evening's chores, securing the work already accomplished. Twisting tight the bolts which held Frank firmly in place for decades. They checked the tension on all the lines and only had to adjust a few. After that, they began to probe anything with any life. They gorged themselves on what made Frank, Frank. He was delicious and had much more to offer the forever-hungry Leech than they had expected, especially from someone with so many Anchors secured. As they ate, the slight moan of each Leech gave away the only true joy they could ever experience here on Terra, gnawing on the soul of a captured Prode.

FIFTEEN

STUCK

Clicking the mouse one last time, the twenty-four-inch screen snapped to black. The familiar wave of shame washed over him as the images drove him to fulfill the decades-long compulsion. The internet hummed in his ears, and he felt dead. He was worn out and looking for his phone, as he found it under a napkin on the desk. Chuck was shocked to see it was 3:45 A.M. He had to wake up in three hours for work.

"Where had the night gone? What am I doing with my life?" These questions bounced through his tired mind and deadened heart.

He wasn't going to bother to walk all the way to his bed, so he flopped on the dark brown sectional couch ten feet away from his computer screen, threw a pillow over his head, and yanked on a grubby blanket that was bunched up in a ball in the corner seat. As he lay down, he hoped his alarm would be loud enough to wake him from the stupor in the morning. Chuck could sleep anywhere. He has proven that over and over in his life, and off he went to his favorite place in all the world.

The phone hid beneath the couch cushion next to his ear, shocking him to attention at 6:45 A.M. The theme song from one of the Rocky movies, "Eye Of The Tiger," blared. He thought the song was cool when downloading it a few days ago. Now, he wanted to throw it through the window and out onto the front lawn, or weeds, he meant. Working on a day like today was the last thing he wanted to do.

"Do I have any sick time left?" He wondered through his foggy mind, thinking it would be best for everyone if he could just call in and get the day off. He dozed.

85

"Hey Sally, this is Chuck," he said using the most pathetic voice he could muster forty-five minutes later. "Hey, I'm not, feeling well this morning, like I ate something rotten. Could you tell the Boss Man I won't make it in today?"

"I'm not telling him that, Chuck. Today is inventory, and you have to come in. You are supposed to be here in twenty-eight minutes! Don't you remember the meeting we had last week?" She said with disgust.

"Yes, of course I remember the meeting Sally. It's just that I must have picked up food poisoning from somewhere," he pleaded his case to the unimpressed secretary.

"Listen you have missed too much time already Chuck, if I tell Ed that you are going to miss today's inventory, his head is going to explode. He will fire you for this. Is that what you want?"

After a few seconds of silence, Chuck replied, "No, Sally you are right. I will just go throw up now and bring in extra clothes in case I uhh, well you know. In case I have an accident or something."

"Gross. You are really gross, Chuck," Sally said and hung up.

Chuck looked with hatred at the screen, which for a split second, simply said, "Work."

Rolling off the couch onto the brown carpeted floor, Chuck landed with a heavy thud— he was more tied up in the old blanket than he thought.

"You got twenty-eight minutes, Chuck," he said with a distorted mouth and a snide attitude while wagging his head from side to side.

"Sally, if you weren't so hot I'd like to beat your face in," he said as he searched for clean clothes in the pile on the recliner next to last night's convenient bed.

Inventory would mean he would be working at least twelve hours. It would be a long day to be sitting at the computer and inputting data.

"It's a long time to be doing anything," he thought. He knew he was getting way too old to be going to work on three hours of sleep, let alone an inventory day.

"Why am I such a retard?" He asked himself out loud as he went into the galley kitchen, pulling on a wrinkled dark blue hoodie with a large yellow "M" on the front. He had yet to change his pants, figuring no one would notice his pants since they would be under his desk all day. He smelled at his armpits and acknowledged he needed to stop in the bathroom and apply some deodorant before he left. The fridge had no light. The bulb had burnt out months ago, and seeing anything was almost impossible as the dirty mini-blinds were drawn closed on the window. He searched around and found some lunch-looking thing in a plastic zipper bag.

"Oh yeah, the chicken from Franks last week," he remembered. He ran to the bathroom at the end of the dark hallway and brushed his stinky teeth and tongue. Grabbing the deodorant stick, he smeared nice-smelling white goo under his arms to replace the shower for the day and ran his fingers through his greasy hair. He hoped he had something to drink in the car.

"Keys! Keys! Keys," he said aloud like he was calling out to a pet dog to come in and go in the kennel.

"Where did I put my dang KEYS?" He was becoming enraged, mostly at his lack of self-discipline, but internally blaming everyone else.

"You are such an idiot, Chuck," he barked at himself as he tried to retrace his steps from when he got home yesterday. Looking over, he noticed the target by the computer keyboard. Then Chuck stumbled into his day, hating what he was, and what he was forced to do to make a living.

Fourteen hours later, Chuck slammed the door on his tiny yellow car hard enough to make the steel sound like it had buckled under the pressure. Instantly he regretted abusing the piece of crap, but not too much. Chuck remembered his mother had left him the car and the house over fifteen years ago. He hated the place and cursed her for leaving him in a money pit. The run-down house was the last house at the end of a dead-end road, which felt like the perfect metaphor for his pathetic life.

It sat back off the road and was hidden by a couple of acres of woods as the driveway snaked through the trees at the end of the cul-de-sac. It looked like the dark, wooden-sided house was shoe-horned onto its foundation between several large maple trees. The gutters had fallen off a few years ago, and bees made several large basketball-sized nests under the soffit. The front screen door had been ripped off its hinges during a wind storm last spring and was leaning against the house next to the front porch. He had manually finished the "ripping off" process when the squealing metal rubbing on the concrete kept him awake for a few nights after the storm.

The lawn no longer existed, only weeds, which were rarely mowed. The 1960s black pickup truck rusted away next to the house and had many items simply thrown into the bed. It was, after all, a very convenient trash can. The growing mass included a torn garbage bag raided by raccoons a couple weeks back, and Chuck simply threw most of the items into the truck bed. Two flat tires on the same side caused the old beast to list awkwardly toward the house.

"Thanks, Mom, for giving me such a dump to live in," he muttered as he carried a fast and ready pizza he had picked up from the gas station. He was starving and was itching to get back on his computer. Work had been such a hassle. He just wanted to escape for a while. OK, maybe forever. The "Maybe I should burn the place to the ground and get the insurance money," thought passed through his mind as he walked onto the porch. He filed that thought in the 'consider later' bin. He wanted some stress release right now, and that was all that mattered to him.

As the computer booted up, he remembered that he wanted to text Frank so they could figure out if the Vegas trip would happen next month. He needed to get some cheap tickets nailed down. Or were they just going to do the fishing thing again this year, out on the Bay, like they had done with good old Larry almost every year.

He scrolled through his phone's contact list to "Frankie D" and quickly texted his best friend. His friend that he hadn't heard from in about a week. It was unlike Frank to be silent for so long. He was way too fidgety to sit still for so many days. Maybe he had found himself a woman to hang out with. He considered it for less than a second and pushed the send icon.

He cracked one of the two tall-boy malt beverages he had bought at the station and flipped the lid open on the pizza box as the monitor finally came to life. The ritual that ultimately caused him to hate himself, even more, every time he traveled the disgusting road was well on its way. Dopamine surged inside his head for three hours as he sought even more raunchy images and stories. The chain to the "depravity" Anchor was twisted even tighter. Chuck was stuck, indeed.

Sixteen

Take The Advantage

"We hear you chewing, where are you?" asked a slender Leech into the darkness.

"I'm over here by the "Loner" Anchor," said the fat Leech, wiping his mouth.

A few moments later, the giant plump Leech was joined by two other lust-filled maniacal brothers who had slipped in unnoticed through the eyes of the target Prode and down into the depths of his darkened heart.

"Whoa- YOU are a big fella," said the first in surprise.

"What do we have here Bud?" Asked the darker of the two intruders.

"What we have here is my Prode," said the Plump, with emphasis, and disdain flowing from his bloody lips.

"What makes you think you two can just invade my territory? This is my Prode," he said, sticking his chest out in defiance.

"Orders," was the quick retort from the lighter One.

"From whom?" Demanded the older Leech. "This wretched Prode has been mine for almost forty years. You think you city boys will just come in here with your fancy slicked-back hair and polished shoes and push me out?" His eyes almost bugged entirely out of his head as the volume of his voice soared, and spittle shot out from his mouth with every exaggerated syllable.

"General Von Jamin orders, sir," announced number One.

Pop, the air was let out of the big Leech's argument.

"Wha-wha-what does he want with me?" Asked the suddenly much more somber and stuttering Leech.

"It's not you he wants, it's the Prode. He wants it for a big job," Number One continued with all the confidence he had just gained over the shaken country bumpkin of a Leech.

"Don't worry, you don't have to leave. Well, at least not until he is sent home," Number Two smirked with absolute arrogance as he spoke.

"Apollyon, already?" Big Leech wondered aloud.

"The job first, then home," Number Two emphasized the distinction slowly.

"Don't worry, you've got some more time to eat," quipped One as he bubbled out his cheeks, poking fun at the outnumbered and now outmatched Leech.

"We may need to set a couple more Anchors to bring it to Completion," said the giant Leech to the slick pair standing before him.

"We are working on it Chubs," said One, just to tick off the deflated Leech even more.

"Newsflash, Bubba! We've got a class "A' Whisperer moving from Sally, the sexy secretary, and transferred to Boss Man Ed tonight," said Number Two. "Ear to ear, if you catch my drift, fatty."

"Which happened in his office just a few moments ago," said One as he checked his device for the interdepartmental memo and the current time.

"That should produce some pressure on good old Chuck, especially when they see what he has been looking at on his work computer," the three erupted into frantic laughter as they considered the possibilities.

"Well he is almost open to the next level of depravity already, this should motivate him to step on up to the next level," said the now smiling "Plumpy" to his new best friends.

"If this goes the way you think, we may even get the Feds involved and that would put it over into Completion in a hurry," cracked the Plump, looking for approval and getting none.

"Whoa, you gotta slow down, Chewy. Our mission needs him mobile, not in prison," said Two, as he tried to come up with as many different insulting names as he could for the fat, lazy slob of an inbred country bumpkin Leech standing before him.

We can't say too much here," One said while looking around as if someone may be listening. He leaned in and lowered his voice to a whisper.

"The best outcome would be old Chucky spending more time with his buddy Frank."

"We can't say anything more, you understand?" Two followed.

"So we should get ready. We could use your help," said One to draw Plumpy close to the conspiracy.

"We brought the most advanced mind drill and the strongest Anchors we could carry, so let's get set up for the crash that should be happening in the morning," said a happy Two.

"Woot, woot," said One as he did a little drilling dance, and opened his bag of tools.

The phone rang as Chuck returned to his computer from the bathroom. Finding it on the recliner, he saw it was "Boss Man Ed."

"Why is he calling me at eleven O'clock at night?" He wondered aloud.

"Hey Ed, whats up?" He said as he put the phone to his ear.

"Chuck! Sorry to call you so late, but I really need to get some stats off of your computer," said the direct voice.

"Ah, OK," Chuck said, wondering if he had deleted his search history lately.

"Sure I will get you those first thing."

"Well I am still here at the office trying to get this put to bed, so to speak, and I need access to your computer Chuck," said Ed plainly. Ed always had been a direct boss. Telling you exactly the way he saw things without hesitation or reservation.

"Sure thing, Ed," said Chuck while hiding the certain trepidation he was now feeling. He gave him the password, and that was the end of the conversation.

"Thanks. See you tomorrow Chuck," Ed said as he hung up.

Saying Chuck didn't sleep well is an understatement of cataclysmic proportions. The guy who can sleep anywhere slept nowhere. As the morning light tried to break into his dilapidated house, he was just beginning to break free from the grip of an all-night fantasy excursion and smell less like all the booze he had consumed. Thanks to Frank, he had found a couple of Uppers on the table next to his bed, which had increased his anxiety.

He knew he had to get his act together, so he shaved and showered. His iron didn't work, so he simply hung the clothes in the bathroom as he showered, hoping some of the wrinkles on the nice pants and collard shirt would come out. He really needed the job to not go away.

"He just looked at the inventory stats, that's all," he said to calm himself as he drove up to his usual parking space. He was early by over twenty minutes, which had never happened before. Only a few cars were in the lot on this side of the beige building. He grabbed his man purse from the back seat and headed in like he was shot out of the car.

"CRAP!" He screamed to himself through clenched teeth as Sally sat at her desk, the closest to the door. Luckily, she had her back to him as he slid through the door like a ninja. He passed the entryway and made a beeline down the hall to his tiny office. The plate on the door still said "Chuck Powell -I.T.," And he allowed himself to breathe for the first time since he exited his crummy little car. If he could just get to his computer and clear his history, his day would be made, his job would be safe, and all would be well in the world of Chuck.

As he pushed his wooden door open, pulled his key out of the lock, and flipped his light on. The first thing that jumped out at him, like a baseball bat to the face, was the pile of wires on his desk. His computer was gone. He slumped into the guest chair before his desk, wanting to scream. The knock came within the next two seconds. It was not an inquiry to ask if Chuck was accepting appointments—but an authoritative knock to get his attention to the fact that someone was breaching his doorway.

"Chuck, we have to talk in my office, now," said an insistent Ed.

"Don't bother taking your coat off son." He turned and left.

One minute later, Ed described his disappointment in his I.T. guy. Telling Chuck he had pictured him lasting a long time with the company. Ed told him how shocked he was at the sheer volume of pornographic images he found downloaded onto Chuck's computer, which was the company's computer. Ed hoped that Chuck hadn't opened him up to some sort of legal issue.

He was holding out a payroll envelop to Chuck when he said,

"Son, I think that you have a real problem and you should use some of this money to get yourself some genuine help. I know all of us men face challenges with this stuff, but you went way too far at work. Chuck, I think you may be a sex addict."

Tears ran down Chuck's face as he slumped in defeat in Ed's comfortable guest chair. He was busted. The one thing he had kept hidden since he was fourteen was now out for everyone to see. The one uncontrollable thing now made him feel like a real piece of work. Inside, he knew it was more than just one thing that was out of control in his life. There was a whole litany of vices controlling him. He was just too afraid to admit any of this to anyone.

"Isn't that what a real man is supposed to do?" He wondered.

"Didn't someone tell me to never admit to my weaknesses and mistakes?" His head was swimming, and his body was numb. Ed's voice was at least a mile away.

"Chuck!" Ed shouted directly at him. "Did you hear me?" His face was stern.

"No, Ed, I didn't," Chuck said.

"Tommy from accounting is going to take you back to your office so you can gather your personal items and escort you from the building," Ed said in a sympathetic tone.

"OK," is all Chuck could muster at the moment.

He stood and didn't know what to say or do, so he just turned, dropped his head, and quickly exited Ed's office, the newest place of maximum shame.

Within two minutes, he had what he wanted out of his office and was guided by the prominent accountant to the front door. Sally was on the phone but glared at him with a "you are a sick pervert" stare as he passed her desk. She had done this to him, he decided! The only thing he could think to do was flip her off as he trudged by. He let the bird fly without even watching for a reaction but heard a scoff from behind her desk as he passed through the front door.

In the car, he opened the envelope to find that Ed had given him four weeks of pay as a severance. It was over twenty-five hundred dollars. He figured it was because he had been in their employ for four years.

"Well, he owed me way more than that," is the feeling that accompanied the fleeting moment of excitement after seeing the amount on the check. Then, a deep and sickening wave of emotion began to overtake him as he wondered what to do next.

"You are such a loser, Chuck. Such a—." The thought was interrupted by a firm rap on the window. It was Tommy, the escort.

"Mr. Powell. Mr. Powell, you will have to move along now, sir. We need you off of the company property," a muffled voice said from outside the window.

He left. Four years of his life up in smoke.

Within a few moments of driving, he had a plan. He was going to take the money and go to Vegas. He thought a vacation would be best for him, a time to break away from all the stress and enjoy life for once. Now, finally, some sunshine broke through his gray existence. Screw the job. He was going to party large!

SEVENTEEN

DEEPER

"You see, Plump-ster," said the overly excited and supremely arrogant number One to the dumb Leech.

"We Leech like to get in early and set as many Anchors as we can before anyone comes along with the bright idea to screw things up," he continued. "When we are able to bust in and nail them young— it is easy to drill into their souls."

Two jumped in. "If we have to wait until they are older then we have to break out the heavy equipment. And you know what a pain in the butt that is."

Chubs had no idea what they were rambling on about, but he didn't care because a new feast was in his future. As soon as they were done drilling, he could eat!

"Or if you wait for a traumatic event in the Mark's life, then you can be more successful with a smaller machine. But today, right beneath our feet, old Chucky Boy is having a rather traumatic event. Is he not?" Two asked, One in comedic fashion.

"Indeed he is, fine sir!" said the happy Number One.

"Chucky just lost his job in a very public and embarrassing fashion, so he is feeling really crappy about that and who he is in general. Now, instead of doing something to get his act together, he is going to indulge his inner carnal beast."

"Beast!" One roared for effect.

"So we brought the big drill, and he is going to wallow in his stink out in Vegas, so we will be able to set a huge Anchor in that mess and bring him flying into Completion!"

"Just one question remains for old Chubs here," One said as he looked at the old Leech with a big smile.

"What's the question?" asked the old Leech to One.

They both answered simultaneously, "How are you with flying?"

On the way to the bank, he dialed up Frank again. No answer, so he left a short "call me" voicemail and hung up.

"Where is that guy hiding?" He wondered aloud as the pretty girl smiled at him through the teller window.

"I want to cash my paycheck," he feigned a smile as he endorsed the check, hoping she would believe the paycheck was for one week of work. Forgetting two essential things, Chuck grabbed the pen from the tube. One, the slender twenty-three-year-old blonde had access to all his abysmal banking records, and two, she could see the twenty-year-old piece of crap he was driving. He was fooling no one but Chuck. He never had a chance with her, not in a million years.

"OK. Just include your licence and your account number and I would be happy to take care of that for you, Mr. Powell," said the teller with the perfect smile.

"Thanks," is all Chuck could say as he put the items into the tube and sent it on its magical journey. But he was thinking, "Wow, she remembers my name!"

"I'm going to Vegas. Yeah, taking a little vacation," he was talking to the post on which the microphone was mounted, holding the talk button in and carrying on. He wasn't exactly sure where the sudden burst of confidence came from, but he was ridiculously attracted to her.

"That sounds nice," was the official reply in return.

A few minutes later, she returned with the tube filled with a thick envelope and sent it back through the drive-through roof to his pathetic car.

"Thank You, Chuck. I hope you have a nice trip," she said with a professional smile.

"Thank, uh, thanks," he stammered a bit. "You wouldn't want to go with me to Vegas, would you?"

She laughed nervously.

"Thank you, but I can't get away right now, work and all," she said, and was becoming even more uncomfortable at that point. She reminded herself how much she loathed the lustful looks and outright improprieties she had to deal with all day from men like Chuck Powell.

"Just go away," she thought and simply turned away from his gaze. She knew that getting out of this flea-bitten town would only happen if she looked amazing for the right guy. Her right guy was the man in the little office across the lobby. Yeah, he was married to some bimbo, but not for long— if she got her way.

Chuck knew he had crossed the line in a desperate attempt to feel better. He was convinced she would have made him feel much better about himself. With the emphasis on "much." At the moment, he could not handle the renewed feeling of rejection that washed over him again. So he just drove off in a hurry, without responding, the rusted yellow car puffing copious amounts of impressive blue smoke from the tailpipe.

"Vegas," is all that he muttered under his breath.

EIGHTEEN

LARRY

"Larry!" She waited a moment for a response.

"Larry, honey, it's time to get up!" Wendy Shields called up the beautiful walnut staircase in the foyer of their stately home to her sleeping husband. Knowing that guy for almost thirty years, she was convinced he had pushed the snooze button one too many times and drifted back to sleep. She made the snap decision to ascend the fifteen polished stairs while considering the condition of the pan of oatmeal, she had just put on the stove.

"Hey, honey, it is time to get up," she said quietly, entering the under-lit room through the mahogany-stained wooden door. She made her way to the old-fashioned silky tan window shades. She gave one of them a quick downward pull to release the internal stop, allowing them to magically rise toward the vaulted ceiling. Wendy loved those shades from the moment she saw them in the city five years ago. They matched everything they had tried to make their master suite say. She smiled as she freed all three front windows from the darkness. The room was bathed in early morning light as she glanced out the window down over the front porch roof and onto the lawn. Opening the center window, a puff of fresh air enveloped the room. A few cars meandered down the main street of the small Michigan town of Pigeon, which was right in front of the house.

"The lawn was getting very long," she thought, noticing her favorite mommy Robin, digging for a worm.

"Maybe they have hatched," thinking about the nest on the top of the eaves, where the gutter tucks under the roof at the west end of the front porch.

"Hey, Mister," she said as she grabbed her husband's butt through the blanket. "You have to get up." He didn't flinch, which was a bizarre response to the overtly sexual greeting. Moving toward his head, she pulled back the blanket from him.

"RAAAAAA!" Larry shot forward, grabbed his beautiful yelping wife by the waist, and threw her on the bed next to him, planting a big, wet morning breath kiss on her surprised lips.

"Larry you turd!" she squealed and still loved every second of attention he gave her. Hugging him with a genuine desire for him even after fourteen years of marriage, she whispered into his ear,

"Breakfast is on the stove, and I have to make sure it doesn't burn, so you have to let me go," he squeezed her tightly. She didn't really want to leave.

"I'm not letting go of you, ever," he whispered through her red hair as he found her neck. Blowing hard through his lips on her skin just north of her collarbone, he made a gross farting sound with his mouth, causing Wendy to wiggle and push away with both hands. She went right for his only weakness, digging into the tickle spot on his neck with her fingers. It was her best defense against the attack and his hideous breath.

"Hey, what is going on in here?" The inquisitive, almost middle-school voice said as Mary stuck her head into the room.

"Your dad is being a big jerk!" Wendy tried to get away, but the onslaught continued.

"Ewww," said two younger girls, their voices suddenly joining the audience.

"Mary, please run downstairs and check on the oatmeal I put on the stove," said Wendy to her oldest daughter.

"OK," she responded as she ran down to the kitchen in her freshly laundered plaid school uniform.

"I'm so glad she is a morning girl," her Mom thought while trying to flip her husband onto his back. He finally relented, and she kissed him gently on his forehead, keeping clear of the pungent dragon breath.

"If you would just brush your teeth you just might get lucky once in a while," she whispered into his ear. She quickly pushed off and jumped away faster than he could grab her with his burly arms.

"Come on, babe, we can lock the kids in the shed for an hour," said the smirking X-ray technician to his wife's backside as she made for the door.

"Sorry, hon, I really don't have the one whole minute to spare," she said with a loud laugh, getting in the final word as she left the room.

Larry just flung his arms out like he had been shot through the heart by his quick-witted wife.

Turning to the two girls in the hallway, Wendy, now Mom, spoke:

"Alright, Boo-Boo, you must get dressed for school and let me brush this craaaaaazy hair, girl." As she lovingly stroked the blonde hair of Melissa, their middle child.

"Mommy, I am dressed already," Sunshine quickly pointed out. Sunshine was little six-year-old Megan, the youngest of the brood. She looked adorable in her dark blue uniform, curly red hair, and bright green eyes.

"I know, and I am so impressed," Mom said, as she bent down and kissed her nose.

"Father, I am so blessed," she thought the prayer on the way to the bathroom.

"Mom, the Oatmeal is ready!" Mary, the ten-year-old, shouted from the kitchen.

Larry grabbed his phone off of the nightstand next to the bed. He knew he couldn't delay the inevitable any longer. Work was calling, and he had to get dressed, eat, brush his teeth, and leave. The sixteen-mile trip was bound to be interrupted by at least two school bus stops, but hopefully not the train in Bad Axe. The freight train only ran occasionally in the springtime, yet it could make him late if luck was against him.

He pulled out the charger plug and noticed that his game was still running in the background, accumulating needed points. Larry was a game nerd, with several on his phone and his fantasy football leagues. They just had the football draft, and he thought he would be a contender for the championship again this year. He had won over two hundred bucks in one league last season and loved the friendly competition with a group of his friends.

Noticing he had a new message, he clicked it open. It was from Chucky Boy.

"Hey Larry, this is Chuck. I am in Vegas, dude, on vacation for a bit. I was looking around on the web for something and I got a text from a number I didn't recognize. Some guy was given my number by Frank. He wanted me to know that he had just got out of jail where he was serving time with Frank! I can't believe he's there. I had no idea. I looked up his charges and it was like three different things, all from the same day and all in Huron county. He's going to be in lock-up until July sometime I guess. I didn't know if you knew. Hey, could you grab my mail every once in a while. I am going to stay out here as long as I can, PARTY ON! Thanks Buddy. Oh yeah, I won over three grand on the slots dude!!!! Who is the man now? Go to work you loser! Ha ha ha ha!"

"What?" was all that Larry could say about all the weird information. He found some clean green scrubs and got dressed.

"Wow!" Wendy mouthed over to her husband, sitting at the table eating breakfast with the girls. She re-read Chuck's email.

"I know," he said back silently to Wendy as Sunshine elaborated on what she had to do in school today.

"Well that sounds like it is going to be really interesting, honey pie," Larry, now dad, said as he stood and rubbed her head as he passed to get more coffee.

"This is nuts, Larry. I didn't know anything about any of this. How did Chuck get the time off work to stay as long as he can in Vegas?" she asked.

"I have no idea," Larry said while pouring the steaming black juice into his white "World's Best Dad" mug.

"I think I'm going to try to see if I can get in to visit Frank at lunchtime," he said, trying to figure out how to make it work.

"The jail is only a mile from the hospital, right?" Wendy was trying to remember where the detention facility was in downtown Bad Axe. There were few places to hide in the small city, but it was huge compared to their tiny, one-street Pigeon.

"Yeah, it's like two miles away, over by the place I get coffee sometimes," he said, rejoining his daughters at the kitchen table.

With her ten-year-old all-present and ever-listening ear, Mary asked her father who he would see at the jail.

"Um, well, it's Frank," he said over this mug, lifting it to slurp in its life-giving goodness.

"Uncle Frank is in jail?" She was shocked by the thought. The two other girls were stunned into silence by the abrupt statement.

"We aren't sure what happened and that's why your dad is going to visit him just as soon as he can," Wendy said, hoping she had explained enough to satisfy her inquisitive daughters curiosity.

"Can we draw him a picture daddy?" Asked the shocked little Sunshine.

"He would love that Megan!" Larry said humbly.

A tear gathered in the corner of Wendy's eye, thankful for the gift of a child with a tender heart.

"After school, we can all write to Uncle Frank to tell him we are praying for him," she told the girls.

Larry arrived home at 7:20 pm, which was his usual time. Megan heard his car door and ran down the stairs to greet the only man of her six-year-old dreams.

"Daddy! I am so gl-gl-gl-glad you are home," her brain was running so fast it caused her speech to stumble a bit, as she threw her arms around her favorite man in the whole wide world, as she sometimes said.

"You know, Sunshine, you give Daddy the best welcome home hugs ever," he threw her squealing body into the air and began to chew on her belly. Laughter echoed throughout the house, spilling out onto the sidewalk. The intensity tripled as the other two girls made a frontal assault on the unsuspecting dad.

"Oh no! They are ganging up on me," he said in a wildly exaggerated voice, falling to the floor in feigned weakness.

Wendy loved watching this play out every time Larry came home from work.

"He was such a good and loving dad," she thought as she descended the stairway. Another set of tears welled up inside her as she thanked God for the madness taking place in her foyer. It truly meant so much to have a man like this for her husband.

"Alright girls it is almost time to get ready for bed," she said over the roar.

"Dad, did you get to see Uncle Frank today?" Asked Mary from the bottom of the pile of children.

"We wrote letters to him," said Melissa proudly.

"I, I, I drew him an angel to watch over him while he is in jail," said little Sunshine.

"Well I went to see him but I didn't have an appointment so I couldn't get in today. But I have a time to see him tomorrow during my lunch," he reported gladly.

"Will you give him our letters?" Melissa wanted to know.

"Of course, honey, but the officers have to look through them first, and then they will give him the letters tomorrow night after dinner," Dad explained calmly.

"I just asked him what it was like being in jail and how the food tasted," Mary said, looking into his eyes.

"Thanks, guys. I am sure he will love hearing from all of you," Dad said as he got up, wanting to get something to eat.

"Alright kidos, why don't you get some reading in before we take baths, I have to talk to dad for a minute," Wendy helped them up and watched them ascend the stairs while she turned for the kitchen.

"How was your day?" As the two talked while Larry heated up the leftover spaghetti from dinner, it was the first question of many.

They were best friends now and could talk freely at any time. It had taken a lot of work to get to the point where both felt they had been heard and validated. The weekend seminar they had attended over a year ago made a difference. Sure, there were still those days of selfishness by one or the other. Still, they seemed to have turned a corner after fourteen years of marriage and seventeen years of being together. They didn't count the tumultuous high school years of on-and-off dating and hating. Only after they had grown up and started serious dating when they were twenty. It seemed like a lifetime ago now and yesterday in the same instant. Funny how time was like that.

Larry loved the times they spent looking into each other's eyes and sharing what was happening. She was still so beautiful. He knew he had married a woman well above what he deserved and was thankful. She was smart as a whip and kept him in line in many ways. That usually meant stopping him from brooding over things for too long. Depression ran in his family, and he could fall into the trap during great stress or uncertainty. So, she was on the alert to keep tabs on where his mind was spending time. It was the nonnegotiable reason she insisted that they went to her church most Sunday mornings.

Looking at him now, she was so thankful to God that He had kept them together through their turmoils. Losing the jobs, watching his Mom die, and almost losing the house they had worked so hard to restore. It was hard not to think of everything they had lost during those times instead of seeing what they still had together. It had brought them to a crisis. It was during that time she turned back to God. Yes, it was motivated primarily out of fear and desperation, yet the change inside her was still monumental. She found peace in the cross of Jesus and forgiveness for her rebellion. Healing for her immense pain and searing loss. Those things gave her the strength and faith to cling to God during her trials, despite the horror of losing a child through miscarriage. She knew she would not have made it without her faith. They would not have made it either. Now, when she looks at Larry, she doesn't see him through the eyes of fear anymore— she asks God to help her see him through His eyes.

"Let's get the kids to bed," she told him as he finished his late dinner.

"Maybe we can go to the shed?" As she passed, he playfully swatted her on the backside, smiling that husband smile.

"Yeah I think I have got a couple of minutes to spare," she quipped as she sped up her pace to get to the stairs before he could get up from the table and catch her.

"Very funny, very funny. You better save three whole minutes tonight girl," he called after her, laughing.

"Promises, promises, Promises," she laughed at herself as she climbed the stairway.

Nineteen

Jailbird

"Mail Call!" The Deputy announced over the intercom speaker in the "B" block of the Huron Country Detention Center. The inmates immediately went silent. Letters were the lifeline to the inmate's real life and were highly coveted among all the ninety souls inside the county jail in Michigan's Thumb.

The Deputy droned on through the names in alphabetical order.

"Conrad,"

"Here!" said the almost gleeful inmate, a newbie for sure.

"Conklin,"

"Yep," was the one-syllable answer a definite jail veteran offered.

"Draper,"

No response. . .

"Draper," louder now.

No answer. . .

"Draper, Listen I know nobody loves you Draper and you probably had to pay someone to actually write you from the lonely guys website or something, but you got five seconds before this goes in the trash," said the annoyed Deputy.

"Here, Boss," said the clearly shocked inmate. Who would have written to him? The Deputy handed him not one but three identical white envelopes.

"It must be your lucky day, Draper," said the snarky elderly man, looking over his reading glasses which desperately held onto the end of his red bulbous nose.

Checking the testy Deputy's accuracy, he quickly glanced at the mail. They all had his name and inmate number. They were slit along the top, indicating the

107

safety officer had done his due diligence by looking through the letters. Frank decided to play it cool on the way back to his bunk by combining the three letters to make it look like there was only one. Inciting jealousy in a place like this was not a way to keep the peace. Even though he would fight if he had to, there was no sense in begging to get jumped over a few stupid letters.

He jammed the white envelopes under his white blanket on his bunk, deciding to read them after the peering eyes had something else to gaze at. Guys in jail can act like such resentful and suspicious little girls sometimes. It was always better to let someone else take the heat. So, learning to bide your time to do what you needed was always prudent. Frank was thinking a little more clearly as the effect of the drugs and alcohol had subsided with time, even though the craving persisted.

After losing a chess game in which he was soundly beaten by a kid almost half his age, he retired to his bunk. He had the lower bed in the stack and had always thought there was more privacy on the lower level. So he grabbed the letters on the fly and laid down just a few minutes before lights out. Opening the first letter, blue, green, and yellow crayon crumbles fell out on his chest. The picture from Larry's little Megan stabbed him right through his calloused heart. Tears welled as he studied the image of the angel watching over a stick man on a bunk behind bars.

"We are praying for you, Uncle Frank," was scribbled across the bottom half of the page in blue crayon by a young hand. He ran his finger gently across the crayon, reading and rereading the words. He had to suddenly turn to face the outside wall so no one would see the tears freely fall from his weathered eyes. He bit down on his finger to try to stop those image-killing tears from rolling midstream, but it was useless. That little girl hit a chord inside him, and something broke loose.

The lights went out, and he was still sobbing as silently as he could. Everyone around him assumed he was sleeping off a lousy letter from home. The following two letters were more of the same but somewhat less intense.

"Larry, you didn't tell me about the letters," he whispered, and a smile formed.

"Why those kids looked up to a loser like me, I will never understand," he thought and dozed off to his best night of sleep since arriving.

The foundations of Frank Draper's heart were shaking violently. One Anchor, the Anchor of "Never Been Loved," busted its chain in two by a single picture from a precious little Carne. Four other old Anchors had their chains stretched to the limits.

"It's the tears. You have got to stop them!" Screamed Mortic to the two other Leech as they tumbled back and forth in the heaving chest of the Prode. One grabbed the "Loser" Anchor and began to twist the nut slowly with the wrench he had seized on the way over.

"Mortic, we can't lose this Anchor, it is the key to his heart," screamed the tan Leech to his partner in crime.

Mortic also made his way over to that Anchor and began to help twist the wrench that was slowly re-tightening the chain.

"Keep going," encouraged Mortic.

"I think I have got the "Unlovable" Anchor under control," now called the other.

The heart began to stabilize as the little Leech was worn out from the excitement.

"I haven't had that happen in quite some time," Mortic whispered through tired little Leech lips as their emotional Prode finally dozed off.

"What's your problem, Draper?" shouted the big man with the breakfast tray at Franks's back.

Spinning around to see who was in such a fuss on this fine morning, Frank caught the tray as it slammed into his face, sending food flying and spinning away to his right, grabbing for the left side of his smashed face. A significant body dressed in the same black and white vertical striped pajamas drove his shoulder squarely into Franks's unsuspecting stomach, instantly evacuating all the air from his lungs as he landed hard on the polished concrete floor. His head whiplashed violently backward. Frank heard a loud hollow sound close to him as his lights went out.

Deputies rushed in, restrained the assailant, and cuffed him as they held him down, one with their knee in the small of his back as the other, the more prominent man, just sat down on his shoulders. Blood oozed out from Frank Draper's skull as a third Officer came from behind the watch desk to give first aid to the injured inmate. Within a few moments, an ambulance was hailed to rush Frank with a guard to the local hospital.

<hr />

"IDIOT! You blathering Idiot," the tiny Whisperer cursed the big dumb inmate as Frank's head smacked the ground hard.

"You were not supposed to kill the Prode, just piss him off!"

Twenty

Outside

The dusty beige speaker mounted high on the sky blue break room wall crackled to life.

"Larry Shields please report to the E.R. Larry Shield's to the E.R.— Stat."

Larry left his delicious homemade blueberry muffin and a carton of cold chocolate milk on the table as he made a mad dash through the double glass doors, turning right and accelerating down the empty hall to a full-out run.

"Almost never," he thought about how often he had been hailed over the intercom while on break. Slowing to dance past a few people in the E.R. entryway, he headed through the archway, wiping the crumbs from the corners of his mouth and breathing heavily. Moving around the busy check-in desk, Larry saw Sonya, the black nurse who had summoned him.

"What's Up Sonya?" Larry asked.

"Two things, same patient," she said, half smiling and two fingers extended on her right hand. She held her hand up, pointing toward the ceiling like she was giving him a peace sign.

"First," she said, pulling her middle finger down on her right hand, "You have an inmate who needs an emergency C.T. Second," she returned to having both fingers up in the air, "That same inmate says he knows you."

"Really?" Larry said, confused, as his blue eyes began to move side to side, trying to quickly scan his memory, forgetting about Frank's plight in the intensity of that moment.

"What kind of people you been hanging around, Larry?" Sonya asked, now with a full smile.

"He's in Two," she said to Larry's backside as he walked to exam room number two.

———◦———

M-142 was free from traffic on the early summer morning. Larry was traveling east into the intense and beautiful, multi-colored sunrise. With shafts of orange and yellow light knifing through the early morning clouds. He was familiar with the route because it was how he went to work every day and why he knew to take along the worn-out sunglasses. He loved mornings like this and had always wondered how many amazing sunsets or sunrises he would see in his life.

"How many does anyone get to witness?" So, with that thought in mind, he had decided many years before to be grateful for the scene whenever he was privy to happen upon one. Now, he would often pause for a few extra moments while in the presence of the grandeur of those everyday miracles. It had also bolstered his wife's argument for God's existence over the years. Who could argue with such beauty?

Bad Axe was in the middle of a stretch of road that traversed thirty-eight miles east to west across the tip of Michigan's Thumb. Ironically enough, it connected M-25 on the east, in Harbor Beach, with M-25 on the west, just south of Bay Port. M-25 follows the coast around the Thumb, the peninsula that makes lower Michigan look like a mitten on the map by pushing some sixty miles northward into Lake Huron.

Larry loved the summers here. He spent plenty of time on the lake fishing from his boat and camping in the woods in their pop-up trailer. His schedule allowed him to do these things for four days at a time after working four days in a row of twelve-hour shifts. He tried to take advantage of all his "weekends" during the summer, regardless of the day of the week.

Unfortunately, this would have been one of those coveted "weekend" days for early morning trout fishing on the Saginaw Bay up by Caseville. Still, his friend needed him to pick up his sorry butt from the county detention center in Bad Axe.

"This is what friends do," Wendy reminded him early this morning as she stretched out in their cozy bed and her exaggerated joy by being able to sleep in later than he could.

"But getting released at 7 a.m. was kind of brutal," he said.

The jail is two miles east of his job at the Huron County Hospital, just a block south of 142 and across the street from the Little League Diamonds. Larry wheeled his dark blue Saturn in at 6:59 a.m. with two hot coffees in tow.

Eighteen minutes later, Frank Draper was coming across the parking lot.

"Hey buddy," Larry, now outside the vehicle, said, offering the coffee and a hug.

"How are you doing brother?" he asked sincerely.

"Man, I am sooooo glad to be outside! Thanks for coming to get me. I appreciate the ride and the coffee," he said cheerfully, lifting his coffee to thank his childhood friend.

"Watch out, the Joe is smoking hot. I got it from that coffee shop around the corner," Larry said, noticing the familiar but worn cowboy boots.

"That truly was the longest ninety days of my life," Frank admitted to his buddy as he entered the front passenger seat.

"Hey, there is a letter from Chuck," he said while looking around the gray interior. "Here it is," Larry said, handing Frank the sealed envelope.

"It came in the mail a couple of days ago. Chuck had it stuck inside a letter to me asking me to get it to you as soon as you got out," Larry explained.

"What's in it?" Frank asked, curious at the same time.

"I have no clue," Larry said, looking a little closer at Franks's face, his medical curiosity kicking into gear.

Frank noticed and rubbed it instinctively,

"It's a lot better now," Frank said.

"How are the headaches?" Larry asked, knowing he had two concussions in the past three months.

"They're good." He lied because he did not want the attention.

"Wanna grab some breakfast?" Larry already knew the answer before he asked.

"Is the Pope Catholic?" Frank grinned his stupid grin while looking sideways at his chauffeur and beginning to salivate at the thought of real food.

An hour and a half later, Larry pulled into Franks's place on the gravel part of Sturm Road about five miles south of his house. It was an actual dump of a trailer on three acres sandwiched between a couple of farm fields. But the surprise waiting for Frank was the old, familiar green Chevy Pickup with the blue hood in the two-track drive.

"Awesome!" Frank was touched. "How did you pull that one off?"

"Hey a mover and shaker like me can't reveal all of his sources," Larry said with a laugh.

"I appreciate it, and I will pay you back, brother," Frank had zero money and knew he was not sure when the payment would happen.

"We will go fishing real soon, OK?" Larry was sincere as he said those words.

"Sounds great man. Thanks for everything." They met in front of Larry's vehicle. They hugged a brief man hug, with a double pat on each other's back.

"See ya and stay away from that old farm house, you big dork," Larry pushed the tease button one last time before exiting.

Frank just flipped him off in jest with his stupid grin as Larry left him standing behind his truck with his unopened letter in his other hand. As he stood and watched Larry disappear down the road, he was hiding his growing desire for some medicine with a drink chaser. That compulsion had been stirring in his belly for days. Now he knew just where to find it.

Twenty-One

Fixed

At 3:30 am on a moonless night, a dark figure walked through a row of overgrown maple trees. He had trekked across corn fields from a road more than a mile west. His tattered black tennis shoes were filthy from the journey. His eyes had adjusted to the darkness thirty minutes ago, so seeing the way up the driveway was easy. He crept up the concrete porch, noticing the screen door leaning against the front wall of the dark house. The hinges of the discarded door were bent beyond repair. He took a careful pause, making one last sweep of the area, checking for movement in the shadows, and stood silent for a few moments, listening to the night before he proceeded.

Crickets bleated their one-line love song. An owl hooted somewhere off in the blackness, but everything else was quiet. Not even a dog was barking as far as he could hear. This house was isolated, the last on a dead-end road, and the perfect target with the homeowner out of town. He leaned into one of the nine small panes of glass on the front door, the one closest to the lock, and it quickly gave way, splashing the rug inside the door with some sharp shards of glass. He paused to listen.

Then, he reached one of his gloved hands through the shards and into the room. With a click, he relieved the deadbolt of its essential job.

Searching his black backpack, he found his second pair of shoes because he had removed his dirty shoes and left them on the grass in front of the porch. Stepping into the house, he avoided the glass as he looked around to understand the layout of the interior. It was a tiny house with few desirable resale goods. Before proceeding, he produced a roll of clear packing tape and a small square of cardboard, which he used to loosely "fix" the small window on the door— at least, that was the look he was going for if viewed from the outside.

Moving with purpose, he took the computer apart. He carefully slid the desk-top unit into a black duffel bag he had removed from his backpack. Going to the bedroom, he used a mini-flashlight in his mouth to see while rummaging through messy drawers. Discarding the unnecessary contents all over the room, he searched for valuables. He systematically searched the entire dwelling from top to bottom, gathering various items and transferring them to the black bag in the living room. The mysterious man moved as if he had no fear. He was businesslike, quick, and quiet. He occasionally paused to listen for signs he had been discovered. The only thing to be heard was his own measured breathing.

He located a small toaster in the kitchen and moved it into the living room. He assembled a pile of blankets on the couch and set the silver appliance on top. Grabbing an extension cord off the T.V., he plugged in the timer he had found connected to a living room lamp. Turning the dials to set the timer to go on in 24 hours. Wadding up a pile of papers he had grabbed off the desk, stuffing them into the slots at the top of the toaster, and he plugged his creation into the timer. Sliding the switch upward, the unit came to life, bypassing the timer setting. Then he pushed both toaster levers on the front of the appliance down to "on" and watched the coils turn red. As soon as they started to glow bright, he flipped the switch on the timer to "off" and then back to run. He rechecked the clock. The show was set to begin tomorrow at 4:05 am.

Removing the final item from his backpack, he flipped open the round red snap lid. He used a large bottle of lighter fluid to soak all the papers in the toaster, the blankets, and the couch. The couch was on an inside wall that backed up to the kitchen— with the gas stove on the other side of the plaster. The four stove burners were clicked on, past the igniter stage, and set to run on low. The rotten egg smell rose to his nose. His time in the house was almost done.

Dark man pulled the door closed and maneuvered over the porch, stepping down and bypassing the two steps to the ground. He slipped out of his clean shoes and returned the dirty black ones to his feet, tying the laces. Placing the clean shoes in the pack, he zipped the backpack shut, slung it, and grabbed the duffel with all the new treasures. He paused and reviewed the detailed plan, not wanting to miss even one small thing. He had remembered to turn the hot water heater off. Check. Item by item through the list, he proceeded. This took a couple of still moments standing in the shadows to accomplish. He confirmed that he had completed the entire checklist and retreated from the property in the direction he had come.

"Oh my gosh! Larry, have you looked at the paper yet?" Wendy yelled from the kitchen table for her husband. Larry was out on the front porch swing enjoying the waning moments of the hot summer evening, an ice-cold adult beverage, and most of all, watching his girls ride their bikes up and down the narrow city sidewalk. They giggled and vied for his attention with their newly acquired bike-handling skills and tricks.

"No, not yet. Why?" He asked, craning his neck around so his voice would be better projected through the open windows into the house.

The wooden screen door creaked as Wendy pushed it open, still holding the small Bad Axe paper in her right hand. She had gotten up from the kitchen table as the words from her initial question had left her lips.

"Do you remember meeting that couple last summer at the barbeque up in Caseville? They had recently moved into the area from Colorado. Remember the guy had taken the job to run the quarry, and she was working as a secretary at Chuck's old place?" She was excited now her free hand was moving like a maestro directing an orchestra.

"Uhhhhh," Larry tried hard to force his worn-out mind to remember.

"Yeah. Yeah, she was pretty and uppity, and her name was....." Long pause, like he was digging and waiting for help from a game show host to break the tension by scraping the name off his tongue's end.

"Sally!" He said. "And Jeff!" Remembering names was a substantial part of his job and one of his strengths. He was smiling for the victory over his weariness.

"It is her!" she said, her eyes opened wide as she read the story on the front page again.

"She was killed in an accident yesterday, coming home late from work. Her car crossed the center line on 142 at the curve south of town and was hit head-on by a semi.

"I heard that story at work today but didn't catch the name of the victim," Larry perked up, putting both his feet down and stopping the slow, hypnotic movement of the wooden swing.

"Man, he has got to be crushed. I heard that it was a ugly crash," Larry said.

"Get this, the article said they were separated about a month ago," Wendy said while making a distorted "Oh my gosh" face over the edge of the paper.

"Whoa," he said, taking that in.

"I wonder if Chuck knows?" He considered calling him but realized that Chuck-O had taken a job for a few weeks and would still be working.

"I think I will message him later," he said.

"Hey, I am going to call Jessica from church and see if there is something we can put together for Jeff, the poor guy," she said as she turned to leave with her mind moving a hundred miles an hour.

"Hey, does it say if there is an investigation into the accident?" He wondered out loud, pointing his face at her retreating frame.

"I didn't read anything like that," she said, simultaneously thinking about the new widower and planning ways to help.

Eight hours later, Larry, Wendy, and the entire family were sleeping because it was still an hour and a half before his alarm was set to go off...

"WEW- WEW- WEW- WEW," Firetruck sirens rang out loud. They shot past the front of their house on a mission, causing a stir in Larry for a moment, like an internal, ingrained, automatic response switch for a medical professional had been implanted in college.

Two hours later, as Larry danced around the house getting ready for work while all the girls enjoyed a sleep-in day, there came a gentle knock at the front door.

"Hey Ron, I mean, Sheriff," Larry said, pulling the door open wide. He asked the tired-looking Officer to come in. He knew Ron from many run-ins at the hospital and was very curious about the house call.

"Morning Larry, sorry to bother you," he said as Wendy stole a look around the corner from the top of the steps. Still in her pajamas, she remained hidden.

"How can I help?" he asked the immense cop.

"Hey, we were wondering if you knew where we could find Chuck Powell?" The Sheriff removed his hat and held it in clinched hands.

"Chuck? Yeah, he is in Vegas," said a very curious Larry.

"Las Vegas, Nevada?" asked Ron for clarification.

"Yes. He is supposedly coming home in a few weeks." Larry said.

"Oh, do you know how long he has been in Vegas?" Ron asked.

"Uhh," said Larry as he searched the early morning memory bank. "A couple of months now, maybe a little longer, like three months. He went out there after he lost his job and had won some money at the casino, then he picked up a contract job in the city for a month or so," Larry explained.

"OK," Ron was thinking now.

"I just texted him last night," Larry remembered.

"What's this about, Ron?" Larry folded his arms and leaned against the side of the open door.

"Well Chuck's house burnt down last night and it looks like it was arson."

"What?" said Larry.

"Yeah, it's a total loss. We didn't know if we should be searching for a body."

Twenty-Two

Burnt Ends

"**H**ey, Chuck. You have got to call me right away. Something serious has come up," Larry said in a frantic message, still unable to process what had happened.

Ten minutes later, Larry called Chuck's number. It rang many times.

"Hey," said the sleeping voice on the other end of the line.

"Chuck, sorry to call so early," Larry said.

"How early is it Larry?" Asked the confused voice.

"Hey, I got some terrible news for you, buddy," he said, trying to break it gently.

"Whats up?" Chuck perked up a little.

"Are you awake?" Larry wondered.

"I am now Larry, what's going on?" He said.

"Is it about what we talked about last night?" He sounded distraught.

"No. Dude, the Sheriff just left my house looking for you." He was trying to keep his voice low to not risk waking the kids. Wendy stood beside him, trying to hear the conversation behind the phone.

"What? Why? What did he want?" Chuck's voice was palpable with fear.

"Your house burnt down last night. Sheriff said it looks like arson." Larry said.

Encrypted. "Supreme Commander of the Lakes Region Cryptus: To General Von Jamin, TOB. Stop. Plan is unfolding perfectly. Stop. Received confirmation on Carne Mark movement north. Stop. Gathering three weeks hence. Stop. Herd in play. Stop. Report on progress with Prode. Stop. Need plan B to be in place, if necessary. Stop. End." Encrypted.

Encrypted. "General Von Jamin, Thumb Operation Base: To Cryptus, SCLR. Stop. Prode in play. Stop. Carne in play. Stop. End." Encrypted.

TWENTY-THREE

ENTER ENDS

T he white and black Sea Ray fishing boat slipped through the clear water of Saginaw Bay almost without effort. A thin fog hung above the flat lake as the twin 75-horse outboard motors hummed like a throaty baritone in the early morning light. The fishermen were on a mission and knew where to go. They had fished these waters together since they were boys. It was northwest of the marina by fifteen miles out into the open water. The craft, aptly named "X-RAY," was in hot pursuit of a daylong assault on underwater entertainment. This joy came with culinary benefits, which all considered a bonus to the fact they were getting to be on the water again.

The soft buzz from the line running out of the reel was music to the three guys' ears. The gentle plop of the lure hitting the glassy water reassured them they had returned to the place they all had loved for a lifetime. The sun was just going to break the horizon on the calm and alluring July morning. They were far enough out in the bay that the land to the southeast, where they had journeyed from, was now just a sliver in the distance. Above that horizon, hundreds of windmills peaked over the forest's shadow, all stalled in this morning's windless sky.

The island was just a mile and a half to their north. According to inside information, this location was where the fish had been hammering lines all week. The guys at the marina are known to run their mouths when they get a few beers in them, and apparently, the fish have been hot through this area. The scuttlebutt was they were heading into the rivers to spawn, which would be a week early.

"So, how are you doing with the whole house mess?" Larry asked his buddy Chuck as he sat back down after an excellent long cast.

"Well, living with Frank is a real pain," he said, trying to pry under his other buddy's skin while slowly bringing his line in.

Frank responded by whipping a donut hole at his head but missing by three inches. It plopped in the lake to become fish food.

"Man, don't waste my vitamin "D," said Larry in a hushed tone.

"Yeah, you didn't buy those, Wendy's gonna kick your butt." Chuck said to Frank.

Chuck told Larry, "No, the house was a dump, so I will get over it. I think I will just sell the land and do something different."

"What about the insurance, I mean you had coverage right?" Larry pressed a bit as Chuck put his rod into a holder.

"Yes! I'm supposed to get the fat check for a cool sixty-five thousand this week," he said, while rubbing his hands together in anticipation.

"Yeah, your first rental payment on the bedroom suite is for that exact amount and is due this week too!" Frank chipped in, laughing out loud.

"Suite! Funny, Frank. You gonna use the money to delouse the joint?" They all laughed.

"Maybe with some dynamite," Larry pounced.

"Isn't it beer thirty yet?" Frank asked while making eyes at the big, heavy cooler.

"Draper, you got a problem, man," Larry poked while placing his rod in another holder. He opened the treasure chest and tossed one to the other two men.

"The only problem I have out here is where I am going to store all of my fish," he said with a smile and a crack of the day's first beverage.

"That would be in MY freezer, since neither of you have one," said Larry.

"Well, here's to getting paid," Frank led the cheer.

"Here, here!" They responded by tapping their beers together, and off they went.

Twenty-Four

Claimed

S wimming through the deep waters comes naturally to the Leech. It is their preferred area of operation, so keeping up with the two Prode and their Carne friend in the boat was easy. What was difficult to swallow was the fact that a Prode would choose to hang around the vile Carne. It was the center of many discussions on the trip out to the lake. The other point of consternation and constant chatter was the soaring squad of Angelus Mortis. There were ten flying in formation in the sky above them.

The "Reapers," as they were referred to, scared the Leech to death because of their power— outranking all except HE. So, the pressure to not screw up this operation went up— way up. Reapers loved to escort the Prode to Apollyon. Usually, they made a big production out of it all, with their black masks to hide their identities and their long black-handled Scythe to escort the pathetic, helpless Prode home to be slaves until judgment day. Like the sarcastic Leech always says, "Better to be a Prode on Apollyon than a Carne anywhere!" The Prode may disagree after crossing over, but no one asks.

The Reapers thrive on intimidation because they answer to no one but HE. They choose to work with the Generals and Commanders here on Terra and only communicate with them. The rest of the Legion could only hope they were performing up to the wishes of their overlords. They are here as enforcers of the will of HE, with no regard to how the operations get accomplished and no regard for Leech, who are grown in pools of sludge by the millions and are not named. The Reaper's single focus is the KSD— their prime directive on Terra.

As the ten special slimy Leech got into position by slithering up into the "X-RAY," they found a temporary home under the console behind the cooler. They were all outfitted with glass eyes to operate more efficiently in the scorching sun of Terra. They were chipped in to hear all communications from Command. Today's operation was all business, and the Reapers watched every detail.

When the Leech took up their position, half of the Reapers swooped in behind the boat by fifteen yards and stayed on station. Their multi-layered transparent black robes floated around their ten-foot frames and functioned as body armor. The favorite weapon of most Reapers was the eight-foot-long, razor-sharp Scythe, which eight of the ten had in hand. Now, it was a matter of timing for the Completion ritual to begin.

----------◄◊►----------

The fishing continued throughout the morning with only moderate success. The drinking was extra successful, to say the least. As the sun warmed, the three men decided to check out the island for a while, then return to the hunt.

"Right over there, Larry. It looks like a clear spot," Chuck pointed north. He was directing the craft toward the south shore of the island. It looked like there was an opening near the forest. Taking their party to the beach to escape the glaring heat seemed like a good idea to the tipsy trio. They waded in, sitting on a massive boulder beneath a tree facing the lake and nursing another cold one.

"Don't get much better than this," Larry muttered to no one in particular.

"So Larry," said the now-slurring Frank. "We got some big plans, old Chuck and me," he said, employing his stupid smile.

"Yeah, and we want you in on the ground floor with us buddy," said Chuck as he leaned forward, too close to Larry.

"OK, what's the big plan guys?" Larry asked.

"Well, Chucky here has just come into a bit of money, you see," said Frank, flailing his arms.

"Dough, money, cash, Benjamins, dollars, greenbacks, you get the idea," said Chuck, who was more drunk than the rest.

"So we are going to invest that capital into an up-and-coming revenue stream and make a fortune. So we can do this kinda of stuff all the time," explained Frank, arms extended like he was trying to sell the island to Larry.

"We are gonna fish that revenue stream to death, Larry!" Chuck said, laughing while spilling a little beer on himself.

"You're an idiot," Larry said, smiling. "What's this grand plan?" Larry asked.

Frank reached into his pocket and found the new metal tin of mints.

"Well we need for you to experience the potential my friend," said Frank, as he sparked his lighter to life.

The marijuana for that day had been selected for its potency. Frank had decided to kick up the effect by sprinkling in a few other things as well. The three old friends got so high that afternoon that they opened their souls. The Anchors held fast as the invasion was about to begin.

<hr />

"NOW!" All the communicators sparked to life in the Leech at the same instant.

The Leech walked right in through the wide-opened doors and began to drill the final hole in Frank Draper's soul. The ground was hard and crusty, but the new custom drill was up to the task. After a minute or so, Mortic was getting antsy. These Completion rituals were always so nerve-racking. Who could tell if one of those invisible Pluck Warriors might be watching the progress of all their work and waiting until the last second to drop in and destroy the whole lot of them? He was strangely comforted by the presence of the Reaper squad and simultaneously agonized by their presence.

"Check your depth!" Shouted Mortic into the face of Leech number three, wanting precision.

"Almost there," was the reply, muted by the roar of the drill.

"Ten seconds, Mortic, get the Anchor ready," said number two.

"Make sure you get deep enough; you don't want it to come loose during the ritual," yelled young Mortic to the drilling Leech while waving away the billowing smoke.

The seconds ticked as the Reapers readied for the final move. The five circling Reapers were still in formation, indicating that all was well in the heavens above. The band hovering low and directly over them was preparing one Reaper for the ritual. They removed his flowing black garments and doused the Reaper with a good measure of shimmering liquid that ran down its entire length, causing him to sparkle even in the shade.

———◄O►———

Frank stood up a few minutes after finishing his joint and started doing some "Tarzan" yell while pounding his chest like a madman.

"I love this stuuuuuuuuuuuf!" he screamed as loud as he could out into the lake. "I am king of the world! Can't you see that now?" he strutted and asked the wind.

"Let's go!" It was his last scream before he collapsed to the ground. The two other men laid back in a glazed-over stoned stupor, not caring their buddy had fallen.

"What was in that stuff?" Larry mumbled as his head swirled and the boulder beneath him floated.

———◄O►———

The gangly undressed Reaper rose above the screaming Prode and simply threw himself into the man in one smooth motion. All ten feet of Reaper penetrated through the top of the human head in less than a flash, causing the Prode to fall to the ground. All the Anchors held fast— the possession was complete. Frank Draper was now claimed. He was no longer himself but could be used for whatever HE wanted, whenever HE wanted. Frank's open eyes glossed over with a shiny sparkle that faded to black.

The Leech were busy drilling in the next Prode to undergo the Completion ritual as the second Reaper was getting ready for its new assignment. Controlling a Prode was a great honor for any Reaper, one for which they trained for many years. The shimmering liquid cascaded down the second Reaper, which meant it was almost time for Chuck to be Completed.

A first-class Whisperer buzzed the Prode to make way for the final move. It sang songs of delusion and drew pictures in the man's eyes, which caused him to see visions of grandeur for his future. The drugs had opened this portal wide. He would be the king of weed, untouchable and above the law of natural consequences. As the final Anchor was set, more singing and visions opened the last door. Chuck smiled as he lay, waiting for his new life to begin. Chuck wanted the newfound freedom he had been promised and was convinced awaited him. The freedom to rise above this paltry world and reach for the next, where he was confident he would be god over his destiny.

The Reaper was lightning-quick and entered with complete authority. Chuck Powell's freedom had arrived. As reality washed over him, he tried to scream and turn away from the darkness which held him. The Anchors stretched but, in the end, held firm enough. He was a prisoner in his own skin, having surrendered himself to his soulless Reaper. The invasion, which had begun many years back, had reached its culmination on the minute island. Chuck was under orders now, and he would comply or die.

TWENTY-FIVE

PREY

Something did not feel right to Wendy. She was at the church, planning the fundraiser to help Jeff Somersly, who had lost his wife Sally in a tragic auto accident— when a powerful and sickening wave came over her and spilled out onto her face.

"Pray for Larry," she heard from somewhere deep inside her.

Wendy looked at the other two women, and tears fell— unexplainable tears— as she covered her face with her hands. Her sisters rushed over to her side and began to hold her, and they soon prayed with her.

"Pray for Larry," is all she could manage from her quivering lips.

Thinking something had happened in their marriage, the women stumbled and stammered to know what to ask God for. They prayed in general terms for a few minutes.

"Pray for Larry's protection," was whispered to Wendy from a messenger at her side.

"Could you just pray for Larry's protection?" she asked her friends.

"That's right, he's out on the lake today, isn't he?" Julie said.

"Yes, but it seems like it is more than that. He is hanging out with his high school buddies, and he tends to give into them and do stupid things." The messenger had not brought a word of comfort on this day.

"Father God we lift up to you Larry right now in Jesus' name. He is your child even though he may not act like it all the time, heck none of us act like your children all the time," said the woman with a southern drawl. "He is out on the lake now with his two buddies fishing and carrying on. Please, Father, send your warriors to protect those men, especially Larry, Lord. Please, be gracious to them today. Surround them with your mercy and your grace. Cover them with your love Lord. Help them right now, Father!"

Julie Mills had an intimate connection with her Father, and Wendy was thankful she was her friend.

The band of Leech was drilling down on Larry now, expecting a breakthrough any moment. Not that there would be a Completion ritual— you cannot have one of those with a Carne, but you can still set as many Anchors as you can inside their hearts. Which messes with their ability to walk the way they should. Many Anchors set in suitable locations can cause a lifetime of pain, derailing the Carne's entire purpose. The Leech would not end up with a meal from this drilling since a Carne soul is not appetizing. But it would get them some bonus time on the next Prode they encountered.

The sky exploded with a vast, intense blue fireball, sending waves of panic through the Leech, causing them to drop the drill and take cover. The Whisperer shrieked and darted out toward open water northeast of the island. The remaining eight Reapers tried to form defensive ranks.

The pair of time-shifted Pluck Warriors fell like lightning on the Reaper squadron, with violence never before witnessed on the island. In less than a second, three Circling Reapers were cut into four pieces, each by one Warrior's flashing sword. The second Pluck dove to the ground in a streak, eyes blazing red, and landed on the boulder next to the three men, smashing back to liquid two Leech in the process. He drove his sword up and through one stunned Reaper, evaporating him. Another Reaper swung his scythe and put a large gash in the Pluck's thigh, causing him to reel back and to the right. As he stumbled, a different Reaper struck down with his razor-sharp weapon and took a piece of arm off the Pluck with a scream.

The Warrior jumped and pulled hard with his wings against the air to gain an altitude advantage over the more numerous Reaper squad. As he did, the Reaper that had landed the blow to his upper arm fell back by a few yards, but not far enough to avoid the slash across its midsection, which destroyed its black armor protection and pushed it wildly off balance and out of control.

The second Pluck dove from the sky and landed on the boulder. He reached Larry Shield's heart and yanked out four slimy Leech. He crushed them on the back of his golden shield. Peering in, he located the last Leech, Mortic, next to the mind drill. He grabbed both the Leech and the drill between two fingers and popped them like a blueberry, dispatching them into the deep. He leaped into the air beside his wounded comrade with the immediate danger eliminated.

Seeing this, the remaining Reaper decided to withdraw to fight another day and streaked into the lake.

Knowing the Whisperer was just gaining speed away from the island, the uninjured Warrior willed himself up above the dragonfly-looking beast and flapped his wings down with such a force that he knocked the Fly into the lake. Then he dove in and split the demon in two with his massive weapon.

━━━◆━━━

Larry sat up as he grabbed his aching head. It sounded like a million screaming birds had invaded his throbbing temples. Still, they were all behind them, carrying on in the trees. Looking at the other two guys sleeping on the massive boulder beside each other, he shook his head, frustrated with himself. He wanted some water from the boat. Splashing through the cool water made him feel better, but something inside of him ached. He was ticked off that he had again fallen for his buddy's shenanigans. Those two had always wanted to party like rock stars since high school, but he was never into it.

But this was different. What was this grand plan his derelict buddies had? He wondered as he reached for the cooler and a cold drink of water.

Looking ashore, he noticed Chuck sitting up and showed him the water, to which Chuck responded with a weak thumbs up. Frank had smoked more than they had because he was still down for the count, but he grabbed him a drink, too. The bag of chips was taken hostage as he turned back to land.

"Dang dude, what was in that pot," Larry asked the two of them as they munched on the chips.

"Something special," Frank said.

"So, what is this plan of yours?" Larry was tired of waiting to hear their pitch, emphasizing the 'what' in the question.

"We are going to use some of the insurance money to grow weed on this island and get connected with some new friends I made in Vegas to supply a large distribution network on the west side of the state," said Chuck with a gleam in his eyes.

"We are coming back to the island in a couple of days and spending some time out here thinning out these dumb birds and we need you to drop us off," Frank stated plainly.

"Why are you thinning out the birds? Larry needed help understanding the logic.

"Just too many of the stinky things, they are poisoning the ground," Frank answered.

"Their droppings make awesome fertilizer, but with so many birds it's too much, and is beginning to screw up the PH level in the soil on parts of the island already," Chuck said.

"That's all you need from me is a ride on my boat?" Larry asked.

"Yes for now, and when we have product harvested a ride across the Bay to Au Gres so we can off-load the goods." Frank said.

"And this would only be a couple of trips, then we plan on getting our own boat, unless you like the extra cash and want to continue," Chuck chipped in.

"I will give you the ride out and back then we can talk," Larry decided.

Twenty-Six

Home Front

The girls were playing in the sprinkler in the yard when Larry arrived home with his boat in tow. He backed his favorite toy between the shed and the pop-up trailer in the back yard which was open to prepare for their vacation to Michigan's Upper Peninsula in two weeks.

Larry was looking forward to getting away with his family. His head was throbbing. He knew he had failed them again as he unhitched the boat. Larry decided he needed to bury the shame and guilt right then and there. He did, or at least he hoped he had.

"Hey, Dad!" Came the three-girl chorus as they waved to him while he carried a pale full of fish to the table on the back deck.

"Hey mister," came Wendy's sweet voice through the screen door.

"Hey," Larry said, trying to fake "happy" and "no, I am not guilty of doing anything stupid today," in reply.

"Did you have a good time hanging out with the guys?" She asked in a positive, non-judgemental tone, remembering what she had read.

"Yeah, it was a long day and I am fried like a lobster," he said to her, holding up his burnt arms.

She pushed through the door and tried to give him a real hug. He was going for his fish cleaning stuff in the cupboard under the sink and almost pulled away but then gave her a clumsy, halfhearted, one-arm hug in return.

"We caught a few nice fish," he said, trying to deflect her inquisitive gaze after the awkwardness of the attempted affection. He entered the house and retrieved his knives and cleaning tub for the mess he was about to create.

135

"Good, can we eat some tonight for dinner?" She asked.

"Sure," he said, surprised, "I was hoping you would be up for that."

"It sounds good to me, but the girls may want something else," she said.

"So, how is Chuck?" She asked. Wendy sensed there was a cloud over Larry right now. He seemed to always come home from a day with the guys in a funk, and she was not sure why. Her suspicions swirled. With today's thing at the church, and that was the only way she could currently describe it as a thing— she was a lot more tuned into Larry, trying to understand if he had been in real danger or if something else had happened. Confusion reigned. She wanted to tell him everything that had happened to her, but she knew he had no desire to talk. Tonight, there could be a marital ambush after the girls went to bed. He may be willing to talk about the day. Wendy hated feeling like everything had to be pried loose.

"He's a little weird, actually," Larry confessed.

"Oh? What does that mean?" She asked, hoping there was a glimmer of hope to have this conversation sooner and not later.

"Well he's gonna sell the land from his mom's old place and find something different, which is OK, I guess. I don't know exactly, but there is something weird about him since he went to Vegas," he said. Larry felt he was losing his friends.

Twenty-Seven

Used

F ive days later, Larry was piloting his boat across a much rougher Saginaw Bay in light rain with Chuck and Frank in tow. Along with them, the boat carried a few hundred pounds of camping gear, a roll of black construction site barrier, water, food, rifles, and ammo, which left little room to move.

There wasn't much said between the three of them, knowing this grand plan to become weed barons was pushing the limits of their friendship. The two camouflaged passengers glanced at each other amidst the roar of the motors with renewed excitement over the growing possibilities.

Chuck reviewed the simple plan in his head. First, they kill all the birds they possibly could, and second, they plant their special weed seeds. The weather looked like it would cooperate after this morning's light rain moved out; if not, they had their new camouflage tent. The pair hoped it would warm up to average summer temperatures before their vacation time was up. The sky was filled from horizon to horizon with low gray clouds, and the water spray was downright cold in the wind.

"You guys be safe out here," said Larry as his two buddies walked away through the lake with their last bit of supplies on their backs and in their hands.

"Thanks, Larry," said a waving Chuck. Frank stuck his arm up in the air to express his gratitude.

"See you in a few days," Larry said as he fired the boat up to leave.

The next four days for Larry were spent expelling his nervous energy in many ways as he kept busy late into the evenings. He was isolating. Wendy was more than aware he had been a different guy since he first went out with the boys.

Something was out of kilter, and she was fighting hard not to step into a worrying mindset. It never helped her feel any better in the past, and Wendy was sure that was still valid. She was striving to be attentive to Larry without trying to freak him out and drive him further into himself.

"Please God bring him back to me," Wendy was praying constantly.

She was surprised to find a note on the pillow on his first day off.

"Gone fishing," is all it said, except a smiley face was attached to the bottom of the sticky note.

She sent him a "Be careful" text and began crying out to God on his behalf right there on her pillow. Then, she thought about sending a prayer request text to her faith sisters.

"I am just going to get through this part, and then they can get their own boat," Larry thought as he left the marina.

It was a beautiful morning on the water, and that was the only thing that relaxed him as he sat down for the thirty-minute ride out to the island. He was working hard to keep his mind from racing. He forced himself to think about other things, like what he needed to do to get ready for the vacation, which lasted five minutes because he was ahead of schedule with all his newfound energy over the past few days.

"Wonder how them Tigers are doing?" He thought but did not know. He liked baseball and understood you followed the hometown team. It was the question his father-in-law used to ask out loud when he was trying to change the subject.

His phone buzzed in his pocket. He had put it on silent so the fellas would not be encouraged to ask him any questions when he got to them.

"K" was his only response to his wife's text. It was sent just before he was too far out into the lake. He thought fifteen more minutes in the danger zone as he raced past a couple of boats fishing in the early morning light.

"You made it," said a happy but scruffy Chuck as Larry walked up onto the island boulder they had all slept on five days earlier.

"Yep."

"You should come see what we have done with the place," said an excited Chuck.

"Alright, but we have to get going soon, we don't want to get caught out here with our pants down," Larry said.

"Come and see. You can help us get the stuff we are taking back and we can get going sooner," Chuck said, looking back over his shoulder as he walked over the familiar ground.

"Man, it stinks up here," said Larry, wrinkling his face.

"Yeah, the sun is baking them birds we shot," confessed Chuck.

"Hey, you made it back," Frank said. He was stuffing the tent into its sack.

"Look, we planted all of our stuff in the pen we built," said Chuck, pointing through the trees to the black sectioned-off area.

"I thought it would be bigger," Larry said.

On the ride back home, the two guys would not shut up. Like they had been isolated on an island alone or something. Larry was shocked into even more profound silence by some of the things they had wittingly, or not, let slip out of their mouths. He was not sure what to do with any of it, so he buried it behind a smile and an excuse that he had to go home and take the girls to their 4H group. Larry would have said anything to get out from beneath their clutches. He felt smothered when he was with these two. Trapped. They were becoming something Larry did not like.

Now, he was fighting a growing panic about what he had done to aid these guys. He was afraid he had exposed himself to legal issues when these two dopes got caught, and they would get caught. He was sure of it and had to figure out what to do next. They wanted to pull him in close by telling him secrets, but it had only succeeded in pushing him away, maybe for good.

He hoped that in another few days when he left on vacation for those twenty glorious days, most of this new ambition would fade away; these dreams would die, taking their secrets with them. He knew after his trip to the U.P., he had to cover a one-week vacation with twelve working days in a row. That would allow a month of separation from Frick and Frack and perhaps enough time to return to normalcy and sanity.

Encrypted. "Supreme Commander of the Lakes Region Cryptus: To General Von Jamin, TOB. Stop. Are we a go? Stop. End." Encrypted.

Encrypted. "General Von Jamin, Thumb Operation Base: To Cryptus, SCLR. Stop. Yes we are go. Stop. End." Encrypted.

TWENTY-EIGHT

FULL CIRCLE

After waiting for a raging storm system to clear the area, Frank and Chuck rode in Chuck's new, three-year-old pickup truck. They backed down a driveway next to a restored old Victorian home and entered the backyard. The house was dark in the predawn moments. Frank grabbed the bolt cutters behind the seat and snipped the lock off the trailer. Chuck finished backing the ball under the hitch. Frank cranked the handle, lowering the black and white boat onto the ball hitch, while Chuck plugged the lights into the round outlet on the bumper of his new black GMC. He hung the safety chains and jumped back into the vehicle. The pair eased out of the driveway, casually turning left on 142 toward Caseville. The island was calling. It was time to check on the progress of the crops, as they called them.

"You brought the rifles, right?" Chuck asked Frank as they drove west and then north on M-25. They decided to go to the closer Bay Port launch instead of up to the marina at Caseville, not for the miles but because there were fewer eyes.

"You know it," Frank said.

Out on the lake, Larry's borrowed boat ran like a champ. The excitement was building inside them even though the lake was rough and the air was cold again. This was an unplanned trip to the island, almost like she had summoned them. She beckoned them home because they had a job to do.

They stalled the motors out away from their boulder and coasted in close, as close as they dared, with their friend's boat. They were protected from the wind on this side of the island and set anchor just twenty yards out.

"Grab the guns and ammo, something doesn't feel right," Frank said while he scanned the area.

Walking over the boulder and toward the pen, the pair heard some female voices talking low in the morning air. The wind carried the words to them, so Frank was confident they had not been detected.

"Get down." Frank mouthed and waved his hand in one single motion.

"Load up," Frank whispered back to Chuck.

He dug for the ammo from Franks's black backpack and handed it over his buddy's shoulder to his waiting hand. Grabbing a clip, he slid it into his gun's bottom, ensuring it clicked. He pulled the charging handle on the black AR-15 and slowly led a shell into the chamber. Chuck was doing the same.

After a couple more minutes of kneeling and listening, Frank decided to act. Sneaking up to where he could see their pen, he saw two women yanking the black barrier plastic out of the ground. He could not see anyone else around and did not know if they were there alone. He got up and pushed forward. They still had not seen him.

"HEY!" What in the hell do you think you two are doing?" Frank shouted, startling women, causing them to both scream, stumble back, and nearly fall.

ACT III

Twenty-Nine

Traveling Light

The island below continued to shrink as Bruce and I were carried heavenward. All the intensity of the battle hung on us. The images we were shown in those few moments of struggle ran like electricity through us as we held on for dear life. During the ascent, there were no thoughts or feelings of fear. We watched the ground disappear below us as we ran through a thick layer of clouds. Above the storm, we could see the flashes of lightning from the top side of the clouds contrasted with the deep blackness of the intense storm. We were held firmly—without feeling trapped.

At a point in our ascent where we could see the far-off cities of Bay City and Saginaw, I laid my head on Jesus' shoulder with an overwhelming sense of relief and appreciation. He selected us to go with him on this journey. Any words I could ever write down here cannot describe the overwhelming joy I was given. I overflowed with gratitude that welled up in me. My desire for the former world faded as our altitude increased.

At that moment, wonder exploded as I was lifted out of the fog of carnal life and ushered into eternity. I could see the blessings given to me throughout my life. It was not a specific event-by-event recounting but more of an overview of mercy and grace that was shown to me. Another gift from the gracious nail-scarred hand holding us while we soared.

"Why are you so wonderful to me, Jesus?" That was my immediate thought.

"Yes, Lord, why are you so amazing to us?" Bruce asked in my mind. I was able to hear what he thought.

"Is that you, Bruce?" I asked myself tentatively, or I wondered through myself.

"Yes brother I can hear you!" he replied.

We both just started laughing like we had never laughed before, and Jesus laughed along with us and revealed new truths as we flew higher still.

"I Am because I Am," was his calm response as the laughter subsided.

When we crested the horizon, where Bruce and I could see the bend of the Earth's atmosphere, Jesus told us that he had to return to work. But it assured us that the next leg of the journey home would become one of our favorite memories. It would be a time of new understanding, insights, and growth like we had never experienced. We would begin to know our true Abba Father and see how he was at work throughout our time on Terra. We would understand fully the things that held us back from Him, all our wounds, Anchors, and unbelief. We would face the pain of those things in a way that would grow us more into who we really are. To accomplish these things and prepare us for our time in the next world, we would have to walk alongside a unique Guide that had been chosen. His name was Andreas.

Jesus lifted his head up, and we followed his lead. As we looked into the black void of space, it took a second or two for us to adjust. Perhaps it was not our new eyes but our ability to use them. I imagined that infants on Earth experienced the same realization of things like 'mom,' 'bed,' and 'food.' Seeing things with new eyes would take some getting used to.

There was a shimmer in the blackness of outer space. Peering above, for a long time, I was becoming more confident.

It began like a ripple in the fabric of space. As we gained altitude, the blackness of the environment started to become pierced by pinpricks of light. Then, millions of tiny lights appeared above us like someone had turned on a galactic switch. Never could we have imagined this beauty and glory was living right above our heads for our entire lives! All the space travelers had talked about this after returning to Earth.

Again, the shimmer happened, and we were heading right for it. It was growing, and what appeared to be random edges became distinguishable for brief moments, hiding many stars.

"That is where we are headed," Jesus said in us.

As we gained the same altitude as the bottom of the strange craft, he swung us in a tight arch over the outside edge, and a new scene opened before us. We now flew toward what appeared to be a ship meant for travel in outer space, but it was beyond anything humans used. The black shimmer was like a gigantic textured shield, almost as if it had been modeled after a piece of some mountain face on the Earth with angles and outcrops in random places. Now, on the other side of the shield, there was a shining golden globe-like area where we were speeding.

The area was part of an object with three long tubular sections intersecting through the top of the globe-like portion's top. In front of the three gigantic tubes was connected an area larger than the rest of the ship by four times. That section was constructed in a vast swooping arc that started from where the tubes ended and joined into a large portion of another globe-like area that shone. Thousands of tiny lights emanated from the crystal hull, projecting beams of multicolored shafts from every angle possible. The ship resembled a gigantic jellyfish.

Jesus made the final approach toward the back of the golden globe, swooping in with extreme speed. He left us standing up on the white stone-like deck as he blessed us and left— all in one motion. We both knew the flight had been for our benefit, perhaps to give us an overview of the massive ship. We were certain we could have appeared in this place immediately after departing earth.

"Welcome new arrivals Bruce and Craig from Michigan," was announced among a hail of applause from other people who emerged from our mental fog and were standing all around us. It was surreal.

"I am your Auctor, Andreas, and you have been transferred to us here on the loading deck of an Inter-Dimensional Transfer Ship. This ship has been tasked with transporting you and all of today's Transfers from Terra," Andrea said. He was stunningly tall with pleasant features and dark eyes. Andreas was a young man with shoulder-length, slicked-back black hair and spoke to the entire group. At least, we thought he was talking to everyone— but, at the same time, it felt as if he was speaking only to us.

"We welcome you to the IDTS Galaxy Rose," said Andreas while clapping. The roar was almost deafening, echoing off grandiose stone walls— which looked as if they had been quarried granite.

147

As we began to gain our bearings, Bruce and I started to notice the glorious detail of the ship.

"Welcome three new arrivals, Boon-Mae, Chet, and Han, from Bangkok, Thailand," was announced to applause.

Bruce and I looked at each other, puzzled, wondering what was happening. I noticed the floors on board this ship were gorgeous. They appeared to be polished white marble with large ebony and gold veins flowing through each section. The pieces were twenty feet squares across the room's expanse. The room was two hundred feet wide and double that in length. The granite walls were on two opposing sides of the area, extending up twenty feet. The ceiling was open, vaulted, and transparent as the stars and the three long tubes were visible. The roof was not sitting on top of the stone walls; it appeared to be another twenty feet above them, indicating a mezzanine level at the top of the walls. It, too, was glass-like.

On the far end of the grand hall, a waterfall dropped over the edge from the upper level. That wall was deep brown in color, and green leafy trees sat off to the left. The forest floor was dirt-covered, with patches of grass, but it was a long way off. The light in the whole place was warm and bright, as sparkles of colored light beamed in from the back of the colossal crystal section of the ship.

"Welcome two new arrivals, Austin and Mark, from El Paso, Texas," was announced among a hail of applause.

"OK, every time new arrivals show up, they are announced to the group as a whole," Bruce said in hushed tones.

"They must then give the 'Galaxy Rose' pitch individually after the introduction," I said. "This place is amazing, Bruce." I pointed out things I had noticed.

"Did you see the stained glass back behind us?" he asked.

"No," I said. I turned to look, and Bruce pointed it out with his shiny spirit arm.

"Man, I am going to have to get used to seeing you like this Bruce," I said.

"I know what you mean. How did we even 'feel' ourselves land on the floor of this ship?" Bruce asked.

"How are we talking?"

We did not understand this new world.

"Welcome fifteen new arrivals from the bus trip in Argentina....," was announced among a hail of applause.

I later learned the name of the place we stood— the Grand Meeting Hall. We were allowed to roam freely. I went straight to the waterfall. The ice-cold water felt like it had melted off a glacier high up in the Rockies. How I felt something flowing through me was beyond my ability to understand.

Bruce moved to the stained glass masterpiece suspended from the granite wall by two posts resembling giant ivory elephant tusks. The intense artistic rendition was of Jesus carrying a lamb, and the piece measured fifteen feet high. As I caught up, he stood before the image, crying. Of course, there were no 'spirit body' tears, but I knew Bruce was having a moment. Then it hit me; I remembered he had crafted the same image into the stained glass for my parents' church over forty years ago. I joined him in the memory.

"Welcome another new arrival, Mohammad from Tunisia," was announced among a hail of applause.

The arrivals and announcements went on for hours, sometimes in rapid machine gun fashion. The Great Meeting Hall was filling up quickly, but I had spoken to no one other than Bruce. In fact, I could not remember even seeing someone up close. It was strange to have so many beings around without interaction. I would not call it uneasy, but peculiar, would be a better description of my feelings.

Another massive announcement brought several hundred people in, and I went looking for Bruce. He was touching the rock carved into a stunning abstract piece.

"Wow! Amazing!" I said as I approached.

"Yeah, and the texture is so familiar," he said, touching the art.

"Hey, have you noticed we are with these people but have had absolutely no conversation with anyone other than each other?"

"Yeah, now that you mention it," he said.

"Well, the room is almost full, so something has to happen soon," I said.

Another period of time passed that felt like an hour of Earth time.

"Welcome to our very last new arrival Amy from the Philippines. Amy is from Georgia and was doing mission work in the Philippines," was announced among a hail of applause.

Then, a four-sided screen appeared above us in the middle of the crowd of several thousand people from around the Earth. It was magically suspended above our heads, floating so everyone in the room could watch. It felt familiar— like being at a rally in a convention center.

"Greetings, Transfers! Yeah!" Andreas shouted from a place at the top of the stone wall, and his image was projected onto the monstrous screen.

"We are so glad that you are finally with us!" More applause circled the room. The area above the granite was also filled with people, a different kind of people, but easily identified as people. All around the room from above, they watched over the top of the wall as the new transfers were welcomed aboard their magnificent ship.

"This is your new day! The beginning of the rest of eternity, what we would say is your best life and it starts now!" Wild cheering and applause from all the people filled the room with a sonic boom. It felt like the floor shook at the celebration.

"My name is Andreas. I am the Auctor for this voyage-voyage-voyage. I am not from Terra or Earth, as most of you would call it-it-it." He said, waiting a moment for the echoes to quiet.

"My role as Auctor -Auctor -Auctor is really one of a mentor and guide -guide -guide for this brief moment of transition for your entire graduating class of "20 August 2023, which is 7,652 souls -souls -souls.""

A long, proverbial "wow" echoed across the hall, followed by clapping. The noise did not come from the folks on the floor— they could not make the clapping sound— but it came from the beings above on the mezzanine.

This was new information for Bruce and me. All these people died on the same day that we passed. It was our forever connection with all 7,652 of them.

"I was born on Para, -Para -Para, and was created to help Terrains transfer from life on earth to their new life, -life, -life," he said, pausing to let it sink in.

"I have much to explain to you, and this way of communication isn't very productive, so I need to tell you a little about how we Auctor are gifted by our Creator.

"Who is forever to be praised!" The sudden, explosive, responsive shout from the mezzanine to the mention of the Creator was accompanied by loud shouts of joy that went on for at least a minute.

"You'll get used to that," Andreas said, pumping his fist to the cheers.

"One of the gifts I have been given as an Auctor is the gift of "Speculum." He repeated the name slower and continued.

"Speculum is the ability for us Auctor to appear to everyone of you at the same time and hold personal conversations with all of you and remember the entire experience," he waited.

"So in just a few moments, the screen will be gone -gone -gone, and I will be next to each of you so we can talk face to face -ace, -ace. It's much more personal. We need this personal time because I have much to tell you about the next twenty-nine days of your new life. We will walk about the Grand Hall, and I will share with you what you can expect to happen. Some life-changing events will occur within the next month. You need to be prepared to get everything you can out of them," he said in his chopped-up stadium-speaking voice, trying to overcome the resounding echo.

"At the end of the explanation, we will have an open discussion to put at ease any unanswered questions about the exciting process in front of you. These will be process questions only at that point," Andreas said.

"Are— we— ready?" He shouted, emphasizing each word. Then he asked the question again, trying to put the souls at ease and energize the ship's staff.

THIRTY

ANDREAS

The screen disappeared, and everyone in the hall faded into the background. Andreas, my Auctor, stood in front of me. He was over six feet six and had a climber-thin body. His skin was a perfect olive color without a wrinkle or blemish. His high cheekbones, prominent nose, and lips were not unusual for someone from Italy or Greece. What was different was his substantial dark brown eyes, at least half again as big as human eyes. Yet they felt inviting, disarming, and welcoming. His slicked-back hair made him appear in his mid to late twenties. The caring tone of his voice was unencumbered by an accent and soothed my mind as it passed through. He was dressed casually in a wrinkle-free plain white t-shirt, khaki hiking pants, and dark brown deck shoes that showed some wear around the toes.

"Craig, I am so honored to finally meet you, brother," he said, embracing me. I was trying to figure out how to respond. I thought I should just return his embrace.

Boom! The embrace was a turning on of a switch. It allowed me to see with unrestricted intimacy into Andreas and him into me. There was nothing between us then, and I understood his life, motivations, and purpose. It was such an intense feeling, like a massive dopamine dump into a human brain that I no longer possessed. Nothing was sensual about our exchange; it was just an overwhelming ability to see someone for who they were created to be and who they were.

"That, my new friend, is your first taste of genuine next-life intimacy, and I am so honored to have met you. I am so blessed to have been selected to be your Auctor on this part of your journey." He said, his hands still resting on my shoulders as he peered into me.

I could not put words to what was happening inside me. I overflowed with emotion, bawling like a baby. It was a holy cry, a cry that was moving me more into the place of acceptance. A realization washed over me, and I knew the truth that had lived inside me for over thirty-five years— the truth that God himself chose me before the foundation of the world to be his very own in Christ Jesus. Gratitude exploded from my heart.

To think that Andreas was doing this intimate thing with all the other 7651 class members simultaneously must have been quite the experience for him.

"Yes, Craig, it is an honor to have been selected to guide this beautiful group home," he said with humility.

"You have loved nature during your time on Terra, I mean Earth," he said over his slip of the tongue.

"Yes, it was a place I was able to experience the majesty of God," I said.

"OK. Let us walk through some as we talk," Andreas said. In the next blink we were on a trail that cut through thick woods which felt familiar.

"This feels like a trail along Lake Superior!" I was transported back to the place I had loved for many years. The smell of the woods, the cool breeze from the water, the birds singing in the trees, and even the rich black dirt beneath my feet. I was there in that split second, and we were standing on my trail.

"Yes. It looks beautiful, Craig. I can see why you would experience the majesty of God in a place like this," he said. Then he stepped over a large rock in the trail.

"I need to tell you about your new life Craig. The life you spent on Ter., sorry, Earth," he caught himself in error, "was lived out according to a definite constriction of time. If you would imagine time as a trail that we are hiking on, it would only and always allow you to be in the now. You had lived in those past days, but those days were gone and only reviewable in your memory. The future was dreamed about but wasn't yet there. So the only concept of time all Earthlings have is right now. The immediate moment which is clicking away one second at a time. It is, at best, limited view of reality." He said, looking over at me as we came to a place that allowed a clifftop view of the beautiful blue lake stretching to the horizon before us.

"Wow," he said. We paused to take it all in.

"I love this place," is all I could say as a summer breeze swept up the cliffs and into our faces.

"Being here again triggers memories and with them feelings. But they are past," he said. "The earth is always 'Now,'" using his slender fingers to make quote signs.

"It was hard remembering whose I was in the moment by moment life, but in reality, that is all I had. Truth is He was all I needed. Yet, the daily distractions were powerful," I said.

"Or, perhaps you gave the power to the distractions in the moment rather than living in the truth of the now and the reality of Jesus being in each now with you," he said as he pulled away to continue further down the trail.

"You are right," I said, amazed at his insight for such a young man, as we stepped back onto the trail and into a thick wood.

"So there are two other worlds, Craig, you have not been able to see when you lived on earth." he said.

"OK," I responded, trying to understand his meaning.

"You can't see them because they exist twenty-eight days into the future," he tried to see into me to understand what I was thinking.

"I am a person who needs to internalize, Andreas," I explained. "It takes me some time to process before I am able to give much back, it has nothing to do with you."

"I understand," is all he said. We came to a narrow spot in the trail and had to climb over an immediate rise. Using roots from the trees as steps because the incline was sharp, we started up.

"OK, I think that I get the idea," I said to him at the top of the hill.

"I am from one of the worlds that, according to Terrain time, lies twenty-eight days ahead. It is called Para, and it is where we are all headed," he said as if he had delivered the earthshaking news a thousand times before.

"Jesus talked about going to prepare a place for his people to be able to come and be where he is," he said, knowing I knew the Scripture reference.

"Yes He did say that," I admitted. "He also talked about a new heaven and a new earth," I threw out.

"Absolutely, and that is what is being prepared for all of us. At the end of time as we know it, both worlds will be brought to unity and the new Jerusalem will descend from the heavens and God himself will live with us," he proclaimed with a look of wonder.

My head swirled with the new, unconsidered possibility.

"So, what about this other world, the third one?" I asked.

"That is Apollyon and is the place reserved for those who rebel against God," he said with the slightest air of authority.

"Apollyon is also twenty eight days ahead in time," he explained.

"Alright," I replied, trying to wrap my brain around that one.

"All three worlds orbit the same sun, as a matter of fact they are almost the same distance from that sun. Apollyon is directly opposite from Terra in its orbit, so the sun is between them, while Para is one month ahead of Terra in the same orbit," he said while using his hands to help in the description.

"Got it, that makes it a little clearer," I said, as the idea had clicked on a theoretical level.

"So the mission of the Galaxy Rose is to get this class of transfers from Terra, twenty-eight days into the future and one month ahead from Terra's orbit.

"This must happen every day of the year," I said as it dawned on me from the announcement earlier.

"Yes there are fifty ships in the fleet all working on a rotational basis," he said.

"So why don't we just show up in heaven? The whole 'absent from the body is present with the Lord' thing. I asked, confused.

"Abba is with you on this journey in ways that are much more experiential than on Terra, so both those things remain true. With so many coming during the last days, this was the process Abba chose," he said.

"How long of a journey is it to get twenty eight days into the future?" I asked as I navigated through the edge of a large puddle.

"Excellent question," he shot back as he jumped over the water on the trail. "It takes ten days to make the passage to Para."

"In those ten days you will be busy preparing for what comes next in your life," he said.

"Busy doing what exactly," I just wanted to cut around the minutia.

He stopped walking and leaned against a downed tree to take a break.

"The first thing that happens is that you will be outfitted with your very own EED," he said it like I would know what it meant.

I wanted to put my hand up like I was back in school, but he sensed the objection.

"Sorry, an EED is an acronym for Essence Encapsulation Device, basically you will be slipped into a suit that was made for you and is completely unique in all the universe. That suit, which was woven together from dirt, will contain your essence, everything that makes you, you. Your spirit, soul, and everything you have learned in your first life," he explained.

"After you are in the suit, it is then filled with a liquid that is lighter than water and the Holy Cru'or is added." He looked into me to gauge whether he should continue straight up the information mountain or if we needed to take a break and go downhill for a few minutes, so I could catch my breath.

"Do I feel like I am drowning in this suit, which I am certain has to be zipped closed somehow?" I asked.

"No," he said.

"I can see the picture you are drawing for me."

"May I continue?" he asked.

"Yes."

"The one," I cut him off. "Will you explain what the Cru'or is?" I asked.

"Yes I can Craig," he said to reassure me that all questions were valid.

"Can I share that question later with the whole group?" he asked.

"Sure, I guess that would be fine."

"The Cru'or is simply one molecule of blood taken from the cross of Jesus Christ that is added to the processing liquid. Cru'or is a Latin word that communicates the idea that the blood was taken from a wound that flowed. The only thing that takes away our sin in this universe is the blood of the perfect Lamb of God. He paid for our rebellion, and our personal sin keeps people from knowing

God. So when Jesus was crucified on the cross of Calvary, a squad of hidden Angelic Warriors gathered enough of his precious blood to be used in the final application of the sanctification of the elect."

"The blood payment for your sin was by faith, and today will be, in fact, reality. The Holy Cru'or is used to wash away all the Anchors that have held us from seeing who we are created to be. It destroys the strongholds that have blinded us and kept us from seeing ourselves and others from how our Abba knows us. It vanquishes the lies we have held onto, in some cases, our whole lives. This Soaking happens for everyone in your class as we travel to Para," he said as he took a deep breath.

"Wow," my mind clicked now like someone had opened the door of understanding.

"You are telling me that the same blood of Jesus that justifies us before our Holy God is what also sanctifies us for our next journey? The blood of Christ rids us of all of the deception which has plagued us for our entire walk on earth. Will all the sins that entangled me vanish through this Soaking time? Will we be able to interact with others without the lies, the pretense, the distractions, the pressure to conform to other people's expectations?" It felt like all the questions came from outside me, being downloaded into my heart and out of my mouth.

"Yes and more," he explained. "Your expectations will be broken down, and you will be able to walk as you were created to walk. Your unique life will uniquely glorify Abba. Along with that, all those being transferred, along with all of their unique gifts, will be merged into the Holy Assembly as we await the Day of Unity! Glory to Him alone who has washed us and set us free!" He bowed low as he gave praise to Abba.

"Where is the Holy Spirit in all of this?" I asked because I had yet to hear His name mentioned.

"Great question Craig!" he said while smiling at me. "As you know the Holy Spirit has been working on Terra," he looked at me to see if I objected to him calling my home by his name, which at that point I did not, "to bring people to faith, to grow their faith and to make them more like Christ. When your class is Soaking you are held in an area of this ship that is a Holy place. There are only a few who can enter because it is a place the Spirit of the Living God dwells with power, because it is only through his power we can be changed into our true selves. He uses the blood of Christ to make those changes."

I let that whole exchange ruminate inside me for a few moments. I realized the blood of Jesus was the key to everything, even here.

"Can I be taller, in my new suit, I mean?" I was laughing while asking.

"It has already been made for you my friend," he said as he chuckled.

"But the way I was killed on Terra, you know, the measurements they may have taken would be different than the actual pre-tree smashing event height," I was almost crying from laughter and snorting.

Andreas joined in my fun for a moment. He seemed somewhat awkward.

"What happens to the suit at the end of the Soaking time?" I wondered.

"The suit becomes part of you like your body was part of you on Terra. It's where you will wait for the resurrection of your perfect body after unity is complete.

"So, during the Soak, what will I be doing?" I asked.

"You will simply be," he said.

"What does that mean?" I asked.

"Just being in the process of cleansing is enough," he explained. "You will be silent throughout the journey, and there will be moments when you can record thoughts and emotions. Some people write volumes about the experience like Mother Teresa— now that girl was a writer!" he said, trying to bring some levity back.

"I think I will love that time," I said while holding back an emotional waterfall.

We walked along, beginning to descend as the trail switched back and forth. It was narrow and clumsy hiking as we came to an opening in the trees that allowed us to overlook a beach from a tall cliff. The long white sandy beach was nestled between a high hundred-foot cliff on the south where we were and a smaller fifty-foot outcrop on the north. It was my favorite beach in the world, and no other soul was on it.

"Can we sit for a few moments," I asked as we reached the warm sand.

"Absolutely."

Watching the gentle waves roll onto the beach, breaking before us, was perfection.

THIRTY-ONE

RED CARD

Sitting in the shade of a mature oak tree, he repaired his torn net. The day was warm, but the air was moving across the lake, making it perfect. He held a round wooden frame with a long pole attached by wrapped twine. The structure was in a teardrop shape as two ends ran up along each side of the dark wood of the handle. The cord secured the wooden dowels, which connected the two pieces. The binding rope wore out before the net more often than not. He replaced it many times over the years. On this occasion, the net itself is the problem.

Every time he went to dip beneath a fish he had caught, it found its way free. You cannot provide for anyone if you let the dinner swim off with another fat worm. After fishing all morning, he found himself in his quiet spot on the lakeshore.

His hands were cracked and dry from fishing. It was his livelihood in the remote village. Restringing the net would not do anything to help the conditions of his hands as the rope sucked more moisture from his fingers.

He felt alive as he worked. He loved living here in this place he called home for over sixteen years. He felt fortunate to be placed there. The people were good folks, most working with their hands. Many of this fishing village's thirty houses hugged along the only street through these parts. The stone-covered road was behind him by a few hundred yards. Far enough to avoid the noise of village life and avoid distractions.

He was hairy and had earned his nickname based solely on that fact. Everyone around the fishing village called him "Bear." Although he was forty, there wasn't a hint of gray anywhere. Even in his thick mustache and straight sideburns, not one off-colored hair, just how he liked it. His hat covered the only part of him that was not covered by a curly black rug, his bald head, and the top of his ears. The cap, which did not come off his head, was sweaty, with white stains circumnavigating the entire crown, almost like one of those sand paintings in a jar. Sweat was evident on the bill. He loved his dark blue hat almost as much as his bright blue and white fishing boat.

Sitting under the tree, he could see the skiff at the end of the dock. The wooden wharf jutted about a hundred yards from his shade tree into the calm waters. Two younger, shirtless, tanned men from his crew were washing the blue and white boat. They were emptying five-gallon buckets of water across the wooden deck, cleaning up from today's catch. Six other boats were tied to the dock, with a few of their crews finishing the day's work in the mid-day sun.

"Hey, Bear," called the familiar voice. She was walking over the grassy rise, about twenty yards away and coming from their shared home. Neeve had a plate in her hand with some food on it. Her long blonde hair was hanging down today, unlike when it was hoisted high on her head. She had a relaxed gate about her as she strolled along. He was glad she had sought him out because he was hungry. He knew he needed to take time to sit and enjoy a good meal more often.

Neeve was always watching out for him these days since her arrival. She had tried working in the big city at the end of the road for a few years, but there needed to be a better fit for her skill set. They sent her up our way to be a cook for Bear's fishing cadre. The reunion was lovely, and the familiar company was even better. She had whipped things into shape in a hurry in the house, holding everyone accountable for their issues and their stuff. Her laid-back style had put everyone at ease, but no one got fooled into thinking she was weak and a pushover. She was neither.

"Bear, you gotta eat something today," she said in her smooth southern way.

"Thanks, Neeve. I appreciate you looking out for me," he smiled as he looked up.

"Again!" she said, teasing him as she smiled back.

"Why don't you sit down with me?" He said as he made the room so she could use the tree to lean against.

"Break a net, did you?" She inquired about the project that he was working on, and handed him the glass plate draped in a cloth.

"Just wore it out again," he said, setting aside his stuff and eagerly taking the dish.

"It's just some fresh bread and sausage," she said, sitting beside him.

"Oh, and I have some water in my pocket, too," handing him the glass bottle.

"Thank You, Neeve. This looks good." After pausing for a long minute to give thanks, he dug into the delicious meal.

"My word, it sure is a beautiful day, Bear," she said as she leaned her head back and tried hard to absorb the entire scene into her thankful heart.

"Thank You, Lord!" she shouted in deep gratitude.

"Hey guys, I thought I might catch you over here," said the middle-aged letter carrier, Vaughn.

"Vaughn, what is happening exciting in the letter carrying business today?" Asked Bear in his usual comedic fashion.

"Well, same stuff as most days," he said as he searched his big leather bag.

"How was the fishing today?" he asked. "Still coming up empty?" He poked fun at the hungry fisherman.

"What brings you over here?" Neeve asked as she pulled at the grass beside her legs.

"Is that the best you got, letter boy?" Bear asked, smiling and chewing. He always gave the teasing back even more than he received.

"Well, every once in a while, I get to be the bearer of some good news," he said with a pun-intended smile, just as he found what he was looking for. He pulled out two red postcards.

They knew what that meant, and excitement shot through the air.

"Really?" Was all that Neeve could say, staring at the cards in his hand.

"Red! Red means first priority, right Vaughn?" Bear tried to remember. It had been a while since he got a red one, which was only once in sixteen years.

"Sure does, Bear. That means you have to be there on the first day, and you get to stay all week.

"And we both got one?" Neeve asked.

"No, Neeve. You didn't get one arrival announcement," ..... "You got two, each!" Vaughn played with them as they all stood and hugged, dancing and yelping.

The invitations were certified as Neeve and Bear stared at the official seal embossed into the card's background. All the information was given, even down to the departure times for the trains. It would be a day's travel and seven days of the world's best party, then another day to return.

Bear could not hold back the tears of excitement while Neeve wondered.

"TWO, TWO!" She said placing her empty hand on the top of her head, amazed.

"Thank You Lord!"

Thirty-Two

Known

"There are a few more things we must talk about before we have to return to the hall," Andreas said in hushed tones, just over the sound of the waves.

"Sure," I said as another curl of blue-green water overturned and crashed into the sand.

"After we are done here, the whole team is going to spend time getting to know each other," he said, talking a little louder now.

"OK," I said, but I didn't understand the 'why' of it all.

"This will be the only time that this group is gathered on this ship. There is great benefit to your shared story and besides, it is an excellent way to practice getting to know people on a deep level." He was pumped about the upcoming gathering. I hung on every word.

"So, there is a bit more," he said, pressing a bit.

"OK, go on," I said, as I was almost to the point of overload. Alright, I was already past that.

"I will just give you the highlights and the rest you can get at the question and answer session which is going to start in ten minutes," he said as he stood with his shoes in his hands.

"You do remember about the whole internalize thing?" I asked.

"I do," he said, moving back toward the trail.

"After the Soaking time is complete, when we arrive at Para, there is a Purification Ritual that is very stirring and inspiring. You won't want to miss that," he caught himself and laughed out loud at the thought.

I smiled as it took an extra second for the humor to break through the busy circuits in my mind. I did not have much of a choice in the whole ritual matter.

"Ohh, tough crowd," he said as he slapped my back, laughing as we walked along the beach.

"What will we look like after the Soaking is complete? I mean, after being in the water for that long I would imagine that we all resemble a bunch of walking prunes." Now I thought I was being funny.

He did laugh.

"You will recognize yourself for sure. Some have said it ends up being you at your prime," Andreas said, smiling.

"What about hair? Can I get a little help on that issue?" I smiled at the extraterrestrial leading me back to an Interdimensional Transfer Ship so I could go live in another world after I got a new body. A little extra hair on my head did not seem like a big request. It was a heck of a day.

Thirty-Three

The Soak

"And we are back!" Andreas said through the screen to the whole gathering of stunned humans in the Grand Meeting Hall back on board the Galaxy Rose. All the personal meetings with our Auctor were over. We had to return to reality and our new circumstances to hear about another unique situation in front of us all. My proverbial head was exploding.

"Question number one comes from..." The questions continued for a while. Andreas wanted to answer all the concerns he could. Then, a loud clunk and sudden shake came from below us.

"Not to worry fellow space travelers, we are just uncoupling from the loading barge and getting towed out to cislunar space so we can begin our journey home," Andreas said to an eruption of applause from the mezzanine.

"And so those guys can get back to work," he said, laughing and pointing to all the folks on the second level.

"Right now, we will kick off the party with a mixer. You are tasked to get to know someone from every continent. Ready, set, go!" He clapped and cheered us on as dance music was piped into the hall.

Our ability to see the people around us was turned on by some master switch. As you can imagine, people were tentative about this new level of being known. It was awkward for most of us in the room. The noise level increased as people learned to share initial greetings with complete strangers. The laughter was evident as we tried to figure out a new set of social parameters. This was about something other than gaining approval. That was deconstructed during my time with Andreas. Now, it was about knowing and being known. It was about learning to appreciate our Creator's propensity to the unique attributes of individuals and how that all works together for his glory. I could better understand other perspectives on things by experiencing their story. The longer I had with someone, the deeper the sharing went— the more profound the sharing, the stronger the bond, even in a few moments of an embrace.

I imagine Adam and Eve must have experienced it in the Garden so many lifetimes ago. Of course, that had led to sexual intimacy for the purposes of procreation. Here in this hall, in this new life, there was no sex drive. Sharing lives was much more profound and satisfying than a romp in a bed, even with a lifetime spouse. That pleasure only lasted a few moments. This new level of knowing each other and understanding how we fit together was mind-blowing.

No one had any perception of time, and it was a day later, in old Earth time when everyone had finally met and shared.

"Ladies and gentlemen," it was Andreas on the screen above.

"Ladies and gentlemen, thank you so much for this time of sharing so openly. Isn't this a great class?"

Booming applause echoed again.

"Excellent! Excellent! We are going to move from the hall and starting the process of getting all of you into your E.E.D.'s. We need you to start moving back through the doors and up the stairs to the mezzanine." Andreas explained while we moved arm-in-arm to our next adventure with seven thousand new, intimate friends.

Thirty-Four

Anticipation

Bear held Neeve as they stepped onto the train. Officially, the Magnetic Lift Railed Transportation System was being constructed across the entire planet to connect everyone. The cars designed for people were wide and warm, with relaxed seating, allowing the adventurous to remove their shoes and stretch out. Resting was encouraged throughout the train. The sporadic stations still had generous distances between them. Traveling over four hundred miles an hour, most stops were separated by an hour or more.

Neeve grabbed the first empty booth she came to and sat beside the window facing forward. She hoped not to have to deal with any motion sickness this time. Bear left a chair between the two of them and sat down. There were four seats on each side of the booth. He knew if the car filled up, he would have to squeeze in closer, hoping for some alone time during the day-long ride.

Bear was still thrown by the reality of two red invitations last week. He had not been able to concentrate much at work since then, looking forward to the Arrival celebration. It was all their little village had talked about the entire week. Scarce, indeed, was the idea that one person would get two red tickets at once. What were the odds that two people from the same cadre would be handed a pair of red slips together? Neither of them had been able to sleep. Bear appreciated the fact the notices did not arrive a month in advance. Then, there would have been a fish shortage during those days of anticipation.

The trip to the arrival center on the west side of St. Luke would take them all day. It was the regional hub in this northern territory of Para, known as the Great Water. It was recognized for its massive freshwater lakes and rivers fed by the glaciers on the mountain ranges encircling the area. It was typically cooler here, and they liked it.

Bear wondered deep inside himself how weird this double arrival thing would be. Who else was coming had been the question most asked by his curiosity and everyone else. The speculation was driving him crazy.

Neeve was so excited she sat on the edge of her seat. She was looking forward to the first embrace, and with as much enthusiasm would be the updates from Terra. Not that she spent any time worrying about such things, but she often prayed Abba was with those left behind and He would bless them with knowing Him by faith. The rest was out of her hands, yet it would be exciting to hear.

"Steady for Departure," said the voice over the intercom.

The train lifted a foot off the ground with creaks and groans. With a tug, it rocked into forward motion, pushing the two excited passengers back into their seats.

Thirty-Five

Hunger

The silence was over as I woke up on a gurney in some type of medical unit. I was groggy and chose to lay there, gather my thoughts, and pray. I was grateful to be alive. Blessed by my Soaking time. I expressed my joy to Abba by singing a song of praise in my mind. I had been doing just that for the last ten days. The experience had been an incredible journey of washing, cleansing, and renewal.

Almost sixty-one years of crud was scrubbed from my soul. All the thoughtlessness, selfishness, and lies I had clung to were melted away by the blood of Jesus working its way through every part of my being. I was new in the truest sense of the term— new.

"Thank You Father for your wonderful mercy and grace that you have accomplished in me."

I stretched a loud, obnoxious stretch. In doing so, I felt a new sensation of vertebrae cracking and popping up and down my spine. My eyes shot open to the soft glow of a warmly lit room. I rubbed my new eyes with my new hands and sat up. It was me. As I looked at my new self, it seemed as if everything was normal, not crushed into a pile of broken bones anymore.

Jumping to my feet, the sheet fell to the dark wooden floor. There was a mirror on the wall and some clothes on a small chair in the corner. After running my new body through a visual inspection, I dressed in blue jeans, a blue pullover shirt with two stripes, socks, and tennis shoes. All the way I liked it. I noticed I was feeling an ache I had not noticed since arriving. It was hunger.

"Wait, we have to eat on Para?" I wondered aloud.

171

The door to my tiny room slid open, and a young woman in her mid-thirties walked in. She was thin and tall with a muscular build. Her black hair was shoulder-length, and her smile was infectious.

"How are we feeling, Craig?" she asked as she looked at a chart hanging on the clipboard at the end of my gurney.

"Great, so far. But I am a bit confused," I said.

"That's completely normal," she said reassuringly and stepped close.

Her eyes were cobalt blue and gigantic. They were almost hypnotic in nature as she peered into me.

"It takes some time to get used to the new reality of openness," she said, lowering her gaze. "What else are you confused by?"

"I feel hungry," I said.

"Perfect! Exactly what we wanted to hear!" She emphasized this with her hand gestures.

"You mean we spend time eating in Para?" I questioned.

"Of course, silly!" She smiled, showing a mouth full of perfect teeth.

"But you are fasting until after the Purification Ritual is complete, then the real feast begins!" She was all smiles as she checked me for vitals.

"It is just really different from what I had expected, I guess," I said, as she rapped on my knees to check my reflexes.

"Yes, it's true for every transfer I have been a part of," she smiled even more, lighting up her entire face.

"So, are you Terrain?" I asked.

"No, I am Paraguese," she said.

"What's the difference?" I asked.

"Not much, really. I was created here to help with the transfers and have served on the Galaxy Rose from the beginning of the ship's mission.

"How long ago was that?" I asked without any knowledge of any cultural prohibitions.

"Well you don't just come out and ask a Paraguese woman a question like that, mister!" She laughed out loud.

I was mortified. Then I realized that she was teasing me.

"Hey, I have the advantage here, so I like to tease the Terrains. Here on Para, there are no secrets, only lessons," she was funny and intelligent.

"What's your name?"

"Sam. Here, take my hand," she held out her soft hand. Her fingers were longer than humans.

I touched it cautiously, and the immediate jolt of electricity shot down to my heels. Sam became more known to me, and I to her, as we shared what made us unique. It was a fantastic thought— I could be known by a stranger from another world and be accepted for who I was created to be.

"Wow," is all I could say.

"See, now you know how old I am!" Sam said and smiled again.

"You look good for 247 years old!" I joked and laughed out loud.

"Hey!" She slapped me playfully with the clipboard.

"You're going to do just fine here, Craig," she said, then turned and walked out. Then leaning back and poking her head back in through the magic door, "Almost forgot, ten minutes until we dock, so be ready. You are cleared to go down to the Great Meeting Hall. It was nice to meet you!" Sam left me alone with a smile on my face.

Thirty-Six

Reunion

After the gathering in the hall, we were divided up into teams. The teams were needed because we had to be dropped at different arrival points around the planet. Each team had a specific landing craft, and each ship had various destinations.

Then he walked in. "BRUCE!" and we embraced. Backing off from each other, we looked one another up and down and started laughing like kids on Christmas morning. Tears, real wet and warm tears, tumbled down from our eyes. They were tears of joy. Shaking hands and giving each other a man hug, the knowing opened up for each of us, which caused more tears and even snot to form in my nose.

Someone in a uniform gave us a box of tissues and helped us move toward a line of people. A few others were crying. Still, for the most part, there was overwhelming joy and excitement of being alive with your fellow humans who had all died on the same day— ten short days ago. What a fantastic adventure we were on.

A uniformed person returned and whispered in our ears, "You guys are pretty special to have graduated together as relatives. Your Arrival party is going to be amazing!" She patted us on our backs, then turned and departed.

We were welcomed aboard the new shuttle as we left the confines of the spaceport dock on the Galaxy Rose. As we took our seats, we were told to sit back and relax. The seat beeped and then embraced us for the descent. A screen on each seat back in front of us sprang into action, and a young Paraguese couple began to explain the next few hours of our lives.

We were told in seventeen minutes that we would land at our Arrival port in St. Luke. The city was located in the Great Water territory. They went over everything from the landing to the Ritual, and the party. Details were kept scarce so we could experience our new life in the moment.

The excitement was thick throughout the landing craft. About 250 souls were strapped in and diving into the planet's cobalt-blue atmosphere. Streaks of sparks and fire shot past the outboard portals while the entire craft shook and lurched. I was thankful they had not fed us before this roller coaster ride.

The violent shaking smoothed out in two minutes— as soon as we fell further into the atmosphere. The craft's wings were extended, and we began to glide. A bank right, then left, then back right again. Through the window, the blue water and green forests seemed like a model suspended in the sky. Another bend showed us a white city jutting up from the green forest. It had tall spires casting shadows across other buildings. The roads looked almost like the spokes of a wheel, except for the side along the bluest blue ocean. A sliver of white sand painted the water's edge off to the horizon.

"Final Approach," squawked out over a speaker above our heads.

A thruster engaged; we were pushed hard against our restraints. The ground rose through the window. We were coming in at a tremendous speed. A sudden jerk when a set of wheels reached the ground, then two more in rapid succession.

"Ladies and gentlemen, I wanted to be the first to welcome you home," said a voice. Wild cheers and clapping erupted from all the Terrains on board.

The blitz of the next few moments was surreal, as we were herded onto a large transport bus-like vehicle. Moving off the landing area into a tunnel, the bus silenced everyone.

A young man stood up in the front of the craft.

"Welcome to St Luke!" he shouted. More cheers from the passengers.

"OK, we will disembark row by row into the preparation area, where we will line you up in order. Don't worry. There will be plenty of people to help you through. We will maintain an attitude of prayer as you prepare to step out onto Paradise for the first time."

Behind the curtain, we were lined up. Bruce was a few people in front of me. As they announced the name of the first Transfer over the loudspeaker, music erupted and there was wild cheering. What seemed like thousands of voices sang a song. I was excited, and nervous energy built while we waited.

"Austin from Texas is engendered to the tribe of Esther!" Wild cheers from one direction.

"Amy from Georgia is now with the tribe of Gershon!" Cheering and applause.

The entire group would be called in this same fashion. My new heart was pounding in my chest.

As I walked through the curtain, I did not hear a thing. I was swept up into a crazy scene. I stood on a stage— surrounded by an amphitheater overflowing with people. The Roman Colosseum came to mind as the Transferred gathered into the middle of the enormous stage. The people in the crowd seemed genuinely happy. Different sections would jump to their feet as each person was welcomed home. The final man introduced was Yuri from Serbia.

A leader stepped forward and sought quiet from the crowd by extending his hands into the air.

"The reading from Scripture," he announced.

"They cried out to the Lord in their trouble; He saved them out of their distresses. He sent them his Word and healed them, and delivered them from their destructions, Psalm 107:19-20," the young female voice said.

"Brothers and sisters we pray. Abba Father, we rejoice with what you have done in the life of these Transferred. The blood of Jesus has brought them though the veil of tears. We are here to dedicate them to you once again. May we be one as you are one and walk in the newness of life you have given to us. Help us to hear your voice and help us to be your people. In your glorious name, the Great God and King of all Kings!"

"It is so!" Was the overwhelming thunderous response from the cheering crowd.

Suddenly— cool, refreshing water sprays up from beneath us. It shocks us for a split second, and then we dance in joy like never before, splashing and hugging, crying and singing praise to God our Father, God our Savior, God our Rescue! This continues for fifteen minutes as the whole amphitheater rocks in celebration.

Around the outside ring of the celebrating circle of new inhabitants of Para, a group of people with name cards was gathering. They stood in silence while trying to get our attention. They wanted us to follow them off the stage and out of the arena. People started making the connection to follow, and were ushered out, beginning with a few and then growing in numbers. The crowd above was flowing out through the exits while the singing continued.

The path I followed was only two people behind Bruce. After stepping down from the stage, we went through a tunnel beneath the seating of the crowd. A hush came over us while walking a stone path, even as the music continued at the arena. We were dripping wet from the celebration, but the air smelled like lilac and felt warm on my face.

Climbing a rise, the trail opened into a beautiful tree-covered park. Lush green vegetation was everywhere. Walking the cobblestone path, trimmed by brilliant flowers, fresh fruit hung low from trees, and the incredible scents wafting past my nose at every turn, made me feel whole. As we marched through the garden paradise, some people were led off, one in each direction, onto stone paths to hidden pavilions. The roofs were visible, but nothing else. Cheers erupted behind us.

Much later, we came to a place in the trail with parallel paths. Our silent guides directed Bruce and me onto the narrow walkways. My heart was beating a hundred miles an hour. The attendant directed me to fall behind him as he began up the trail, which ascended a knoll through the woods. Bruce was just a few feet away on the other path. We exchanged nervous smiles as we crested the rise.

The white marble wall in front of me was beautiful, and the arch in the middle was about twelve feet tall and eight wide. The guide went through the opening and announced my name to the crowd gathered to welcome me by holding the name card up high. I walked in, and wild cheers were pressing in all around me. The first person I noticed walking up to me from the crowd was a much younger version of my Bepaw— my mother's father. He had passed, I mean Transferred, back when I was only nineteen. He trotted up and hugged me tight around my new neck— I thought my head might pop off. Tears of joy rained as we shared so many memories during that embrace. He had been convinced all week that the Arrival Party was for one of his two remaining daughters, who were still on Terra. Still, he was glad for my presence on Para.

"How are your mother and dad?" he asked me as he looked into my eyes. I still could not wrap my brain around what was happening.

"They are well, better than most 90-year-olds, and always blessed," I said.

Loud cheers went up in the pavilion beside us, the one Bruce had entered. Music erupted from people playing instruments along the back wall, which was only a couple of feet tall and made from stone. Behind them was a view into another garden which stretched as far as I could see. I noticed the line of Transferees walking off in the distance to their parties. "Over seven thousand parties are taking place across the planet, with 250 in this single garden paradise," said my guide.

An unidentified person grabbed me from behind and lifted me skyward in a bear hug. A young man who had been in church with me for a few years and had gone on a couple of mission trips with me.

"Welcome home brother!" he said, and we hugged again.

Next, a relative spun me again, then a friend, a co-worker, and an old pastor friend from Lexington. I had yet to see the two people who had come through the connecting path from the other pavilion. Until someone tapped me on the shoulder and pointed. I knew who they were immediately.

"Vic!" I ran to him and threw my arms around him. Weeping tears of joy.

"I knew I would see you!" I said as another gush of happy water leaked down my face.

Neeve joined in the hug, "I missed you, Craaaig!" She said in her classic southern drawl and kissed my bald head. I was filled to overflowing, even without the hair. Bruce's party and mine became one massive celebration of new life, and the delicious food made life perfect.

Within a few minutes, a girl, maybe eight years old, approached me while I talked with my father-in-law, Bear. Bepaw, who was close, picked her up in his arms and brought her the final few feet through the maze of people right to me. Her black curly hair, hazel eyes, and beautiful smile seemed familiar. They both put a hand on my shoulder as the precious little girl looked into my eyes and smiled and, with an angelic little voice, said,

"Hi Papa, I am Lilly, your granddaughter. I have been waiting so long to meet you." I was undone as I took her into my trembling arms, held her tight, spun around in a circle, and kissed her for the first time.

"Oh, Lilly, I am so blessed to finally hold you, my dear. I have wanted to meet you for many years!" I said as I lifted her to the sky, letting the joy spill down my face.

The parade of people continued for days. The times spent and stories shared were so amazing and life-giving. Grandparents, a great-great-great grandmother on my father's side, an old boss, and a friend from high school. Aunts and Uncles. The event was awe-inspiring. Who could have ever imagined humans could know such joy? What a perfect entrance into a new life.

Then, on the last day of the feast— the final guest arrived. The one who had carried us out of the raging battle and into the fray. We all went down on our faces to honor the King— as Jesus came for a visit to our celebration.

ACT IV

Thirty-Seven

Charity's Demands

"What? Wait don't shoot us!" Connie screamed out.

"We have been stranded here!" Diana tried to explain.

"What are you doing messing with things that aren't your's lady?" Frank was outraged and used the rifle to point his anger at her head.

Chuck moved in close to the women, who at the moment were trying to get back on their feet, as he leveled the rifle in their direction.

"Stay down!" Frank screamed, cursed, and spit.

"You got them?" Chuck asked Frank.

"Yep," the steely-eyed man's replied as he clicked the safety off. Frank did not tolerate anyone stealing from him, and as far as he could tell, they had caught themselves a couple of thieves in the act.

Connie and Diana tried to convince themselves they were not in another nightmare. That there were, in fact, two men in front of them pointing guns at them. Turmoil and confusion swirled, rescued at gunpoint. These men did not understand anything that was happening.

They began to wonder, "Is this island cursed?"

Chuck moved over close to the women. He thought they both looked pretty and wiped his mouth. That would have to wait for a while. He slung his gun behind him, letting it hang from the strap, and bent down to pick up the hastily discarded black fabric barrier and the stakes. He was doing it slowly so as not to cause any further damage to the crops left inside the pen.

"We are so glad to ...," Nan started to say.

"Shut up!" Frank insisted with a rifle shake.

Connie tried to suppress a yelp and reached out to grab Nan, kneeling beside her. The heavier guy in camouflage looked inside the fenced area at some grass or something growing as the skinny guy pointed the assault rifle at them with cold eyes.

Chuck discovered the women had succeeded in only pulling up half of the barrier on one of the long walls. As he pulled the black material away, he started smiling.

"Frank, buddy, the crops are doing great, man," he said, pointing to the five rows of four-inch-high green sprouts that had pushed up through the black dirt of the pen.

"Doesn't look like any were damaged when they yanked this out," he continued.

"Good," Frank replied.

Looking back at the two startled women, he took a deep breath to calm himself and asked, "So, what are you two doing out here?" Frank asked.

"This is a restricted area," Chuck lied.

"Hey, we didn't even see whatever you are growing in there," Nan said, starting to choke up and stumble over her words.

Connie jumped in, "Listen, we are stranded out here. Our husbands were killed, and we had to bury them with an oar. Our boat was wrecked in the storm, she got a concussion, and I lost my damn flip-flops!" She had hit an angry spot and hung onto Nan.

Frank lowered the gun and sympathized with the concussion.

"What do you mean your husbands were killed?" Chuck asked as if he was confused by the crying girls.

"The storm that came through here yesterday. We were out exploring and got caught in it," Nan tried to gain some composure.

"It was awful," Connie said.

"My Bruce went running back for the boat and ended up either having a heart attack or hitting his head. We found his body and pulled him up to the beach and covered it up with sand." Nan continued. "Her husband was trying to pull a limb off of me and was crushed by a tree that snapped in half. He was dead instantly."

"Holy crap," is all Frank could manage. He slung his rifle and walked closer to the two, both sobbing.

"Sorry to hear that, lady," he said, then realized, "Ladies, I mean."

Connie and Nan shook their heads as they cried. It was even more real now that they had to explain it to these guys. The pain was new and unbearable again.

"What happened to the boat?" Frank asked, trying to figure out what to do.

They were a mess and needed a minute to find a place between the waves of grief to explain. Chuck was trying to set the barrier down without causing any further damage. Frank was closer to them now, having moved to hear better. The adrenaline was causing his ears to ring.

"The storm flipped it over," Nan said while wiping her nose on her arm. It's still out in the cove upside down.

"Have you been alone since the storm rolled through?" Frank needed to know everything. Information is power. His head was clearing up.

"Yes, we had a fire last night and slept under the canopy from the boat," Connie added.

"Alright," Frank said, needing to take charge.

"Chuck lets go get these girls some water and check the radio."

"Check the radio?" Chuck was not following him.

Frank shot him an evil eye, trying to get him to walk back to the boat with him.

"Yes, these women need help, so let's go get them some help," he said.

"Thank you so much," said Nan between sobs.

"Thanks," Connie managed to say.

"Be right back, and please stay out of the experimental area," Chuck said, pointing to the pen.

"OK, sorry about that, we didn't know," Connie said as they walked away.

After a minute of walking, Frank called Chuck to come up beside him.

"Listen, they don't know anything about what is going on here," Frank said into Chuck's ear.

"Right," Chuck agreed.

"So we get them some water, maybe give them some food and get the heck out," Frank said.

"Hey nothing has changed, Frank," Chuck insisted. "Nobody knows they are here, we could just give them a ride back into Caseville," He was trying to figure it out by talking it out.

"The dead bodies will bring the Cops," Frank insisted. "Then the ladies will tell the Cops we showed up pointing rifles at their heads and trying to protect our crops in the pen!" As Frank went on, his frustration grew.

"OK, let's not get ahead of ourselves here," Chuck was trying to calm himself and Frank down.

"What if we leave them here, it may give us some more time to think it through?" Frank questioned.

"What are we going to tell them?" Chuck shot back.

"I don't know," Frank was stuck.

"If we get them talking some more, they can show us around. You know, where they buried the bodies and all that." Chuck was playing the scene in his head.

"You mean all friendly like?" Frank asked.

"Yeah, why not?"

"OK," Frank said, grabbing his chin. "Then what?"

"Well, we give them some supplies, the tent even, and tell them that the radio is broken and that we are going to get help," Chuck smiled at his brilliance.

"What do we do after that?" Frank asked.

"We could do nothing," he said. "Who would know?" It's not like we have given them our ID."

"True," Frank said.

"Then we can go back and figure out what our next move is," Chuck said as they reached the lake.

"What if we tow their boat back and tell them to hang tight for a few hours while we go get the cavalry," Frank suggested.

"What? Are you kidding?" Chuck was livid.

"Slow down, Chucky boy," Frank said, patting him on the chest.

"We cut the boat loose in the deepest part of the Bay, removing the evidence. Plus, it's sitting like a beacon for planes right now.

"If we got caught we could say that the tow line severed," Chuck added.

"We have to make sure our radio is broke for real," Frank whispered.

"I will pull it off its mount, submerge it in the lake, and remount it like nothing happened," he snickered.

"You are going to have to be quick," Frank reminded him.

They got to the boat and went to work. Chuck dunked the radio with the power on while Frank dug out the tent. They found some food stashed for the trip, along with a couple of bottles of water and two emergency blankets from the First Aid kit. The lie was fully formed in their minds now.

"You know," Frank said as they waded back toward the boulder, "knowing the state of mind those two women are in, we could probably tell them pigs fly, and they would believe it."

"Yeah, they ain't thinking right," Chuck agreed.

Their smiles faded as the girls approached to meet them, and they were almost at the boulder.

"Hey, so are the Cops coming?" Nan asked.

"Or the Coast Guard?" Connie said.

"You could take us back right now," Diana offered.

"Well, this is one of those good news, bad news situations," Frank explained.

"Because of the passing of your husbands the County Coroner has to be called in to the scene, I was told. And they are doing that as we speak. Also the Huron county Sheriff's boat is in the marina having some major work done. They want us to tow your boat back in so they can start the investigation right away. Then we'll bring another team back out in our boat with the coroner and get this whole mess cleaned up." Frank explained the bull crap lie.

"That's the good news or the bad?" Diana was confused. Seeing the things they carried in their arms did not match the story.

"That is the good news," Chuck said.

Frank cut him off. "The ball is rolling to fix this situation you find yourselves in, ladies," bending lower to look directly into their eyes to gain their confidence.

"What's the bad news then?" Connie, the skeptic, wanted to know.

"The bad news it we can't take you and tow the boat at the same time," he said, trying to seem apologetic.

"We have a tent and some food to tide you over until we return with the Sheriff," Chuck said, using the 'Sheriff' word to project some kind of authority.

"Are you gonna leave us here on this stinky ass island?" Connie shot back.

"Only because we were told that is what we have to do," Frank said.

"That doesn't make any sense," Nan said.

"They want to question both of you, you can't leave the scene," Chuck said.

"They could be on their way right now," Frank was thinking on his feet. "Them or some other rescue squad, maybe from Au Gres."

"Let's set this tent up by your fire, we have a couple of emergency blankets, some food and water to tide you over while we are gone," Chuck said.

"We probably won't even get the tent up before they show up," Frank said with a fake smile.

Connie did not trust either of the two men. They seemed bipolar to her.

Thirty-Eight

Charity's Threat

"Captain, we, I mean Major," Gilboa stumbled as he remembered yesterday's promotion, "We have a boat approaching, Sir."

"Helek, get comms up," Amadan insisted, "one-klick up."

"Sir." Helek shot straight up like a rocket without a smoke trail.

"Iggy go check the boat, before it gets too close," Amadan said.

"On it Major," said the hulking warrior.

"Let's look alive, 'gents," Amadan told the resting soldiers, snapping them into action.

"Major," Iggy called in.

"Go," was the only word returned.

"How close of an observation post?" Iggy asked.

"Start at fifty yards and report."

"Rodger, fifty yards in ten."

Ten seconds later.

"We have two males in their forties dressed in camo, Sir," Iggy reported.

"Weapons?"

"Searching.... Yes two AR-15's and a couple of handguns. Lots of Ammo."

"Alright take a pass, up close and check for passengers," Amadan lowered his voice.

"Helek, Anything?" Amadan was thorough, even this early in the morning.

"Couple of rats trying for the Shiners, everything else is clear," he said.

"Bapps, get on the rats."

"On it,"

Iggy swung in low toward the boat with his eyes in search mode, scanning the two men. The trouble with operating in search mode is opening yourself up to the enemy identifying you and locking in.

"Major, we've got two riders," Iggy powered off the search and swung back hard toward the rear of the black and white craft.

"Positive ID on two Reapers, one traveling in each, uncertain if they got eyes on me, took evasive action to the rear," Iggy said.

"Stealth, fifty up on the 2-7-0," Amadan said.

"On the nine, fifty yards transparent," Iggy responded professionally and moved to the nine o'clock position, left of the boat from the pilot position, fifty yards above the lake.

"Helek, direct comm," Amadan said.

"Major?" Helek asked him over the private channel.

"Helek, inform the JOCC our situ and tell them I want a Jumper shifted to us ASAP."

"A Jumper sir?"

"Roger."

"On what grounds, sir, they're going to ask."

"On the grounds that I want one. This op stinks all the way to Appolyon and back, the enemy is up to something and I want to insure I have every asset at my disposal. Do I make myself clear?"

"As crystal, on it, sir," Helek was unnerved, not by the tone but by the request.

"There they go," Nan shouted to her sister from the trail to the boulder. She returned to Connie, sitting at the fire, nursing her ankle.

"Did you hear me?" asked Nan.

"Yes, and the more I think about it the more I feel like they are up to something rotten," she said while feeding small twigs into the growing flames.

"Why did they come here with their guns already drawn?" Connie asked.

"They're probably growing something illegal out here in their precious pen," Diana replied.

"Do you think they even talked to anyone on the radio, or just made the whole thing up?" Connie asked with a strained face.

"Got me." Nan was frustrated by the pair as she picked up a branch for firewood.

"Plus, they just drove off with the evidence that anything bad happened here."

"You're right! Except for the bodies." The thought had not dawned on Connie. "But this island holds something they want."

"They probably won't ever come back because they would have to answer too many questions," Diana said.

"What are they doing with your boat then?" Connie said with her brow furrowed.

Thirty-Nine

Hull Hole

Out in the deepest part of the channel, well south of the island, Frank and Chuck towed the remaining hulk of the red boat with the white hull. They had avoided the other seafarers on the water and had put two poles up into rod holders on Larry's craft so it appeared like they were fishing.

"Alright, let's reel this thing in close," Frank said as Chuck killed the rumbling motors and moved back to start pulling on the tow rope.

"Where is the axe?" He asked his partner in crime.

"We only have the Michigan maul or the hatchet," Chuck replied, pointing below the rear seat with his chin.

"The maul will be perfect," Frank said, pointing to the heavy sledgehammer with a splitting blade on one side.

"See if you can get it right up next to us, Chucky boy," Frank said as he stood near the rail, waiting for his target to come into range.

"Now Frank," Chuck said.

Frank raised the maul over his head and slammed the twelve-pound head down into the white fiberglass hull, smashing a hole clean through, sending white fiberglass shards flying. He swung it again. The air trapped below was being forced out of the three spots as the hull sank a little more. The iron motor was now pulling down hard on the bow as it desired to find its rest on the bottom. Five more quick strikes and the boat disappeared below the gray waters.

"Untie it, you idiot!" Frank screamed at Chuck and pointed to the tie-down as the rope ran out of slack.

Chuck yanked hard on the white anchor line, dislodging it from the cleat. This allowed the rest of the line to zip over the edge into the deep. They both watched the evidence disappear into the unforgiving lake.

"Problem number one solved," Frank said, slapping Chuck's back.

———————◆O◆———————

"What's your play here, stinking Reaper?" Gilboa grumbled as he watched the pair from above by a klick. The taller Vanu was beating on the boat's hull, which puzzled him until they finally cut it loose and sent it to the bottom.

"Cap, I mean Major, the Reaper just punched holes into the boat's hull and sent it to the bottom of the lake," Gilboa reported.

"Say again," came the reply.

So he repeated himself with a little more righteous indignation.

"What's their current status Sargent-Major?" Amadan insisted.

"They are now speeding away, back in the direction of the boat launch, Sir," Gilboa said.

"Stay on them. Wait— change that." Amadan was thinking on the go.

"Tic, get out and take over for the Sargent-Major, I want him back here," Amadan said.

"On it, Major," Tic declared, leaving in a mighty swoosh.

"Stay on them Tic. Full stealth, Intel every 30," Amadan commanded his warrior to stay on target but remain hidden and report back with status updates every half an hour.

"Roger," Tic replied.

———————◆O◆———————

Major Amadan sent the JOCC a direct message for a confab with General Sikes. Thirty seconds later, the General called.

"General Sikes, we need that Jumper, sir," Amadan insisted.

"Jumpers don't come cheap, Major," Sikes barked in reply.

"There are only two Jumpers available, Amadan," Sikes pressed his point further.

"Sir, this area is hot, and these Shiners are prime targets. If the Cast was willing to risk their newest ship in the fleet to pull it off, investing that much for nothing makes no sense. My warriors captured that ship, Sir," Amadan knew he was using the fact to his advantage.

"Now we have Reaper using human shields to get close to the Mark after they had harassed them all night with a pack of Rats. This operation is still active, Sir," Amadan was right, and Sikes knew it was proper at some level, but a Jumper?

"OK, Major, if you are so concerned I will push this up the line and see what we come up with," Sikes remained unconvinced.

"Sikes, Out."

FORTY

CHARITY'S FIRE

The girls tore into the food the weird guys had left them as a ravenous hunger caught up to them.

"Nan, I keep thinking about how we will tell Mom," Connie said.

"UGGGG," Diana growled in response.

"Dad, now Bruce and Craig, this is going to put her over the edge," Connie was silent as tears billowed down her cheeks.

"And our kids Con," Diana was tearing up again, too.

"I know, Nan," Connie had been trying not to think those thoughts.

"Remember how we felt losing Dad? Now they have to go through the same thing," Connie snorted up some snot and spit it in the fire, laughing along with Nan about her ladylike action.

Watching the mesmerizing fire for a few more moments and finishing the meal, the girls gained even deeper insight into the impact these last couple of days would have on the family. Everything within the family dynamics dramatically changed in ways they could not anticipate.

"I think the two hardest conversations for me will be explaining it to Craig's parents and the grandkids. Our kids at least have some life behind them and have experienced the certainty of death, but the little ones," Connie shared. That last thought brought on a full moaning cry as Nan grabbed her.

"Craig loved those grandkids, and they all knew it," Diana was trying to comfort her little sis and added, "his parents have such a strong faith."

"Yeah, that's the hard part. Losing a second son is going to kill them.

"Yeah, I forgot about Jeff," Nan said.

197

"Carson is gonna be seventeen, Bry's twelve, Victor is already eleven. They will all remember him I am sure, but the younger ones, may not." This reality brought on another wave for Connie.

"Lord, please give me the strength to do this, I feel so weak," Connie prayed silently.

"Emma will remember him Con, she's almost eight," Nan insisted.

"But Riley, Jaxson, and Noah will forget him in a few years.

"And the Goose is gone now, too," Nan whispered the reality to herself and wept even more. Bruce was known by all the young ones for his funny duck-like voice impersonations, so the name "Uncle Goose" was new.

Watching Charity's fire brought even more realizations and sorrow.

"What about all the guy's siblings?" Nan wondered aloud.

"Yeah, it is all too much to think about," Connie sighed.

"Daphne and Doc are going to be floored," Connie said.

The name sparked a memory for Diana of their younger sister and her husband.

"Did I tell you that Doc hit it big in the stock market?" Nan said, happy to think about something other than death for a moment.

"Really? No you haven't said a word to me, either did Daphne," Connie said.

"Some outrageous investment he bought into recently went crazy high and he sold it and found another one was shooting up in value at the right time."

"Wow," Connie said, not knowing much about that stuff.

"Yeah, it's really big Con, like multiple hundreds of millions big, or more," Nan said.

"Crap, do you think he can buy you a new boat?" Connie said with a chuckle.

"I'm so mad that my Baby is gone, and now this other stuff," Nan was now feeling waves of anger.

At least tending the fire brought calm to both of them as it had for many years.

"This whole thing just feels evil to me," Connie said.

"It does feel like we have been under attack or something," Nan agreed.

"Almost like this stupid island is cursed," they both agreed.

The grief session lasted thirty minutes as they put more wood into the fire. Finally, they both just laid back into the opening of the new camo tent. They pulled a loud and shiny blanket over them sideways. They intended to keep talking but fell asleep, buried under emotional trauma with full bellies. Nan turned on her side to hug Connie like when they were little girls. It was a welcomed security for both.

FORTY-ONE

EVIL CHARITY

The gleaming black GMC pickup truck idled down Sturm Road as it pulled Larry's boat behind. Chuck was driving slow enough to keep the vehicle clean after they had sprayed it off at the do-it-yourself car wash in Caseville. Going up to the small city had been a risk, but they needed to ensure any signs of fiberglass from that other boat's hull were gone. The truck headlights had switched on automatically a few minutes before the gravel road in the growing dusk. The pair was busy munching a sub they picked up at the gas station by the car wash.

"I'm gonna back this thing in to try to hide it behind the house," Chuck said, trying to convince himself that he was getting better at backing up the trailer.

Frank's mind was spinning on high octane, and he missed an obvious moment for a significant rip on his buddy.

"You alright?" Chuck asked as he turned the truck's steering wheel back and forth, straining to see in the mirrors. He was trying to keep the boat out of the ditch and on the driveway.

"Just reviewing our options," Frank said, staring at the dash and chewing.

"We are going to go inside and watch the local news to see if there have been any reports about the four missing people," Chuck said.

"Well, at this rate, we will have to catch the late news," Frank laughed at his friend's frantic attempts to put the trailer where it was supposed to go and mocked him with flailing arms and grunting sounds.

"Shut up," was the best Chuck could do in reply.

Shutting the truck's doors, the two were deep in thought as they walked into the ramshackle trailer. The cold twelve-pack went on the dusty brown flowered couch— along with the massive bag of barbeque potato chips.

"Break out the medicine man, medicine-man. It has been a rough day," Chuck said, and he thought he was funny.

Frank was more than willing to comply. Fighting through all the crap strewn about, he went to his tiny room in the rear. Frank found his supply bag right where he left it when he filled his pocket tin. They had to do a lot of thinking tonight, so he grabbed extra dope.

The TV had been droning for the last few hours as the men waited to hear if anyone knew about the missing boaters. The beer and chips were gone, and Frank and Chuck slept. They were burnt— so stoned out of their minds they never heard reports on anything.

<hr />

"Major, SUSFU," Tic called in, Telling Amadan the situation was unchanged. He was resting on the warm hood of the new truck in front of the trailer— well, that's where he wanted to be— but he was across the street, hidden in an uncomfortable treetop.

"Copy that," Amadan said.

"Bapps, comm check," Amadan called.

"Snug as a bug, Major," Bapps reported that the girls were sleeping in the tent, and everything was clear.

<hr />

"Developing story from the small city of Au Gres. Two couples are reported missing out on Saginaw Bay tonight due to an apparent boating mishap. Names are being withheld until next of kin can be located. Still a dark blue pickup truck and an empty boat trailer sit abandoned for the second night at the public boat launch in Au Gres." A shot of the truck and trailer was shown, and the report continued, "The lakeside home of the owner has also been found empty with two dogs left to fend for themselves. The pets are now being cared for by a family friend and appear to be in good health.

"A neighbor told police that something is wrong," the reporter said as the report breaks away to the interview.

"Yes— they love that little boat of theirs. They use it almost every weekend out in the Bay, but they always come back the same day. Always. I think her sister was up for a visit with her husband. I saw all four of them go out two days ago but no one has come back," the camera returns to the anchor desk.

"So, if you have any information on a missing red boat out on Saginaw Bay, you are asked to contact authorities, and we will keep you updated with all the latest news, weather, and local sports...." The TV droned on and no one in the trailer listened except the growing evil.

"Major, balloon's gone up," Tic whispered.

"Go."

"Full Squad of Reaper entered the airspace above the trailer, they are in search mode," Tic said.

"Go slow to station two klick in their sun, keep eyes, report,"

Tic made his way back through the trees until he had enough distance between him and the Reaper squad. Then he slowly ascended to two klicks in altitude and rotated to the east to be in the sun's light when it came up, to blind them to his presence. He remained transparent. Tic struggled to be 6,300 feet above the target because he could not hear what was said inside the trailer. He knew that was the play of the Reaper to back him off enough to gain the element of surprise. Tic knew the enemy was a pack of sick freaks only looking to kill, steal and destroy, he also knew they weren't stupid.

"On station."

"Copy."

———◄●►———

Four hours later, the sun was peeking over the horizon, and Chuck was still snoring on the couch. Frank was up drinking coffee in his favorite chair. He had already made his decision about the fate of their plan.

"Chuck, time to get up," Frank said from his perch.

"Chuck, Chuck, CHUCK!" He got louder each time, and still no movement.

"What the Chuck, dude," Frank was irritated now and walked over and kicked the bottom of Chuck's shoe as it hung off the edge of the soiled couch.

"Yeah? ... I know... Something." Random words from a half-sleeping man.

Frank held his mug of java under Chuck's nose. Finally, he gave in and violently shook him.

"Hey, yep, I am awake now. Thanks, Frank," he said, rubbing his head and eyes with both hands.

"Well, it appeared you were going to sleep 'til noon! Coffee is right in front of you on the little table," Frank's patience was already wearing thin as he strolled back to his chair.

"Thanks man," Chuck said. "I was having a raunchy dream about Sally from work," he smiled as he tested his steamy mug for temperature.

"I already took care of that situation for you, Chuck." Frank expression was maniacal.

"That was, that was you? Seriously?" Chuck was shocked. "I, I, I had no clue."

"You mentioned it in the phone call, and when I got out, I made sure she had an accident," he smiled, tipping his big black mug up for a draw.

"Did you plan on killing her, Frank?" Chuck asked as he gazed over the top of his mug.

"No, that was a bonus, Chucky boy," Frank smiled and laughed.

"She set me up man, she had it coming," Chuck said, convinced himself of his righteous cause.

"She was hot though," Chuck said and lusted after her memory.

"We gotta make a decision," Frank said, looking straight at him.

"I didn't see anything on the news last night," Chuck said. He was sleeping.

"We gotta piss or get off the pot," Frank said.

"How do you see it, Frank?" Chuck asked.

"Option one is we walk away. We take Larry's boat back and forget the whole thing. Those women were so afraid they knew nothing about us, and we didn't leave them anything that could connect them to us. It would likely be a mystery to everyone."

"OK,"

"Option Two, we take our business to the next level. We show the distributors we will get the job done and they can count on our product. I mean it's growing like gang busters on that over-fertilized island, so we are gonna have good dope. The question is can we deliver, Chuck? Do we really want this thing to happen?"

"Are you saying we should kill them?" Chuck said hesitantly.

"Yes. One bullet through both of their heads at the same time. We do it in front of a tree and dig the round out of the wood after we are finished. No slug to trace back to us. Then we stick them in a hole and walk away for a few weeks. We take the pen down and cover our tracks, put the boat back, lay low."

"You have really thought this through," Chuck said.

After a few moments, Chuck said, "I can't pull the trigger," he admitted sheepishly while staring at his coffee mug.

"I know, that's why I am going to do that part. But you have to hold the rope we tie them up with." Frank was serious.

"I think I can do that," Chuck said, not looking up.

"It will be fine, Chucky boy. We don't know them from Adam. Plus, they are trying to wreck everything!" said Frank. He was trying to stir up hatred.

"Yeah, you're right," replied the not-so-convinced collaborator.

"If something goes bad after, while we are laying low, no one should suspect us of anything. We have zero ties to the island as far as anyone else knows."

"Except one," Chuck said, obviously referring to Larry, as his eyes darted to his friend.

Frank paused, thinking. "I will do whatever we need to do to make this work."

A few minutes passed in silence as they both thought about the upshot.

"For today, I say we go launch the boat up by Hat Point. We'll take the back roads just to stay out of view," Frank suggested to calm Chuck.

"That will add onto the time in the lake by a half an hour," Chuck said.

"It's worth it. We can't let those women screw this whole thing up," Frank concluded the matter, and a Reaper smiled inside.

"Let's go solve problem number two," Frank said as he stood up.

———◄O►———

"Major, the boat was parked outside the LOS," Tic argued.

"You had zero line of sight? You are not certain what, if anything, went into that craft before they left?" Amadan sought clarification from his warrior on station.

"Roger that,"

"Current position?" Amadan barked as the frustration over the lack of Intel gnawed away.

"Lake, plus two, twenty due east, rolling to you, hot," Tic said clearly.

"Air Assets? Amadan said, calming himself.

"Two Shields, ten Birds close, ETA thirty," Tic was precise and had to stay off comm to remain hidden.

"Helek any word from JOCC?" Amadan asked.

"Not yet," he said tersely.

"Advise JOCC on our situation, see if they have another Ready Squad to shift to us. It's going to get hot down here quick like."

"On It."

"Alright, we need a confab. Not you Helek. You go plus one," Amadan said, directing the comm soldier to a higher altitude for better range and stealth.

Helek paged all the non-assigned warriors to circle up. All fifteen anxious warriors gathered close to hear what the Major had to say.

"Men, we have two Human Shields headed our way, I believe to do harm to our Shiners. They have an escort of ten Reaper. I am certain if this is a real shot at bagging their Mark, we will have more Reaper fall on our heads. The call for a

Jumper is going up the chain and hopefully will come through soon." Amadan said.

"With all due respect Sir," Gilboa spoke up.

"Out with it, Sargent-Major."

"Jumpers are awesome, but four of us, four, will have to baby sit him per strict regulation. Are you sure you want the headache?"

"Absolutely sure, here's why, we have been given no authority to shift flesh side. Our ROE is specific— assist and protect only. I don't get to make up the rules of engagement.

"Permission to speak freely Sir," asked Bapps.

"Go."

"Sir if we could better understand some of the thinking that goes on above it sure would make it easier to get behind what seems to be a short-sighted assignment, before it goes bad, Sir."

"Well, Bapps, if we had all the foreknowledge of Abba only then, could we understand. For now, we were created to serve him without questioning. We run on the faith. His Will be done! Enough said?" Amadan oversaw these warriors, and they knew they were the better for it.

"Sir, Yes Sir. Thank you, Sir."

"I have a plan to counter-act...." Amadan went through two options. The warriors drew assignments and waited for a black and white boat to arrive.

———◆◇◆———

The island lay before them; Chuck was nervous about what they were about to do.

"Run this thing up to the boulder, we will tie it off to the tree," Frank demanded.

"Hope we don't get hung up on a rock," Chuck pointed out.

"If we do we'll just get out and push, Chucky boy." Frank was just being a jerk now.

The boat scraped bottom several times, making Chuck wince for his friend Larry. Frank did not care. With a rope in hand, Larry jumped off the bow onto their boulder and tied it off to the tree.

"ETA five minutes, Major," Tic called in.

"Copy."

"Major, Jumper is inbound," Helek said into the Comm.

"Beacon up," Amadan said to Iggy.

"On," was the reply.

"Ten seconds, on point," came the unfamiliar Scottish-accented voice of the Jumper Warrior.

"Roger," Amadan replied. He smiled slightly, knowing the one who was landing.

The special operations Warrior landed without kicking up any dust behind the tent in the island camp. Four warriors came to his side, and they all went transparent. Amadan knew the Jumper arrived at the last possible second, with Reaper and the Shields inbound and close.

"Thank you Abba," Amadan whispered.

"We need the guns, the rope, those two socks for blindfolds, the ammo, and the shovel," Frank pushed Chuck hard. They gathered up the gear and headed out toward the girl's camp.

"Ammo up," Frank said. "Lock and load." They set a clip and yanked the charging arm to load a round as they ducked under some brush. A clear trail was forming from all the traffic on the island lately, so they followed the path, walking right toward the girls' camp.

"Safety off," Frank commanded. He used his right thumb to push the little lever down so the gun was ready to fire.

"You guys did return!" Diana said with a smile until she noticed the guns. Connie turned to look and knew something was very wrong.

"Get up NOW!" Frank yelled and pointed the rifle at their heads.

"Reaper, double squad on your ten," whispered Helek.

No answer. There were already ten Reapers above the warriors crouched low and holding stealth mode. Now, twenty more were inbound from the northwest. The plan was to keep transparent as long as possible in case the Jumper had to be used. Amadan watched as the Human Shields forced the women to their feet. Comms had to remain silent to maintain stealth for Amadan, but he wanted to scream. He knew they only had a ten to twenty-second window to work in, so waiting until the precise moment to execute the plan was the only way it could succeed, but the tension was crushing him. If they were allowed to go flesh side, this would be over in two seconds, but he could not, so they had to play this out perfectly and wait.

Reaper 1 was the kill squad, already inbound for overwatch duty, waiting for Pluck to reveal themselves. They would overwhelm and destroy the vile beast with superior numbers, when that happened.

"Send the other two units in NOW!" Cryptus screamed at the junior officer.

"GO Reaper 2, GO Reaper 3," was the command from the communications officer.

The second soaring squad of twenty Reapers began a steep dive toward the island from five klicks up. Reaper 2 knew their role when racing along over Mach 2, as they shot in from the south. Known as the 'chaos squad,' they used pure speed and howling shrieks to instill panic among the Pluck warriors, slashing through the operational area to dislodge the outnumbered foe from hiding.

Reaper 3 was diving in from the east a little lower and slower. It was seeking to pull some warriors into a fight and lead them away by making a run to the west, then scattering and doubling back to reinforce the main attack.

———◆———

"You are hurting me," Connie said as Chuck pulled the rope tight around her wrists— her arms forced behind her back. This made her want to twist and fight even more.

"Shut up!" Frank screamed and struck her with his fist on the side of her head. She fell to her knees in pain. Diana lurched forward toward Frank, and he brought his fist squarely up into her midsection, bending her in half as she toppled over onto the ground.

As he stood over Diana, he placed his worn cowboy boot on the side of her neck, as his boiling rage enticed him to drive her skull into the dirt.

"Tie her up now," he said to Chuck.

Frank went over to Connie and grabbed her by the face as tears ran down her cheeks.

"Don't worry little girl you won't feel a thing," he said with a smile as he tightened his grip. His eyes appeared dead to her.

"Father, help us!" Connie cried out as she looked up through the trees toward her home.

He pulled the long black sock from his coat pocket and tied it tightly around her head, covering her eyes. She began to whimper as she sat back on her legs. Frank kissed the top of her head, laughed a sick, demented laugh, and pushed her hard.

———◆———

"Two double Reaper squads, one on your six, the other on your two," Helek's voice ran into Amadan's head.

"Ready Squad, four minutes out," comm whispered.

It took every ounce of concentration and discipline for the Major to hold off the attack even another second. The trap was almost set and ready to spring death and destruction— if he could wait long enough. Reapers were so close he could smell their nauseating scent.

The high-pitched screams streaked in from the south. The hidden warriors could hear them popping through the sound barrier as they approached en masse.

Four warriors went red. Gilboa shot straight up from ten yards south of the tent. He rammed a Reaper with his head as he ascended, smashing it across the face with his shield. In the same movement, he yanked his sword out of its sheath and cut the head off another. A third Reaper swung its scythe hard around as Gilboa went past him and hit the rising Warrior just below the knee, almost severing the bottom quarter of his leg. He swung around and shot north with all he had, grabbing his med bag with his shield hand while he sprayed a contrail from his left leg.

At the same instant that Gilboa jumped, Iggy unleashed from his hiding place beneath a bush just east of the campfire. He had three unsuspecting Reapers lined up for the kill. He severed one Reaper head in two with a double overhand downward slash. He twisted violently to the right and used his wing to knock another demon flying as he connected across the chest of another, who fell and thudded on the ground, dead. A fourth Reaper dropped from above Iggy and drove his razor-sharp weapon through the base of his right wing. He sent the giant Warrior somersaulting back to earth with his wing trailing him, held on by just a few ligaments. He landed hard on the ground, and several Reapers went in for the kill.

Bapps was the third Warrior to leap from cover just a tenth of a second behind Iggy and drove his sword up through the midsection of the Reaper, who was right above his position— just north of the tent. His sword stopped after it pierced clear through to the top of the head. He had to shake the Reaper off his weapon and immediately went for more altitude. A streaking Reaper from the south met the edge of his swing and vanished into a mist. Three more screamed by on his left as another was coming up after him from below. Pulling hard up, he turned over and brought his wings in close, sending him into a vertical dive. He raised his sword over his head and drove it through the top of Reaper, who was trying to catch up to him. Another Reaper flashed by, and Bapps raised his shield to defend against his attempted slash, which sent sparks shooting in a halo him.

Tic shot down through the clouds and rode up transparent on two Reapers within ten feet of each other. They had been part of the boat overwatch squad, and he hit them perpendicularly and cut them in two. All four parts fell into the lake at the edge of the island. Tic had three Reapers see his glow as he came out to strike and shoot in close. He knocked one off course with his shield and removed an arm from the second, but the third cut him deep on the leg. He pulled in and dove toward the lake and twenty more Reapers from the Chaos Squad ripped through the air over his head. Stuffing an emergency 'Stop' pack into his wound, he grimaced and pulled hard to gain speed. The enemy was everywhere, and he had to focus.

"END THIS!" Cryptus screamed into the wind as he watched through his goggles.

"Pain is all I feel, Father. Where are you?" Connie prayed through the raging chaos in her soul.

The women were tied facing each other with their heads on each other's shoulders, the long black rope wrapped around them under their arms. Their fighting had ceased, but the trembling had not.

"Shut up! Just SHUT UP! Frank screamed like a madman to drown out their whimpers. He sent even more fists flying to still the thieving bitches. Now pacing back and forth, he was trying to build up the courage to solve problem number two.

A Whisperer sang a song of death in his ears. Ear to ear, the Fly moved quickly from the left to the right and back again, repeatedly telling him to "kill, kill, kill, kill, kill, kill. They are trying to steal, steal, steal, steal, steal from you, Frank. Be a man, a real man. Be a man, a real man. Be a man, a real man, for once in your life!"

"AHHHH!" He screamed as he raised his rifle, pointing to the side of the taller sister's head. The muzzle was only six inches from her trembling temple as tears slipped from beneath the taunt black sock. The scream continued from possessed Frank while Chuck's eyes were wide with fear. He just wanted to fall away back in time.

The mindless bullet exploded forward to pierce the head of Diana at the temple. It carried pieces of brain matter through to her younger sister. Blowing out Connie's skull behind the ear, and followed on to exit the other side of her head, where it lodged in the tree, just below the bark. Blood sprayed across Chuck's face and onto Franks's hands, and two Reapers howled in delight as their sweet mission was accomplished.

"JUMPER GO!GO!GO!" Amadan screamed red-faced, a split second late.

ACT V

FORTY-TWO

WE TAKE

Pushing up through the sandy black dirt of the island, razor-sharp claws were the first thing to be exposed from the underworld. The ground then gave birth to a long snout from a rat-like nose connected to a large round head. The red slits seeming to be eyes were covered by semi-transparent lids that leaked with sticky green mucus— which would clot and drip down a dull black outer coat. The nasty eye boogers provided lubrication for slipping through the soil. Ears were almost non-existent, like holes in the side of their head with a tiny covering flap, followed by stout necks and shoulders. The emaciated body seemed gigantic compared to the head and neck.

With its slender legs and stubby feet, the creature was hideous. Instead of walking, it seemed to slither across the ground with nasty red eyes scanning back and forth. It was soon followed by more that were engaged in an endless search. Being at the bottom of the societal food chain, they were edgy and vile creatures whose singular joy was collecting souls out of the dead. The business of death was booming all over the planet as spawning beds back home were working overtime to keep up with the demand for more beasts to join in the harvest.

They swarmed and grunted in deep, throaty sounds around the collection site. Crawling over the former host, they sought to peer inside to locate the straps. Using their razor-sharp claws, they ripped away the final two connection points of the lifeless physical shells, causing the unformed souls to ooze onto the ground until they looked somewhat like a human slug. Transfer bags, or as some called them, gathering bags, soul bags, or soul socks, were retrieved from below their ever-present and dilapidated cart.

Other workers rounded up the essence of each soul, which was like trying to sweep up oil from the top of the water. Eventually, the whole thing was slathered into the clear sacks for transportation. Each bag had to be shut by securing a metal compression ring with a handheld vise-like contraption. Another type of worker called a Scribe, scurried up close to the bags and scribbled a number across each pouch for proper identification with a glowing black marker.

They were called Takers and had become skilled in stacking the endless bags transported these days. The nameless creatures were developed to collect all the souls who had arrived at the end of their pathetic lives here on Terra for the transfer to Apollyon. The roving bands traveled the planet, cleaning up after death had made another colossal mess.

While most considered them to be garbage men for the dead, they reconciled the nature of their job to be more along the line of setting captive prisoners free and considered it a rather heroic occupation. As for the empty physical bodies— they left those behind. That job was left for the Terrains to do after the souls were gleaned and set free.

As the group wandered to the island in Saginaw Bay, they had yet to be given advanced intelligence on what the scene would be like on this day. The scenario had left two to bag and several Reapers to gather. After the Reaper parts were brought to the cart, the second group of Takers had almost finished up on the two human souls.

The first number the Scribe penned on the island today was "10578122-311114." The second was marked with "10578122-311125." Finally, the two voiceless bags of souls were unceremoniously flung onto the parade of pathetic, wobbly carts with high wood-like sides. The group stole away for their next rendezvous with death.

The stack on the cart was unusually high today. It did not matter to the grungy Takers, for how much does a soul weigh after all? They were paid by the bag and not for the accommodations to the passengers. Takers live in reality— they know where the sacks end up and the journey each one had to make to get them home. So what difference would a four-week transfer in misery make? To the Taker, the bags were freight and nothing more. To the soul stored inside, it was a month of silent claustrophobic hell as each bag crushed in on top of the other, suffocating any chance of hope, and that was just getting to the ship.

The only movement 10578122-311114 knew was the cart's gentle wobble as it moved toward its goal. Unable to breathe, speak, move, or complain to anyone in authority, they were prisoners in stuffed sacks. Terror set in, pushing them on a quick journey to insanity. 114 would have been far better off if it could melt into a catatonic state.

"Maybe we can just sleep away the month?" was the real question bouncing around inside them all.

"Please just let me sleep!" was the frantic, unsteady request.

Meanwhile, 10578122-311125 was on the cart's bottom row of bags facing forward. As the pile rose in front, it could see the panic of the soul in the sack in front of it and notice the compression of its bag from the weight of the others above. The look was the most disturbing expression he had ever witnessed. An intense pressure compressed the fear even deeper into the other unmoving soul. 125 desperately tried to see the other but could not connect, even with the eyes. It was as if the bag's design was made to prevent visual interactions from happening, no matter how much effort was made. Isolation, absolute isolation, set in— like a deep cold on a frigid winter day, as they both lay helpless on the bottom of the rickety collection cart.

Takers also gathered the scattered pieces of Reaper into different bags. The essence of Reaper was contained in its forehead. That part was handled carefully since it would be put into a reanimation pod on Apollyon to grow back into another warrior. The larger the piece connected to the forehead, the faster the turnaround time for producing the new Reaper. Then, they had to undergo extensive training— making the whole process last at least one turn. But the more significant pieces took up more room. Takers were paid handsomely for each Reaper head. If there was any damage to the rest of the body, it was removed at the neck, and careful attention was given to preserving the skull. As for the rest of the pieces, the nonessential leftover body parts were ground up and fed to the help. The entire area was littered with meat today, and they were somewhat happy— at least they would eat.

The remote area the Takers were working in for this job made meeting the daily quota harder because they had to fight through all the water just to get here. There were other gatherings to be made. They were supposed to have stops in four different towns. It was going to be a long day. Rolling into Flint late that night, they had collected everything on their list and hobbled the last five miles to connect with the Drone. They had a whole load of souls and would be paid well.

The enormous black cylindrical ship sat in the parking lot of the abandoned automotive factory on the city's north end. The entire loading process was auto-mated with these newest vessels. Takers would back their carts up to the loading area, and each was grabbed and dumped out into the storage area by robotic arms. All the soul socks would slide down a long loading shoot and, after riding a series of conveyors, ended up joining a growing pile in the belly of the ship. About a million and a half bags fit in the hold— about ten days' worth of gatherings for the entire planet. However, with twenty-five regional gathering centers across the globe, due to the sheer volume of the harvest, most transports spent an average of five months on the ground waiting to be filled, then the one-month voyage home.

Forty-Three

Escape Vacation

The beach was devoid of people as far as the eye could see on this idyllic Michigan summer day. Larry had spotted this stretch of paradise after driving a few days before while everyone else was sleeping. It was only twenty miles from their campsite, so he made a mental note to return, explore, and relax. They scurried down the narrow two-track road which led them into the hidden section of Hiawatha National Forest. At several points along the trail, all the girls screamed with delight as the SUV bounced hard through the ruts and over large bumps. The road ended in a dead end at an iconic lookout over the crystal blue lake. The tattered split-rail fence at the end of the road only warned people to stop just before a sixty-foot drop off the side of the dune. Without stairs to access this rustic area, they all ran out of control as far as they could, then slid down the rest of the sand to get to the bottom and the beach. Returning to the car would be a workout, but that task was later.

Today, the goal was to relax, precisely what the family hoped to accomplish with their picnic on the beach. They spread the large plaid blue blanket below them, surrounded by woods and water, over the warm yellow sand. They had all gathered around the cooler to give thanks. Everyone took a turn thanking God for the trip, the food, and anything else they could think of. Young Megan even thanked her Abba for the turtle she would find later in the day. Then they sat back in relative silence with the beauty washing over them and into them. They ate their lunch beneath the noonday sun while gentle waves from Lake Superior recreated the pristine shoreline.

After finishing their sandwiches, the girls donned their brand-new yellow swimsuits and munched on orange slices. Larry was busy getting a sunburn on his chest while lying on the blanket beside his seated bride in her fluffy white sun hat.

"Do you want any more of these chips, Larry?" she asked as she started to roll up the bag.

"No, I'm good," he said, blocking the sun with his hand so he could see Wendy's face. The thin hat glowed, making her red hair appear like fire.

"Da, da, da, daddy, do you want me to bury you all they way up to your head in sand," Megan was smiling with one less tooth in her head than a week ago.

"Sure, honey, we can do that," he said, reaching for her face.

"I want to help!" Melissa yelped.

"You should help your sisters bury your dad in the sand," Wendy told Mary, who had her head stuck in a book again.

"Maybe," she said.

The two girls jumped on Larry's belly and giggled with glee. Larry wrapped them tightly with his arms and chewed on their ears, bringing squeals of delight.

"I am a big mean bear, RAAAAA," he said as he chased them across the sand, now on all fours, pawing at their legs.

"No, Daddy, no!" Megan ran to the water's edge and stopped. Melissa ran past her into the chilly lake, splashing as she hopped over the waves. Papa Bear followed them and scooped up Megan on the way to chase down Missy. As he reached Boo-Boo, he snagged her and, twisting around, fell into the lake with both on his chest. They all went under together, and then Larry burst upward with a yell, and each girl was under an arm. Screams of delight echoed off the forest walls while Wendy smiled and braided Mary's hair.

"Thank you Father for bringing him back to us," she silently prayed.

"Hey honey, could we put up the umbrella, my ginger self is starting to cook," Wendy asked with her mischievous smile.

"Sure," he said with a chuckle.

"Come on, ladies let us go and block out the gorgeous sun for your pasty mom," he said to them while teasing his wife.

The entire afternoon went on like this, with several breaks back on the blanket for drinks, snacks, and sunscreen. The girls spent an hour burying their father in the sand, using plastic shovels and buckets to make to speed up the job. Even Wendy got in on the action, trying to make a living sandcastle out of her husband. It was a perfect way to spend a vacation day.

Six hours later, the crispy family trudged up a steep dune toward their car. They were all carrying something, so only one ascent up the thigh-burning slope would be necessary. Larry looked like Santa Claus, having gathered the four corners of the blanket with items piled in the center and slung the sack over his shoulder. The climb had them all sweating and wanting to cool down again— in the lake at the bottom of the hill. Instead, they dusted off, dodged some pesky mosquitos, and dumped out the piles of sand— before they got into the car.

As Larry spread his towel over the driver's seat, Wendy caught a glimpse of something in the beach grass behind the vehicle.

"Sunshine, look," she said to her daughter, pointing at a six-inch painted turtle making a break for shelter in the woods.

The proverbial "AWWWW," could be heard for a mile.

"See, I told you God would show us one today!" She beamed a wide, toothless grin.

"How about PIZZA?" Larry asked the hungry crew of kids.

"There was a restaurant just past the campground," he told his curious wife.

"No cooking, woot, woot!" she answered, pumping her fist into the air, and everyone else joined in the spontaneous celebration after the afternoon baking.

The black-lettered sign with the flashing arrow on top in front of the worn red building said it all: "Big George's Pizza and Pasties. Come on in Lumberjack Hungry and let the fat man fill you UP."

Around the campfire a couple of hours later, after the smores' mess had been gathered and the girls had gone to bed, Wendy snuggled up close to her best friend and laid her head on his shoulder.

"Thank you for today. It was perfect," Wendy told him as they watched the multi-colored flames dance in the fire ring.

"It's so good just to get away," he replied, trying not to think about anything except that moment.

"It is," she said as she took his hand.

"Do you want to go make out in the car?" she said, biting down on his knuckle.

"Do you really want to end a perfect day like that?" he asked, emphasizing the last word, thinking he was hilarious.

"Yes," she said as she stood up and led him away by the hand to fold the back seat down. There was no way this would happen inside the trailer, with the kids sleeping just a few feet away. The activity would have shaken the camper, and others would have noticed the ruckus with the other campsites being so close. The dark car seemed like the perfect private alternative, making them feel young again.

Fifteen minutes later, they giggled and chuckled together under a blanket, thankful for the chance to get away and be alone.

"I thought we were going to have to miss out on this," he said as he gently kissed her again. The word 'miss' triggered a memory for her.

"I was checking my phone earlier, when I got the smores', and there was a story posted from home about two couples who are missing somewhere out by the island in Saginaw Bay," she said after remembering the post.

An instantaneous and overwhelming feeling like he was smothering shot into Larry's chest.

FORTY-FOUR

BAGGED

The bag with the ending number 114 needed to find out where they were in the gigantic pile of bags. The nearest they could figure was somewhere in the middle of everything. Nine other bags were touching the bag they occupied, and they could see different parts of the individual souls in each of them. Still, no one could catch anyone else looking at them. They had never been so utterly alone in a sea of people. It made them look inside, wondering how they could end up back in a pile of souls, waiting in the overwhelming silence.

The idea of water somehow wormed into his thoughts. Water nagged and begged for attention. They tried to reason away the compulsion— I don't have a body; how could I be thirsty? The thought grew into an obsession, and a growing thirst overwhelmed them. Nothing to drink and no way to swallow.

"Why would this be an issue here?" They pondered.

"I left my body on that stinking island; why AM I SO THIRSTY?" Screaming at the endless screaming. Then, the chewing away at chapped lips began to go along with the thirst. Burning hot coals were being poured on his face, sizzling, melting flesh in its wake. Agony.

125 found himself pressed up hard against the side of the ship. At first, the metal felt cool and somewhat eased the pressure from the growing pile above. Then, the coolness became a bone-shivering cold during the second night— even without the bones. There was no movement, only waiting and constant internal fluttering. He hoped, even prayed, for sleep, but none ever came. This new existence became an absolute nightmare with no end or pause.

About day four, the hunger pains started to set in. Without a stomach or a way to eat anything, a swelling need to eat and fill up became all-consuming. A growing rage became palpable as many began to moan and scream in their bags. They could not hear each other because they had no throats or lungs to expel air which would cause noise to ring out. No, the rage was internal, as was the expanding hunger.

Several months later, the bleak and ever-dimming light from above became as black as the moon's dark side. Then, several clanks and clunks rattled them out of their delusions. A blinding and blinking green light appeared above. The next day, a large jolt and roar of engines shook everything for several minutes, which caused the soul bags to settle— even more pressure pressing in on all sides of them. Within ten minutes, the force of gravity lifted like a veil, and a wave of relief washed through the speeding ship, except for the push of thrust.

The vibration during take-off caused another issue surfaced for 125 to interrupt the pangs of starvation. The bag's surface rubbing along the outside edge of the hull caused an itch to develop on his back. A deep screaming, creeping, crawling, prickling itch that had no way of being satisfied.

Next, the temperature fluctuation began as the unimpeded solar radiation baked the outer skin on one side of the craft. The ship rotated slowly to keep from overheating one area and warping the hull. For a couple of hours, 125 overheated, and then, for a few hours, the freeze of deep space sent the cold through every molecule. The torture continued without yielding for five months. The itching, the steaming heat, being frozen through, the gnawing hunger, intense loneliness, the constant pressure from the thrust, silence, isolation, and thirst. A fierce, overwhelming, unending agony of always craving and never receiving. Only one distant glimmer of hope remained. Wherever this ship was heading had to be better than the long journey.

FORTY-FIVE

SHIP WRECKED

T he aroma of brewing coffee wafted through the small pop-up camper early the following day. Wendy had emerged from beneath the covers and began the coffee maker. It was a cool morning in the trailer as they had not bothered to turn any heat on. She rejoined her snoring husband in the big bed at the back of the camper without waking the tired crew of sunburned girls. The dripping and cracking of the machine warming up threatened to stir them from their dreams. During the return trip to the bed, Wendy grabbed her smartphone to turn it on under the blankets and out of sight— just for a couple of minutes. Even though vacation time was a well-established no-phone zone, she braved the cold to break the rules, silencing the contraption as it sprang to life in her hand. She snuggled her backside close to Larry's warm body and dozed off again for a few minutes as the phone cycled through its lengthy start-up procedure.

Ten minutes later, the coffee smell roused her awake. She had dosed off with her phone smashed against her face. Looking around, everyone was still out. She pulled the blanket over her head and went to work catching up with her online world. Right away, she noticed there were three, no four, missed phone calls from the same unknown number.

Switching to her text messages, the same number had sent a message. She opened it with growing trepidation as fear grabbed her heart from the darkness of the unknown.

"Wendy this is your neighbor Marty. I know you guys are on vacation with your camper. Last night when I got home from work I noticed that Larry's boat was gone. Maybe you came back and took it with you or let someone borrow it. I just thought you should know. See you later. Have a good trip!"

"Larry, wake up." She shook him gently, not wanting to wake the girls, as she turned over to whisper into his ear.

"Hey honey, I need to tell you something," she shook with more vigor.

Larry could not wake up, so she touched his chest and pressed down.

"Hey, what's going on?" He said as he stretched his arms above his head.

"Marty sent me a text after trying to call me four times," she said.

"Our neighbor, Marty?" Larry asked while trying to get his bearings.

"Yes," she said. Earlier in their marriage, she would have demanded that he pay heed, combined with many irrational judgments and fears. But she had learned Larry needed a few minutes to get his mind engaged with the world and out of dreamland, so she waited for his reply.

"What did he want?" he asked. He was rubbing his face awake and turned toward her. He was trying to pay attention to her face's concern.

"He said he noticed that your boat is gone," she paused and let that sink in.

"What?"

Larry sat upright in the bed, touching the canvas top of the trailer with his head. The canvas hung over the end of the bed and was usually covered with moisture in the mornings. All the exhaling from the five sleeping bodies caused extra condensation to gather on the canvas which could drip down like rain.

"He wondered if we had returned to get it, or if you had borrowed it out." She looked to him for some insight.

"It's probably Chuck and Frank," he said to reassure her as he suppressed instant fear.

"Well you should find out," Wendy said.

"I will call them now," he said, letting some of his fear slip out in a terse response. Wendy said nothing as he moved past her to find his phone in the clutter. Still, she knew that something which she had forgotten was revisiting her husband's heart.

"Please Father protect him in whatever this is Lord, please," she silently prayed as Larry exited the camper while turning on his phone.

"Is it time to get up?" Sunshine was smiling as usual while she propped herself up on an elbow.

"I'm hungry," Boo-Boo shot from her pillow.

"I guess it must be pancake time," Wendy said with a smile, not wanting to give any hint that there was potential trouble brewing on the home front.

"Sunshine, you need to clear out so I can make your bed back into the table. Jump on your sister's bed," she told her. Wendy got busy turning the youngest daughter's bed back into the dining table for the family. She had to put crates on her bed and pull the cushions to get to the tabletop. Then, she set the metal pole in its receiver on the floor and put the table into position on the top of the pole.

Mary wailed in protest as the younger two girls ganged up on her to remove all her blankets and pillow to wake her. This only made her angry, as she flipped Megan over and covered her face with a pillow. as Melissa dove onto Mary's back, knocking her off Little Sunshine. A wrestling match broke out as the three played too rough for Wendy's tastes.

As Wendy rolled up some of the canvas curtains in the trailer, she looked out for Larry. He was sitting at the campfire ring, slouched back in his chair, staring into the ashes with his phone in his hand. He looked defeated, which caused her to bite the inside of her lip to stop herself from rushing outside and demanding to know what was happening. Instead, she focused on what had to be done to get breakfast cooking.

"Alright girls I am going to need some help cleaning up so we can cook breakfast," she announced and began to dole out assignments to make it all happen.

Half an hour later, Larry was still sitting in his chair, gazing into a dead fire pit. Wendy whispered into Sunshine's ear and sent her on a secret mission. She slipped on her dad's colossal tennis shoes and clunked out of the trailer's metal door. Sneaking up behind her dad, occupying space elsewhere, she attempted to tickle her hero under his arms.

"Hey, kiddo, what's going on?" He picked her up and sat her on his lap, dropping both commandeered shoes onto the ground.

"Mommy s-s-s-sent me on a secret mission, Daddy," she whispered.

"Really?" Larry said, whispering into her ear. "What's your mission soldier?" he asked.

"My m-m-mission is to bring you back inside to e-eat breakfast," she said, even offering a six-year-old salute.

"Daddy's not real hungry right now, honey," he said.

"I have to re-re-report to the commanding officer." She jumped down to report back to the general who had sent her.

After breakfast had been consumed and cleaned up, Wendy had the girls march to the campground bathroom together to get their teeth brushed and hair combed in the mirror. It was an excuse for her to go on the offensive.

Larry's intervention had roused the fire from its doldrums again. Wendy approached with a cup of hot coffee, hoping it would open the door for words to proceed through his mouth. She had sent a quick prayer request to her faith sisters before launching the campaign and prayed for wisdom as she approached him.

"Mom," came from behind her. It was Melissa running back into camp.

"Yes," she answered, more than a little annoyed.

"Can we go to the playground after we brush?" she asked with a smile.

"Sure, but don't lose the hairbrush it's the last one we have with us. Take a bag for your toothbrushes. Tell Mary to stay with you the whole time," Missy was already running the other way.

"Thanks Mom!" she said as she crossed the shaded gravel road and reached into their trailer for a plastic bag.

"Don't lose the brush," Wendy said again to the back of her daughter's waving hand.

"Hey Mister, I brought you some coffee," she said to her silent, brooding husband.

"Thanks," he said while feigning a smile and some gratitude.

"OK. What's going on with the boat?" she asked.

"I don't know, they aren't answering their phones," he said while testing the coffee.

"Larry, should we call the Sheriff?" she asked and came around to talk to him from the front with the fire warming her back. She needed to see into his face and read what was happening. Sometimes, it was all she had when he drifted down into his land of funk.

Larry's phone began to light up and vibrate in his hand. He turned it over to reveal the number of the person trying to contact him, and fear shot through him. He slid his chair back as he stood up so he would not knock Wendy into the fire. He set the coffee mug down as the buzzing continued. She wanted to see who was calling, but he turned away. She could not catch the name or number.

"Who is calling you, Larry?" Fear gripped her heart, triggered by his hiding.

He held up his hand to stop her and answered the caller.

"Hello," Larry said tentatively into the phone.

"Hey Larry, this is Deputy Ron from the Huron County Sheriff's office calling. Sorry to bother you while you are on vacation, but we need to talk for a couple of minutes," his voice was insistent.

"OK," he responded while taking several steps away from his wife's fearful gaze.

Four hours later, as the SUV pulled the pop-up trailer over the Mackinaw bridge into the Lower Peninsula, Wendy was seething. The perfect vacation was over, and they headed home as fast as they could. After spending many miles crying in confusion, the girls in the back seat fell asleep. The three-week trip had been cut short by two whole weeks, and they needed to understand why it had happened.

Larry had isolated himself again while he drove. Wendy felt alone and confused. She wanted to lash out at him. She needed him to explain what was going on. He tried to pass it off as nothing but that they had to pack up and go in the next breath. She was done with the partial explanations and the silence. She was going to force him to talk but waited for the girls to drift off before challenging him. Now was the time.

"Hey, you have to talk to me!" She demanded as she turned to face him from her seat.

"Your not going to shut me out anymore. I know there has been something going on with you and the guys ever since you last went out fishing with them. Now you need to let me into what's happening so we can face whatever it is together. That is exactly what the Devil wants, to divide us. Remember I married you for better and for worse. You need to tell me what is going on." Tears began to fall down her face as she spoke. She hated confrontation but loathed silence even more.

Mary was only pretending to be asleep in the back seat, trying desperately to hear what was going on between her parents over the road noise and the radio.

"I know I owe you that," Larry responded as tears rose.

"What is it, Larry?" she touched his neck with her hand, encouraging him that she was on his side.

"The guys are complete idiots, and I let them suck me in," he began to speak, and the floodgates opened as he revealed the whole story to her over the next hour of driving and crying.

Wendy summarized, "Their grand plan for their lives was to grow weed on the island and sell it to some distributor across the state?"

"Yes," he said. Larry was exhausted.

"Now they may have stolen your boat to go back out there?" she demanded.

"It could be them," he said.

"What if its the drug dealers taking your boat and getting you implicated in all of this?" She was reeling, trying to understand why he had not thought this through.

"We don't know any of that," he said.

"Well, you should have thought about what you were doing, Larry," she snarled.

"I know Wendy!"

There were a few moments of silence.

"There is more," he said.

He went on to explain that they had revealed to him that Frank had burnt Chuck's trailer down to get the insurance money for the project and that he had unwittingly delivered the letter to Frank from Chuck the day he picked him up from jail.

He had brought her this far into the story and knew he had to tell all of it now. He continued that he believed Frank had done something to Sally's car to cause the accident when she was killed. It had something to do with the way she treated Chuck at work.

"What have you done? You have opened our family up to so much evil, Larry," she said, stupefied. She wept openly now, and three wide-eyed girls in the back seat did not know what to think or do, so they quietly cried along with their mother.

"I hope the four missing people didn't get caught up in all this mess," Larry lamented even more.

"You mean along with the four of us? Your inability to stand up to those two idiots could put you in prison, Larry!" She screamed her fury at him as her fear Anchor tightened in her heart, and a group of busy Leech happily drilled deep into three young souls in the back seat.

FORTY-SIX

PILES

A few months of continued insanity had brought the entire load of one million four hundred eighty-three thousand six hundred and twelve souls to the brink. Not one remained even remotely sane after one hundred and fifty-three days of inter-dimensional space travel and through the bowels of utter agony. As intense needs, desires, and fears now drove out every thought and ambition, nothing of the old life remained.

As the ship unloaded its unwanted cargo onto the southern plain, another pile of bags grew up from the waterless salt flats. The sun was high in the sky and pierced through the flimsy socks, warming them to near boiling. At that point, the souls inside could only hope to drop on the shady side of the motionless pile of humanity. As the conveyor discharged its load, the soul socks bounced down the growing hill, each adding to the mass of the soon-to-be mountain.

If the individuals on board could see the larger picture, they would have noticed hundreds of hills of bags stretching out as far as any human could see. Off in the distance a black cloud rose from ten smokestacks. They belched fluffy charcoal smoke high up into the stratosphere of the moon-like landscape as it trailed off into the distance and out of sight.

The stacks marked each mobile plant responsible for processing the new arrivals. Every single bag that came to Apollyon went through that single facility. Leadership had tried to expand the intake process by constructing even more plants, but that would take decades. For now, as the new souls were piling up from several different transport ships, the average wait time for processing was six and a half years.

They had seventy-eight months to languish in a pile of souls, with nothing to do and nothing to think about other than their cavernous desires. They were, in fact, now prisoners of their own desires.

Eighty-three months later, the factory rolled up to their pile of old socks and started sucking the bags into several tubes. The vacuum drew them up and deposited them inside the high gray walls of the constantly vibrating vehicle. It had sent them to a large room where they were again put into another waiting pile. This room had slanted sides that drained to the bottom like a funnel, where an auger grabbed the bags and moved them through to a conveyor.

Six days later, 114's bag was touched by something other than the six socks surrounding it for the first time in almost seven years of sitting out on the salt flats in that depressing world. The metal clamp on the bag was grabbed by a hook, and they were lifted off the conveyor belt and elevated toward what was labeled as the Searing Room in red letters above the opening. The line of hooks was in the thousands and stretched as far as they could see through the dark interior.

The bottom dropped out as the bag was released and sent diving toward a large pool of swirling brown slime. The instant 114 splashed into the liquid, a searing pain shot through his entire being as every single molecule was intentionally burned alive, sort of. The scorching pain would have caused anyone on Earth to pass out. But in this world, there was no way to lose consciousness. No matter how difficult something may have been, you were forced to endure the pain.

The Searing was designed to burn off the things of the old world that reduced the capacity to experience pain. Afterward, there would be nothing to hinder the reality of true pleasure and genuine pain. It was as if someone increased each soul's ability to feel by one thousand times. Terrains had been subjected to a dulled life experience ever since the fall, which was now burned away to reveal the true rawness of life. It was an official welcome to Apollyon.

125 went through the Searing fire two days later and was left again in another pile, this time to dry. The Searing had opened up one more thing to each of the souls in the wretched bags— the ability to hear sound again. The sudden renewed input was unnerving as the moaning, screaming, and cursing broke through the silence of almost eight years since the first gathering. Every soul had wrestled

with the idea that maybe they were the only ones suffering through the stark conditions; after the Searing, there was no denying the truth of where they were. There were no covering ears to stop the onslaught as the cacophony of wretched protests assaulted the defenseless souls. The gift of hearing did nothing to alleviate the underlying ache of loneliness. As a matter of fact, the growing decibels of sound drove the agony deeper still.

They were all receiving precisely what they had wanted their entire lives. Every soul had longed for freedom from God, on the one hand, to be a god on the other. So here they sat, waiting again in another pile, free from the tyranny of the Creator. They had been abandoned unto themselves. Their bag was their universe, and the desired control was given to them, except they were powerless to create what they wanted. Nothing is more pathetic than a powerless deity.

Forty-Seven

In Deep

"Your best hope is to be as honest as possible throughout this mess. The only thing you have done wrong is to transport two crazy friends to the island. Then you picked them up, brought them back, and went on vacation," Wendy said as much for her serenity as Larry's.

"I had no idea about any of the other stuff until we were on the way back," he reiterated.

"I am afraid for you, for all of us, and I know our Father wants you closer to him, Larry," she said. "I am sorry I lost it. Abba has got this and I was doubting him," she admitted.

"I have been mad at God for a long time, I guess, but I don't even really remember why, exactly," he thought out loud as he drove the final miles back.

"I know," she said.

His phone rang, and Wendy answered for him.

"Hey Sheriff," she said, "Yes, he is driving."

"Yes, about ten minutes away, you can meet us there, if you like," she explained. He replied in her ear.

"OK, see you then," she said and disconnected.

She touched her husband for the first time in a couple hours.

"I am going to pray right now," she said, turning around to include the afraid girls in the back seat. "Father, we need you right now. Send your Holy Spirit to intervene in this situation. Protect Larry and help him to turn to you in this hour of struggle. Jesus, we need you every single moment of every day to help us to know that better right now as we are going through this trial. Reach out to Chuck and even Frank, Lord, and protect the missing family. We pray in the powerful name of Jesus." Larry was crying.

A moment after backing the camper into the yard and sending the girls out to play, two Huron County Sheriff patrol cars turned in the drive.

"Why don't we have this conversation inside, Sheriff?" Larry said to the two brown uniformed men.

"OK Larry, lead the way," Ron said.

Larry spent the next hour telling the men the tale and answering their questions as thoroughly and honestly as possible. He even told them he did not like partying with the guys, but he just went along for the ride. He felt trapped and tricked by his friends and revealed everything to the police.

"Well, Larry, I appreciate your honesty in this mess," Big Ron said.

"Would you testify to what you have told us in court, Larry?" The sergeant asked intently.

"Yes, I will. I think it's the only way these two are going to get themselves some real help," he said. Larry was sad for his friends.

Wendy had been secretly praying, sitting next to her husband while two dear friends were beating on heaven's door on their behalf.

"Just to be clear, do you have any knowledge about any missing persons out on the Bay?" the sergeant pressed.

"No I don't know anything about that," he answered while looking the Sheriff directly in the eyes.

"Would you be willing to ride along out to the island and give us a hand in trying to figure this thing out?" The sergeant asked as he stood up.

"Anything you need, Sir," Larry rose to his feet.

"Something is telling me that we need to go now," he replied.

"OK," Larry said as he made eyes toward Wendy.

"Ron, get the marine division on the horn and bring them up to speed. Tell them that we will meet them in Caseville at the marina," he said, walking out the door.

ACT VI

FORTY-EIGHT

TWISTED CHARITY

"JUMPER GO!GO!GO!"

Instantly, the tall Jumper warrior began to glow in an intense cobalt blue. He was less than ten feet from the blood-splattered tree as the two sisters' bodies started to spill over. He flipped a knob on his staff using his thumb, sending it into "powering up" mode. The eight-foot-long black, gnarly-looking pole changed to an intense glowing white-hot light. One long second later, an indicator light above the knob went from yellow to red and then to the final color of green. It would have flashed two beats a second, but the warrior had not waited for the flash as he raised the staff when the light had changed to red because he knew his weapon. Having rebuilt the battle-shifting weapon in the field countless times, he understood every aspect of the device. Being an integral part of the elite Jumper Squadron for over twenty-five turns, he had deployed the devastating tool hundreds of times throughout those years. He was the best.

With ruthless and courageous skill, he slammed the staff into the ground not five feet from the lady's bloodied bodies. The thunder that shook the ground sent a wave of intense energy outward from the device. A white-hot flash emanated from the stick's center and pushed out at light speed, piercing everything in its wake. The force of the wave began to rotate counterclockwise with a pulsing, throbbing aura, pushing the circle further and further out. The warrior appeared absorbed into the sea of light as the gamma rays flowed brilliantly. Time stopped moving on that island in an instant. Then, with a determined stubbornness, the swirl of light forced time itself to retreat under its unrelenting power. Everything within the grasp of the unforgiving swirling beam was forced to retreat unwillingly into the past. The wormhole was now opened, and the fabric of time was bent backward for eleven seconds.

For almost two miles in every direction, time was twisted in reverse. If one could see time, one would have noticed the fabric turn, like a spinning drill grabbing a cloth towel. The Jumpers Staff was designed to hold onto the corner of a moment that existed around it before it had faded too far into the past and then force that moment into reverse. The best any Jumper could ever hope for was fifteen seconds. Today's engagement forced back the veil for eleven. That time could be enough for many things to change. The shrewd commander could take advantage of the chance to relive those moments by knowing what the enemy did in the old time and adjusting his strategy. More than anything else, Major Amadan was a shrewd leader.

Out in the lake, at the edge of the swirling light, General Cryptus recognized the potential disaster a second too late and was caught in the maelstrom. His three double squads of inbound Reaper were just outside the ring of transformation. This exact moment was chosen to catch his entire force unaware of the change that had taken place on the island. Amadan's warriors were ready for the maniacal attack and positioned to strike a deadly blow. The time differential of eleven seconds was forced on the open waters around the island and acted as a ripple on the water's surface, confusing many fish but not much else.

The Jumper's light vanished.

FORTY-NINE

BACK

With the flash, the Jumper was gone, his job complete.

ELEVEN.

Amadan powered up red along with all the other warriors, who were uninjured and back on the ground with him again, from the eleven-second jump back in time. All of them were ready to return to the fight with a vengeance. They had been used to draw the Reaper close and chose to undergo the shock and pain to make this mission plan viable. The Jumper had completed its mission and had disappeared along with his time-shattering staff, never to return. He was spun out into the future. Jumpers often reappeared within a week or two of the mission. They would return to base with another confounding story, looking to recharge the staff and do it all over again. These soldiers were the absolute elite, and there were only two available at any one time.

Amadan's team was up to speed on the plan after the Jump was complete since the first action was a ruse to entrap as many Reapers as possible into their web. All the warriors shot into action with renewed fury. This was no longer a drill with the knowledge that one had to redo eleven seconds, which could cause anyone to let their guard down— knowing the time mulligan coming. No, this was the time for intense focus and determination to press the enemy with a vicious and overwhelming force of their combined will. No prisoners would be gathered today, and no mercy would be granted to the evil surrounding them.

Amadan spun up between two confused Reapers and power-sliced their heads clean off with ease. He turned back toward the ground, focusing on the two human shields.

TEN.

Gilboa surged through the air, chopping and slicing everything in his wake as he attempted to get to the same altitude as the 'chaos' squad's speedy approach. Iggy joined him as the Reaper was popping through the Mach window. The warriors smashed through half of the shrieking group as they appeared out of thin air to meet them above the operational area.

NINE.

Four members of Ready Squad One were waiting for the second Reaper unit as they tried to fly through the operational area to distract and entice warriors to chase them away from the battle. Four flashing swords dispatched eight Reapers in less than a second. At the exact moment, Ready Squad Two dove transparent on top of the Reaper Kill Team approaching from the northwest. Seven Reapers were sent spinning out of control into the water.

EIGHT.

The two human shield Reapers had no clue what had just occurred because, to them, nothing had happened yet, as time had been twisted into the past beneath their disgusting feet. Sure, they had caught a glimpse of a brief flash, but nothing more. The weapon had worked flawlessly.

The two Carne women were still directly in front of them. The Whisperer danced around Franks's head, singing songs of death and insanity. Bapps slashed in and smashed the Fly into oblivion with the back of his shield, reducing him to ooze like a bug on a speeding windshield. As he swung to destroy the Fly, the shield passed through Franks's head and knocked the Reaper, who possessed him, unconscious.

SEVEN.

Tic was ordered to prepare some birds still gathered in trees watching the events unfold on their island sanctuary. As he had cruised into the battle transparent, he sliced the two Reapers as he had before, sending them to the sea. Then he went head down toward a tree filled with Cormorants and peered through the foliage toward the shooter called Frank.

SIX.

The women were tied facing each other with their heads on each other's shoulders, and Chuck held the long black rope wrapped around them. Their fighting had ceased, but the trembling had not.

Tic shot visions of tremendous red eyes into the living light spectrum and sent fifty cormorants frantically fleeing the tree just east of the screaming man and in his direction.

FIVE.

"Shut up! Just SHUT UP!" Frank screamed like a madman to drown out their whimpers.

Crazed birds drove through the trees, screaming a real fear that had invaded their peace, and the men were momentarily distracted by the display.

FOUR.

"Father give me strength to fight against Evil," Connie prayed. She burst into action as she spun off the hastily wound rope under her arms and yanked her hands free from the knot wrapped around her wrists behind her back. She turned and used her left arm to hit the side of Chuck's rifle, forcing the barrel's end away from her and her sister. Distracted, Chuck held his finger on the trigger. A reflex reaction to the sudden motion caused him to squeeze his hands as the gun swung away because of the lunge of the desperate woman. Trying to maintain his grip on the weapon, he pulled the trigger. The firing pin surged forward, striking the primer of the waiting round. The bullet left the end of the barrel with haste. The projectile pierced the top of Franks's left shoulder, shattering the end of his collarbone. That same instant, a startled Chuck received a knee to his groin from a screaming Connie, whose black blindfold sock had been yanked off her face.

THREE.

Frank reeled away in sudden pain as the crack ripped past his head. Connie had turned and reached for Nan's face, inadvertently scratching her cheek as she yanked down on her sibling's blindfold. Diana pushed up hard and reached her feet within striking distance of Franks's right knee. Without hesitation, she slammed her foot hard on the outside of his thigh just above the joint. Sending out a sudden pop as the leg went sideways from the force. Frank turned toward the new pain with his rifle and depressed the trigger. The obedient bullet exited the barrel at 3,240 feet per second, whizzing through Nan's unwashed hair an inch from her left ear and lodging into a tree. The round wound up just twelve inches above the impact spot from the same bullet in the alternate reality.

TWO.

Connie screamed with primal fury, inching toward the edge of sanity. She threw herself at Franks's falling body, trapping the hot rifle between her midsection and his chest. As she came to rest, she drove her clenched fist down into the man's nose, causing a spray of blood as bone and cartilage shattered with a quick snap.

ONE.

Raising her fist again, she drove it home onto the nose again. Frank lurched up, pushing the woman off his chest as blood ran down his face. Diana reached for the rifle and yanked up hard on the strap.

ZERO.

Chuck was writhing in pain just five feet away as Frank slammed his foot into the side of the taller woman, trying to free his weapon. She went over with a grunt as the air was driven out of her.

The other sister latched onto his head and began biting down on his neck, trying to tear the flesh free as she stuffed her thumb into his right eye in a ferocious attack. The man screamed in pain and punched his fists at her face in a new rage. Over and over, he swung, sometimes connecting solidly with her head, cheek, and jaw. Finally, after five hits, the stabbing pain from the rabid biting stopped, and the thumb was removed from his bleeding eye socket. At that precise moment, a three-inch wide branch struck him solidly on the top of his head. The all too familiar hollow thudding sound returned inside his brain and, again, darkness.

The women had spent all their pent-up frustration on Frank's face and head. The bleeding lump of a man went limp from the blows. Connie's face dripped blood from her body and the pieces of his neck that she ripped free with her teeth. Her eye was swelling shut, her jaw ached, and her nose appeared broken. Diana clung to the piece of wood as she looked in horror at the motionless body between her and her sister. At that very second, a second bullet buzzed by her head, with the crack of gunfire coming from behind.

Chuck stood up now, looking over the three bodies on the ground. He had witnessed the sisters' ferocity and would not take any chances of them turning on him again. When he had released the round, he did not aim or even care where it went. It was sent on its mission of death without regard for consequence. He was hoping the mere action alone would bring the women into compliance and stop the beating of his friend.

"Enough!" He screamed at them.

They glared back at the gun-pointing, camouflaged, poor excuse of a man with pure disdain. They had given every ounce of life they had left and did not care if he followed through with his apparent threat to end their lives.

Frank suddenly came to with a smelling salt vengeance. He was disoriented from his third concussion but knew he wanted to stand up and find his gun. It was attached to him via the strap and followed him up as he stood. He almost fell back over from a sudden rush of the familiar swirling head that often followed his now frequent injury. Chuck reached him and helped steady his leaning frame. Frank was grateful for the help but enraged at the women. He drove the toe of his worn brown cowboy boot into the ribs of the taller sister and fell to the ground again as his injured knee gave way under the pain. Three of Diana's ribs snapped under the pressure from the boot.

FIFTY

CHARITY'S RAGE

The wind whipped hard at the ears of Larry Shields. He felt uncertain about his future as his body bounced during the rough ride. He sat down with four Huron County Sheriff officers blasting across the lake in a fully outfitted Marine Division skiff. Having just left the Caseville marina, they blew right out of the mouth of the harbor, ignoring all the red-lettered no-wake signs. The bow of the fast boat was pointed northwest on a direct path for the island. It was announced to the team that the trip should only take about twenty-three minutes as the cops strapped on their black body armor vests.

"Larry, when you last saw these guys, what was their mindset?" Ron asked over the roar of the motors and the assault of the wind.

"It wasn't good, to be honest. They've always liked to party, and lately, it felt like they had become fixated on it," Larry was trying to cooperate as fully as he could. He knew he was in for some substantial legal issues.

"Do you know what kinds of weapons they have?" the sergeant asked from behind him.

"I know for sure they have hunting rifles, a couple of .22's, and two handguns each," Larry looked straight into his eyes as Wendy taught him.

"Is that it?" The officer pushed a bit.

"There was talk from both of them that when Chuck's insurance money came through he was going to buy a couple of AR-15's, but I haven't actually seen them," Larry said against the rush of the wind in his face.

Ron tossed Larry a vest just in case. The boat planed out— across the tops of the small waves, which reduced the pounding and increased its speed.

"They have been acting different, weird, lately. I don't know if I can put it into words, ... just not themselves." Larry felt the description was not accurate enough.

"Hey, Larry, we appreciate the help on this. We know that when it's your friends, no one wants to feel like they have to rat them out. So, thanks," Ron shouted.

"I hope you're wrong about all of this Larry. I have always liked Frank, but knew he had big issues stemming all the way back to his dad," the sergeant said over the rear of his seat and then turned to face forward again.

About three-quarters of the way out to the island, the craft's pilot noticed a brief but intense flash that seemed to have come from the growing sliver of land. He shook it off, thinking it must have been off the water. He extended his hand with three fingers, indicating to the crew that they were only three minutes out. Ron opened the metal container, which looked like a footlocker, revealing four AR-15 Police assault rifles held snugly in the case. The three officers removed their weapons, loaded a clip into the receiver, and pulled the charging arm to insert the first shell into the chamber. They did their quick safety check, each double-checking the other's weapon to ensure the safety was engaged. The sergeant removed a fourth rifle and underwent the same procedure for the craft's pilot.

"When we get to shore you have to stay put Larry by the boat until you hear an all clear," Ron explained close to his ear.

"Mr. Shields is that your boat?" The third officer was up and looking through field glasses. He offered them to Larry as he stood, bracing himself against the seat.

"Yes, it is," Larry said blankly. He had wished the thing was all a cruel mistake, but he could no longer deny that things were terrible. Larry slumped back down in the seat with his head bowed low. Praying had been somewhat foreign to him for so many years, but in these last few hours, he felt like he was wearing out a rut to God's door. He prayed again— for these Cops, his friends, and even the four missing people whom he did not even know.

The cops slipped their black assault helmets on as the sergeant said something into his microphone which was clipped to his vest.

"PICCUUU!" Rang out across the face of the lake.

"Shot fired, shot fired, shot fired," echoed through the boat as heads ducked low. Larry was being held down by one of the guys.

"Hey, when we make it to shore, you will have to take cover. Get behind a tree or something to protect you. This boat will not protect you from flying bullets," Ron said into the back of Larry's head, facing down in the seat cushion.

"Ron, get in the bow and provide cover for landfall," the sergeant said calmly.

Larry found himself in the perfect position to pray, and pray he did.

"PICCUUU!" ripped through the air again as the boat rammed the rocky shore harder than the pilot intended. Two men sprung over the sides and took up firing positions next to the boulder. They scanned the beach for movement and then waived the rest of the boat's occupants forward. Larry made a beeline for a tree over to the left. As he arrived, the sergeant waved at him to get down!

Larry could hear the sounds of a struggle in the woods before him. He turned his head and looked at his beautiful boat with less enthusiasm.

"This is so messed up," he whispered to himself.

The four well-trained Sheriff Deputies worked as a team moving into the woods. *"They are brave men,"* Larry thought as he tried to press his frame lower into the sand.

"Enough!" He heard yelled in the distance.

This time, Chuck put his left shoulder under the right arm of his damaged friend's body and got him to his feet again. Chuck's balls were aching more as they stood together, and he still wanted to puke. Franks's shoulder was bleeding along with his neck and nose. The top of his skull throbbed, and he was very dizzy. Still, the rage and the smoldering anger burned inside him like a white-hot magnesium grenade in his soul. He needed to kill these women if it was the last thing he ever did with his pathetic life. He grabbed his rifle and tried to pull it up to his right shoulder. He could not lift his left arm, so he hung the gun near his waist and leveled it at the women. As his finger moved to find the willing trigger, unfamiliar voices broke through the fog in his head.

"County Sheriff! Drop your weapons!"

"Put you weapons down and get on the ground. Now!"

Frank thought that was a ludicrous suggestion. There was no way that Frank Draper would drop his weapon ever again. He quickly turned toward the sound of the voices while screaming with red-faced rage. Chuck was so stunned by the presence of other people on the remote island that he turned to look, inadvertently pointing at the new strangers with his gun still against his shoulder.

The four flashes of light in front of them were the last thing they saw in this Earthly life. Their two bodies slumped back into the dirt with newly bored holes in their skull and chest. They were dead before they hit the ground.

Four armed Huron County Sheriff officers rushed forward as the two suspects fell. Two officers immediately disarmed the fugitives and checked the area for more threats. The other two went to render aid to the injured women.

"Clear! Clear!" It was announced by a couple different cops as concerned faces arrived at the women's side.

Connie and Diana pushed the helping hands away and surrounded each other with their arms, weeping without pride. Their battle was complete for today. Bruised and bloodied, they both thanked God for their deliverance.

Over Nan's shoulder, a somber Larry Shields came through the trees and into view. A sudden shock overcame his demeanor as the bodies of his two best friends lay lifeless on the ground. He bent over face toward the dirt and screamed a curse to Hell itself.

Amadan himself swept in low and stood next to the two lifeless bodies. His chrome sword was still throbbing in his hand, and a determined look was painted on his face. He was here to finish the mission of defending these Shiners. He jammed the tip of his sword up under the ribs of the dead Vanu, and a deep hiss of pain was released from the Reaper that was still inside. The beast was hiding and waiting to be formally released by the Takers. The Major knew that the Reaper would be forced to exit if he could apply the right amount of pressure near the Vanu's spine. He stepped on its back and pushed down hard. The Reaper erupted from the man's back, seeking to ascend above Amadan. He had no idea how deadly of a mistake his choice would be. The Major had one of the fastest swords in the entire Force, flicked his lightning-fast wrist, and cut the demon into two writhing pieces.

At that exact moment, the Reaper in the other body tried to jump clear to freedom. Still, the shield hand of the Major snatched him right out of the air, and he drove his sword up through its skull and dropped him dead on the ground. After he slammed his sword through the head of the first Reaper, he knew his mission was accomplished.

<hr />

Pressing through the curtain, the Takers always lead with their claws, and today was no exception. The grungy horde punched through the ground and scurried into view, their evil red eyes bouncing to and fro. They licked their chops when seeing the clean-up task before them on this island today, knowing that this day would be lucrative. They had brought many bags to fill.

First things first, though, the two Prode with the bullet holes. Six Takers went to the human shells and quickly dislodged the Essence from both, as four others approached with the Gathering bag and scooped them up. The steel ring was clamped tightly around the top, sealing their fate. The Scribe waddled over and applied "10578122-311114" to Frank's bag, then wrote "10578122-311125" on Chucks. The two bags were unceremoniously cast on the pile as the cart was pulled by. Apollyon awaited the arrival of two more Prode slaves.

FIFTY-ONE

EPILOGUE

"I know what I heard them say General!" said General Cryptus through his communication device to his direct superior.

"Yes, Sir, it was six Reaper Squadrons that were destroyed," he said, correcting the record to make himself look better.

"I understand, Sir," he replied.

General Cryptus gave an account of the action completed in the Lakes region. His Commander was reviewing the report recently submitted to his office and wanted answers from the Regional Commander over his apparent reckless application of resources. The view from Command was that the entire campaign had been an unmitigated disaster, and some heads needed to roll.

"The communique that was intercepted Sir, said that from one of those four Carne on that boat was the key recruiter and mentor for the next generation. Stopping that transfer of faith and information in an innocuous setting where we could overwhelm and surprise the Pluck was the single largest motivating factor, Sir," said the beleaguered General.

"Well, we were able to get two transfers. Half of the target is removed as a threat, Sir," Cryptus continued his desperate defense.

"We are not done with this project, Sir. We plan on continued surveillance. The Carne funeral services are forthcoming and we believe that we can gather enough Intel, even if the transfer happens, where we will have identified all the targets in that next command level— which could lead to their complete destruction in this region," he concluded with his trademark cynical smile. Cryptus had played the game a long time and knew he had deflected just enough attention to take most of the heat off his Command. It was not his head that would roll today.

———◆○◆———

The girls were looked over by one of the officers who was First Aid certified. The EMTs had been contacted, and it would be at least an hour before they stepped foot on the island. The sergeant approached both women as they were downing some water and asked them what had happened.

The story was painted with vivid detail as both sisters took turns filling in the blank spots on the canvas.

Connie took some of the men to their campsite and then limped to the grave sites, shedding tears as she answered all the questions she could. Exhaustion was retaking hold of her, and they returned to Diana.

"How did you make it through all of this?" Ron asked pointedly.

"Only by the grace of God," they both said together as a helicopter came thump, thump, thumping onto the scene.

Diana had three broken ribs, a punctured lung from the cowboy boot to the side, and other cuts and bruises. Dehydrated, Connie had sustained a hairline fracture just above her ankle and a broken nose, which drove her crazy. She was kept for observation at a Saginaw hospital for a couple of days. While Diana's injuries were more severe, they shared the same room in silence.

———◆○◆———

One hundred and fifty miles away, in the little town of Marysville, Michigan, a Police sergeant named Jefferson picked up a suit-coat-clad man from a local church to accompany him to a residence in their small city. A pretty woman with brown eyes and dark hair answered the door. She was surprised to see the policeman on her front step. She was familiar with the cop, as their two sons had played baseball together on the same travel baseball team in the area. They explained that they needed to come in and talk for a few moments.

"Your mom and her sister Diana are being flown in a helicopter to a hospital in Saginaw, their phones were lost and had no way to contact you, so the Huron County Sheriff contacted us to come and bring the message. They were found on a island in the Saginaw Bay and are in fairly good shape, all things considered," the officer was uneasy as he spoke to them, having not witnessed the carnage.

Tears flowed from the family of four as they sat shocked in their living room.

"They had only been away a few days. How could this have happened?" So many questions ransacked their brains.

"I am afraid I have some bad news to tell you, unfortunately, your dad did not make it," he said.

"Neither did your uncle," the unknown local Wesleyan Pastor interjected.

Tears flowed, and deep moans could be hard outside the home.

The bodies of both men were recovered from the island and transported to the Bad Axe Medical Examiner's Office for an autopsy. Due to the haggard condition of the corpses, neither would be having open casket funerals.

Ten days later, a peculiar moment happened during the memorial service held in an ancient suburban Detroit church. With her walking cast, Connie limped to the front of the church, touched both coffins and smiled. A new confident determination was brewing inside of her as she turned to tell part of the story to the crowd of over three hundred family and friends who had gathered to grieve.

"Jennifer told me that it was said to her that these men," pointing to the caskets," That these men didn't make it. Well, I am here to debunk the myth! These two men did make it home!" There was immediate applause.

"Not by their strength or inherent goodness, but only by the blood that flowed from the wounds of our Savior Jesus," she had not planned these words, yet she knew from where they came.

"The rest of us," she continued, "the rest of us have to fight every single day to stand in our real identity in Christ." Connie looked around at all the people, enjoying her newfound boldness.

"That may require us to face the things that we never thought we had the strength to endure. It will cause us to have to fight, with all of our might, the EVIL that is present in this world, as we hold on for the next." She moved to stand right in front of her children and grandchildren, looking at them as they hung on every word.

"The best way to prepare for that action is on your knees before our Abba. He will give you the strength to carry on! The strength to endure." She sat down in the front pew as Diana stood up with a Bible in her hand.

"The Word of the Living God," Nan declared by faith. As she read the passage from the Gospel of John, an unseen power shot through the entire room like a beacon from a powerful searchlight, it enveloping every soul in the building. It sent several Leech and Whisperers scurrying for the nearest hole. The inbound Reaper Squad hit the solid wall of faith, broke ranks, and returned to base, unable to complete their mission.

In the rear of the crowd, in fact, the last row, sat a free man, his red-headed wife, and three beautiful girls, all celebrating the last day of vacation together— at a funeral.

After the service, the oldest grandson approached his grandmother, whom he had always known as his Gigi. Connie enveloped him with her loving arms and squeezed him tight.

"Gigi," he said, looking back into her tired brown eyes, "how do we really fight the evil, like you said?"

"That is what we are going to learn to do together, Carson," Gigi replied with an engaging smile as the rest of the grandkids encircled the pair. Looking them in the eyes, she said to them all— "Do not be afraid!" Her smile became intense. She knew that a difficult journey was about to begin for all of them.